Unleaving

UNLEAVING

Melissa Ostrom

Feiwel and Friends

New York

A Feiwel and Friends Book
An imprint of Macmillan Publishing Group, LLC
175 Fifth Avenue, New York, NY 10010

Our books may be purchased in bulk for promotional, educational, or business use.
Please contact your local bookseller or the Macmillan Corporate and
Premium Sales Department at (800) 221-7945 ext. 5442 or by email at
MacmillanSpecialMarkets@macmillan.com.

Library of Congress Cataloging-in-Publication Data

Names: Ostrom, Melissa, author.
Title: Unleaving / Melissa Ostrom.
Description: New York : Feiwel and Friends, [2019] | Summary: After being
    sexually assaulted by a football star, Maggie drops out of college but cannot
    escape the fact that everyone blames her for what happened.
Identifiers: LCCN 2018019376 | ISBN 9781250132819 (hardcover)
Subjects: | CYAC: Sexual abuse—Fiction. | Depression, Mental—Fiction.
Classification: LCC PZ7.1.O85 Un 2019 | DDC [Fic]—dc23
LC record available at https://lccn.loc.gov/2018019376

Book design by Katie Klimowicz
Feiwel and Friends logo designed by Filomena Tuosto

First edition, 2019

1   3   5   7   9   10   8   6   4   2

fiercereads.com

For my friends

Unleaving

1

IN THE SEPTEMBER of her nineteenth year, Maggie Arioli did not cover a slender mattress with an extra-long fitted sheet. She did not thrill over the single dorm room her sophomore status at Carlton College would have won her. She did not buy expensive textbooks. She did not lug books or anything else down campus sidewalks shadowed by trees, their leaves green but leaning toward gold. She did not admire the elegant marble pillars or trust the keepers of the columned edifices to edify her, shape and improve her, deepen her like a well and then fill her with wishes. She did not sidle between young men or young women or gaze up at the mountains of two ranges. She did not walk by McCullers Hall, with its white cupola, or the Stanton Center and its bell tower. She did not visit the musty quiet of Swan Library. She did not enter the electric sparseness of a classroom.

She prepared to leave the valley, put the mountains behind her, and stay with her mother's sister, Aunt Wren, in New York, not the city but the state, a western portion and probably, in general, an infrequently imagined place. The aunt, whose artwork entailed communications with larger, livelier worlds, said as much to her niece during the awkward phone conversation when the arrangements were made ("for your sabbatical," as Maggie's mother had lightly coined it).

"It feels like an apology," Aunt Wren had said, "clarifying not the city, the *state*, pointing out the seven-hour distance between my version of New York and other people's. I'm between Rochester and Buffalo, I'll say. Then it's: Oh. Where it snows so much. That's what we've got—weather."

As if to prove it, from nine in the morning until three-thirty in the afternoon, the span of the September trip, rain fell with increasing violence. Through the initial sprinkle, as her mother drove, Maggie mentally said good-bye to Vermont—Carlton, in particular, not just her college town but her hometown. She was half-mournful. The other half of her: *Fuck this place. I never want to see this fucking town again.*

Scotia. Amsterdam. Green interstate signs, alternately Something-Spa and Something-Falls, signaled her and Mom's proximity to Saratoga destinations. Their route took them close to a hillside town over a river. Dark buildings, severe and brick and incongruously ruffled with gingerbread trim, sat blank-windowed on their craggy inclines above the brown water, like hopeless giants reduced to their lace-edged underwear and contemplating death by drowning. New York, Maggie decided, was bleak and ugly.

Then suddenly, the mountains disappeared. Just like that. The earth flattened. She couldn't see what was coming. She couldn't see what she'd left behind. What she saw was sky, and rain filled it.

Bleak and ugly and *flat*.

The weather worsened after Syracuse. Her mother, leaning forward, gripped the steering wheel with both hands. Like a thundercloud, her dusky hair had answered the moisture in the air with threatening billows, a surge in frizz and curls. She usually would have remedied the anarchy with a hairband and ponytail, but this morning, she didn't seem to notice, not even when she glanced in the rearview mirror. She changed lanes, flexed her hands, and rolled her neck.

"Want me to drive for a while?" Maggie dabbed at her hair. Similarly huge.

"In a storm?" Mom shook her head. Woods lined both sides of the thruway, and the trees drooped in the rain. "Too much of this, and we won't have a pretty fall. It will ruin the foliage."

"Yeah." Good. Maggie pictured her old campus sopping, the leaves ripped off the branches and plastered to the ground. Maybe Carlton College would flood. An apocalyptic deluge.

They got off Interstate 90 at Exit 45 and took I-490 into Rochester. The highway became a dizzying loop that wound around skyscrapers, billboards, river, and stadium. Mom attended to the GPS with the concentration of someone expecting to get lost. Which could happen. She had only a hazy idea of where they were going. Aunt Wren was Mom's twin but, for three decades, more of a distant acquaintance. The aunt had gotten out of Carlton at eighteen, almost as soon as she'd tossed aside the tasseled graduation cap. Her trouble had been with their parents, not her sister, but Mom had never shared Wren's contention with their folks. That difference of opinion had landed Maggie's mother in the disowned camp, until last October, when poor Grandma and Gramps died in a car accident. Mom and Aunt Wren had talked more since then.

Maggie eased back and closed her eyes. She ordered her body to relax.

Cut it out. Grab her hands, Matt. Fucking relax, okay?

Her eyes flew open.

"Lake Ontario Parkway's up ahead. Won't be long now." The traffic had trickled off. Though lightning split the sky and the windshield wipers' speedy sluice could barely keep up with the downpour, Mom exhaled and smiled a little. "Go ahead and take a nap. I can figure out the rest."

Maggie frowned. What was her mother talking about? She hadn't played navigator once.

The implication was nice, though. Her mere presence helping, comforting.

She closed her eyes again, willed her brain shut, too. She didn't sleep. Couldn't. Hardly ever anymore. It was like she'd lost the knack.

Aunt Wren lived at the dead end of a dirt road called Ash Drive. A generous person might have called the place rustic. However, holding open a screen door patched with duct tape, Aunt Wren, herself, hollered through the heavy rain, "Welcome to the shack!" and beckoned with a wave.

Maggie stared at the aunt. This could be no other than the

aunt. She looked just like Mom but also (in the severe haircut, threadbare jeans and flannel, and unmade-up face) totally different. Bizarro Mom.

From inside the car, Maggie's mother smiled nervously and raised a hand. She had her car door cracked, but instead of leaping out with her own shout of greeting, she scanned the property and murmured in hollow astonishment, "Holy crap. What a . . ." The smile looked ready to collapse. "I'm just not sure about this, honey."

This: the aunt's unpainted hovel; Lake Ontario, like a molten metal beast gnawing the pebbly shore that crept all the way up to the porch's crooked steps; the woods on the other side, black and grim and wet; and the yard, oozing mud and collecting puddles, the entire surface looking diseased, covered with lesions and sores.

Mom took a deep breath, like a person preparing to dive into the sea, shot out, and slammed her door. Running in a crouched position, head bowed, arms awning her hair, she zigzagged around the reddish pools that bubbled in the torrent.

Maggie clumsily got out of the car and shut the door. Thunder cracked. Startled, she jumped, lost her footing on the slick ground, and almost fell. *"Shit."* Lightning illuminated the lake. It was an arresting sight, like electricity galvanizing a monster. Maggie hurried toward the porch, keeping her eyes on the muck and sand.

Mom and Aunt Wren had disappeared into the house, and when Maggie entered and shoved the wet hair from her eyes, she found the sisters, laughing and crying at the same time, embracing and rocking together and saying in bursts of emotion, "My

God, you look just like Mom," and "*I* do? Then you do, too," and "Can you believe it, Min? Fifty. When did we get so old?"

The kitchen was plain—no fancy appliances, not even doors on the cupboards—but big, clean, and fragrant with yeasted bread and damp wood. A pendant lamp hung over a farm table. The copper pots above the stove echoed this single source of light and gave the room the warm hue of a polished penny.

A noisy penny. Rain pinged overhead, indicating a metal roof, and thunder rumbled. Behind the crying, laughing, roof tapping, and sky rumbling, something else added to the racket, a regular shattering from a distant corner of the cabin.

It was like standing inside a percussion instrument.

Aunt Wren pulled away from Mom and nodded at Maggie. She swiped her face with a red plaid sleeve. Then her face—heart-shaped, big-eyed, long-nosed, eerily like Mom's—softened. The sweetening of the expression prepared Maggie for something like a hug, so when the aunt abruptly turned and shouted over her shoulder, "Jesus Christ, Sam, will you give it a fucking rest? I've got company here," Maggie actually flinched. Her back hit the screen door. It swung open and banged shut.

The aunt flared her eyes and shook her head. "Sorry about Sam. He's mad and taking it out on the rejects." She made a swiping motion, as if explaining would be a waste of time.

Steadying herself with a hand on a chair, Mom untied her sneakers and introduced her daughter and sister. Then Maggie found her right hand captured and squeezed and patted like a ball of dough.

"I'm so glad you're here, Margaret." Over her shoulder, Aunt Wren said, "She's got our hair."

"And frame."

Aunt Wren raised the kneaded hand, as if to lengthen out Maggie and improve the view. She hummed agreement. "More hair and legs than anything."

"But her dad's brown eyes."

The aunt grunted. *"Him."* To Maggie, she said, "You can keep the Bambi eyes, but nothing else from that one, you hear?"

"Poor Jim. God—since high school!—you've had it out for poor Jim." Mom pulled a band from her pocket and drew her hair into a ponytail. "The nicest guy and the best of fathers."

Bor-ing, Aunt Wren silently mouthed, dragging a wry smile out of Maggie. "An accountant." She announced this flatly, as if the profession said it all. With a final squeeze and slap on the knuckles, she released Maggie. "What's first? Want to change into something dry? Are you tired?" She planted her hands on her narrow hips. "You've got bags under your eyes. A nap sound good? You can put on your pajamas. Or take a bath. Want to take a hot bath? Or eat? I made soup and bread. How about a tour? Want the ten-second grand tour? The best part's outside, but you brought a storm with you, so that'll have to wait." While Maggie was deciding which question to answer first, the aunt asked, "What do you think, Minerva?" Her mouth curled at a corner. "Goddess of wisdom. Patron sponsor of the arts." To Maggie, she said, "Minerva. Can you believe that shit? And here *I'm* the one with the artistic talent."

"Jeez," Mom moaned through a laugh. "Let's not start that up again."

The aunt collected the wet jackets and hung them by the door. "She got Minerva, and I got Wren—a common little brown bird."

"With a beautiful song."

As if Mom hadn't spoken, the aunt said to Maggie, "You can see from the start our folks weren't big on fairness."

Mom's smile wilted. She held a shoe in each hand. "That's not true."

"Says the favorite."

"According to you. For heaven's sake, it hasn't even been a year since they passed. Have a little respect."

"Respect would be hard."

"They didn't love me any more than they did you."

"Want some evidence to prove otherwise?"

"Oh, please."

But the evidence. Where's the evidence? Until the police release their statements . . . Maggie shuddered, pressed her hands to her ears, and ordered herself, *Don't.*

Aunt Wren, poised to snap a retort, glanced at Maggie. She covered her mouth.

Mom gave the slightest shake of her head. "Show us around."

"Good idea. This way. Then you can wash up while I throw together a salad. We'll eat and get you to bed early."

The glimmer of the kitchen died in the gloom of the windowless hallway. Dazed, Maggie trailed her mother. The aunt led the way through the cabin, narrating as she went: "Note the wide-plank pine floors, all carefully preserved with the original dents and gouges" and "Even the paint on the walls is antique, totally authentic."

Maggie tried to focus on her surroundings. They trudged into the living room. Rippling gray and blinking whitecaps filled the windows. Back in the hallway, the aunt swung open a door. It was her bedroom. The woods stood close to this side of the cabin and threw its shade, like an extra blanket, over the small space. The bathroom came next. Mom oohed and aahed at the sight of the claw-foot tub and pedestal sink, then Aunt Wren nodded instructively at an opposite door in the hallway ("Linen closet"), a second door ("Studio"), and patted a bannister. Maggie looked up. The staircase was so narrow and steep, it hardly qualified as a staircase. More like a ladder.

"I've only got two bedrooms," Aunt Wren said, "one below and one above. You're up there, Margaret. In the loft."

Mom, determinedly chipper, said, "Wow. The whole second story—all yours."

"Go on," the aunt said. "Take a look. Watch your step. That one's cracked. Keep meaning to have Sam fix it. No, check the right side. Feel the switch?"

"*Ouch.*" Maggie rubbed her head.

"Whoops. Sorry about that. You don't want to straighten there."

Maggie found the switch. And for the first time in a long while, she experienced a stirring of pleasure. The room was . . . something else. She shuffled away from the light switch, half-bent until she got to the peaked portion.

The space spanned the length of the cabin and held the warm redolence peculiar to attics. Its wooden floors, whitewashed walls, and sparse furnishings—just a dresser, a bedside table, and, positioned under three abutted windows, a quilt-covered bed—were made homey by the pitched ceiling. The room was all roof, and it pinged softly. The rain must have let up.

The short wall to Maggie's right held drawers; the wall on the left, embedded shelves, crammed with novels. But the windows perfected the loft. The ones close to the staircase overlooked the trees, blackish green in the gray afternoon, except where early autumn streaked the canopy with ochre. The room was like a nest. No, grander: an aerie. She crossed to the windows over the bed, where the lake roiled. Now it was the lookout on the mast of a ship.

In her breast, she experienced a tightening—a flicker. Maybe she could do better than just hide here.

When she returned to where the women waited at the foot of the stairs, Maggie gripped the bannister and bit the inside of her lip to stop a tremble. "Thanks, Aunt Wren." She cleared her throat. "I like it."

The aunt cracked the studio door and stuck her head in the opening. "Sam? We're coming in, okay?" She sidled forward and held the door to her side, like one blocking a view into a dressing room.

"Fine." A wealth of not-being-fine crammed into the syllable.

The aunt hesitated. "Where's Kate?"

"With Dad."

Her fingers, curled around the edge of the door, fluttered a tap. "Linnie?"

Clank, clatter, thud. "Take a good guess." A stomping crescendo. Then, closer to Aunt Wren: "Don't tell Dad, okay?"

She shrugged, noncommittal and disapproving, then widened the door with her foot. "Meet Sam, my assistant."

Mom cautiously greeted him.

He offered a dispirited "Hey."

Maggie drew herself in with crossed arms. She scanned the miserable Sam in one glance. He was maybe two or three years older than her and dark in expression and features.

He headed for a rumbling room off the end, saying without turning, "Got the pug mill going."

When Mom, smiling and wide-eyed, stood between the kiln and the potter's wheel, she clasped her hands under her chin and did a slow spin, like a Broadway actress gearing up for a solo. "This is so neat!"

Her aunt grimaced. "Filthy. It could use a mopping."

The studio, a stubby wing off the building, turned the cabin into a squat T. It *was* dusty but very bright, almost fantastically so, and not just because of the lighting overhead. If the kitchen was a penny, the studio was a silver dollar—kilns, wheels, giant roller, shelves, worktable, scale, tools, all in gleaming metal. Then stacked and crowded under and over a long counter were finished ceramic pieces, vibrantly glazed in combinations of dark blue, sea green, speckled cream, thick fog, ruby red. Maggie wanted to see the studio on a sunny day. It had to shimmer.

Mom crouched by a shelf of pots. "Oh, I like this one a lot." She grazed a teapot with a fingertip and straightened. "Where are your sculptures?"

"Yes. Where *are* your sculptures?" The assistant was standing in the doorway of the noisy back room, swinging a kind of wire and eyeing his employer.

"Galleries, mostly."

Mom looked disappointed. "Nothing new?"

The aunt turned. "Not really." She lightly touched one of the

11

dozen pots on the worktable—tall jars, still ragged at their bases with untrimmed clay.

"She's going through a functional phase." Sam's mouth quirked.

"Ha. There's an idea. That'd be a good phase for me."

The assistant nodded and sighed, glum again, then disappeared into the back room.

Mom wandered past the row of windows. The lake and sky cut the world into two bands: bleak gray and bleaker gray. She halted when she got to the garbage bin and pulled out half of a pale-green pitcher. "What happened?" Holding the broken piece with one hand, she reached inside for a curved shard of something else in the same shade of green.

"Bad firing." The aunt made a face. She went to stand by her sister and toed a cardboard box on the floor. "These all have to go."

"*What?* That's nuts." Mom let the broken pieces drop back into the garbage and bent to inspect the box's contents. She pulled out a mug. "Goodness gracious. Don't throw these out."

"They're rejects."

Mom thumbed a frozen rivulet of glaze at the mug's foot. "They just dripped a little. I'll take them."

"Don't worry, I'll send you home with a shitload, but not these." The aunt took the mug from Mom and threw it into the garbage. It landed with a loud crack. Aunt Wren scowled at the box. "Too much flux in the glaze. Thought I had the recipe down, even added a few minutes to the firing hold, but the celadon's still giving me crap."

Mom clucked. "I hate to see them destroyed."

Aunt Wren crossed the room. "I don't believe in giving away seconds. Seconds stick around as long as the firsts do. For years and years, thousands of years. So no. Those are garbage. But these . . ." She picked a mug out of her inventory and waited for her sister to join her. "How about this one to start with? You can have your morning coffee in it. See this?" She thumbed the lip. "I call it cream-breaking-red. Sam calls it blush."

"So pretty."

"It's yours."

She thanked her and pressed the mug against her chest. Her smile disappeared when she glanced at Maggie. "Why are you way over there?"

"Oh." She straightened from the wall and walked over.

Mom held out her new mug.

"Beautiful."

Aunt Wren selected a second cup in earthy browns. "And for Margaret. To go with the Bambi eyes."

"Thank you." It was curvy and big, the browns in matte and gloss, and with a perfect ribbon of a handle. Maybe not the kind of sculpture her mother was looking for, but sculptural in its own way.

Inspecting her mug, Mom asked, "You don't use any lead glazes, do you?"

The aunt made a squawking sound. "What kind of question is that?"

"Well, I was just wondering . . ."

"Jesus, Min. This isn't the seventies. No one uses lead glazes anymore." She snorted. "Unless you've got an enemy you want to poison."

Mom smiled, abashed. "Sorry."

Aunt Wren met Maggie's gaze and rolled her eyes, as if to include her in her exasperation. "Should I throw together some killer glazes, Margaret? Might take a few decades to finish off our target, but what the hell. Got anyone you want me to get rid of?"

"That's okay."

The sisters laughed, easy with each other again.

Maggie turned. Did she want to get rid of anyone? Not anymore. She already had.

Quilt to chin, eyes on silvered shadows, Maggie listened.

The tumble of lake: up, down, *get up now*, fall again, *turn, I said, before I do it for you*, crash. Foliage pattered in the woods. More rain or wind in the leaves? They sounded the same. The house was asleep. If Maggie listened hard, she thought she could almost hear the sisters in Aunt Wren's room, the slow inhale, exhale, snuffling murmur. Did their twinness synchronize their breathing? Would they touch in their sleep? Did some deep troughs in their brains magnetize them, turn the faintest recollection of shared enwombing into a lasting pull? A tidal pull, a lunar listing. Lunacy. Enwombing, wounding. Felled and wrenched.

Wretched.

Getting hurt required planning. Or no planning. Maggie realized this after the fact. She was told how this was so.

There were variations on procedures she should have considered before the bad thing happened. Shower. Did she shave her legs? Condition? Exfoliate? Makeup. Red lipstick or pink? Eyeliner or mascara? Body. Lotion? Serviceable white underwear or satin or lace *and* satin? Sports bra? Sexy bra? Hair. Ponytail? Loose?

Clothes. Tight shirt? Tight jeans? Loose? Loose. Sneakers? Flats? Heels? Friends. Alone? With one? Or two? Single girls? Searching girls? Pretty girls? Ugly girls? Loose girls? Doing. Drinking? What kind? How many? One, two, three? Four? Sober enough to remember? Too drunk to know? To know to say no? There: That was it. Speak up, loud, even louder, scream the word, or not a person will believe it. Practically a rule. Too softly spoken, and any word must count as yes.

2

MOM HAD TAKEN the week off from her job at Carlton Library. When she returned to Vermont, she'd go back alone. Maggie was staying with Wren for however many weeks or months she wanted. She wasn't sure *what* she wanted or what she'd do while she stayed. Currently, she had no interest in deciding either. She had, however, formed a hazy notion of how this stint would begin: She was going to wander by the water, unthinking and uninterrupted, while Mom and Aunt Wren went off and did whatever—shopped, visited a museum, ate out.

But they didn't. Instead, *they* took over the beach.

The weather had turned beautiful. Morning after morning at the breakfast table, while drinking her coffee out of the new mug, Maggie would eye the bright sunshine over the sink. She'd mention taking a walk by the lake. And Mom would beam and say, "Oh, that's wonderful, honey." Then: "You can join us." As if she'd already called the lake but was willing to share.

Four days of this, and Mom never took the hint: Maggie didn't want to join them. She wanted to be alone.

She knew it was stupid to act like the aunt's stretch of shoreline could hold only one, two people max, and the first morning, when the dawn had broken over the water without a hint of the previous day's harsh weather, she *had* ventured out with them. But she'd slipped back into the house after twenty minutes. She'd felt like an intruder.

Mom and Aunt Wren must have decided to avoid whatever issues they couldn't agree on, because after that initial tension in the kitchen, they got along fine. Remarkably well, in fact—talking, sprawled side by side on the sand, or walking slowly through the surf, heads down, or in the water, slim sisters wading into a mirror of light and sky.

Maggie mostly stayed in the loft. Under the windows, curled up on the iron-framed bed, she read Aunt Wren's old gothic romances, not her thing but a distraction.

The books didn't always help. When the words, rather than marshaling her thoughts, began to fray and untie them, she'd sit up quickly, turn around, press her forehead against the window screen, and find her mother and aunt below, their wind-whipped hair, the waves washing away their footprints in the sand.

Every day, the lake matched the sky in blue, pink, or violet, however the sky was feeling at any particular hour. Every day, the seagulls flew in shattering reels and echoed the whitecaps in flash and color. It was a landscape orchestrated in doubles and rhymes.

And Maggie would slouch down to the bed, leaving the twinning world to the twins, and go back to a novel that, when looked at as yet another example of the romantic-suspense genre, also seemed afflicted with redundancy: the same male lead, brooding and curt, dangerous and private, violent but ultimately tender; the same female protagonist, recklessly inquisitive and full of longing; and the same storm-wracked, gabled Victorian, teetering on a cliff, sinister and beautiful.

With the raucous water and birdcalls and wind sweeping in through the loft windows, Maggie read mechanically. When she finished one book, she promptly started another. She read to blot her mind, to not remember. She read for the settings—the eerie mansions, with their hidden chambers, dark passages, and countless windows. The settings were the real characters—multifaceted, many-eyed monsters. They swallowed their inhabitants. They housed secrets.

Maybe Wren's cabin did, too. Maggie was getting that impression.

On Friday afternoon, her fifth day at the aunt's, she heard the rumble of a pickup and the spit and crunch of gravel. A door slammed. She lowered her book.

It was probably Sam, the assistant who kept to the studio. Something was going on with him; Maggie just didn't know what. He was like a phantom who made himself known with sounds, the cracks and thuds of his labor and, once in a while, a question for the aunt, who'd taken the week off from work. Just through these sounds, the sharpness of some, the heaviness of others, Maggie could tell he was unhappy. And why was that? She thought back to the first time she'd met him. Who were Kate and Linnie? What didn't he want his father to know? How did the aunt figure into these situations?

And Aunt Wren. What was up with her?

Maggie could see why Mom had picked *here* as the place for her and her daughter to go. It was the solution on which she hinged hopes. For Maggie, healing, and for herself, the same, only with her sister in mind.

What Maggie couldn't understand was why Aunt Wren had agreed. Why would this woman—the runaway, the recluse—open her house to the sister she'd spent most of her life avoiding? Open her house to a niece she didn't even know?

Maggie dropped her frown to the novel in her lap. The characters in this one were especially aggravating—the protagonist, silly; her love interest, a total jerk. And yet Amanda Darling was convinced Colt Manning harbored a sensitive core.

Maggie snorted. *Sure, he's just pretending to be an asshole.*

Exasperated, she slapped the book shut, slid off the bed, and grabbed her cardigan.

Downstairs, she opened the screen door. Mom and Aunt Wren were crouched by the water, as if they were searching for something. *Probably my beach glass*, Maggie thought gloomily. "Mom!"

The wind and water half-muffled her call, but her mother still heard it. She looked up and smiled.

Maggie dangled the keys she'd found by her mom's purse on a kitchen chair. "Mind if I borrow the car?"

According to Aunt Wren, Maggie had two options for bookstores, one twenty minutes southeast in Allenport, the other twenty minutes southwest in Kesley. "I always go to the one in Allenport," the aunt had said. "So do Thomas and Sam. It has a nice selection, and it's bigger and busier than the other one, probably because of Allenport College."

"How do I get to Kesley?" Maggie had asked.

She drove with the windows down and followed the parkway, with Lake Ontario's brilliant blue rippling on her right. After taking the County Line exit, she headed south, turned right onto Ridge Road, and, down ten miles or so, took a left onto Maple Grove. She had the roads almost entirely to herself and passed sweeping fields, orchards, a farmhouse dwarfed by its red barn, pecking chickens, penned goats, a John Deere tractor, a combine harvester, another farmhouse, another barn, more fields, more orchards . . .

She drove fast but could have been speeding on a big treadmill, so repetitive was the landscape. *I've found the middle of nowhere.* The thought gratified her. Nowhere was exactly where she wanted to be.

But Maple Grove eventually became the Main Street of a town . . . of sorts. The business section—from the looks of it, just Main Street itself—had beautiful buildings, elegant and ornate, one after the other, but except for a few, they were relics, their windows either empty and blackly glinting the late-afternoon sunshine or filled with junk. A canal cut through Kesley. The Erie Canal, Maggie guessed.

Tree Hollow Books appeared on her right, near the end of the block that came after the canal's lift-bridge. She pulled into the municipal lot and had her pick of parking spots. After crossing the street, she hesitated outside the bookstore and admired its swirly-lettered sign, the window display (neat and colorful with new releases), and the beveled glass door, its woodwork trim painted a glossy red.

She was prepared to find the shop as empty as the parking lot, all the storefront's charm and effort wasted, but when she entered, jangling the bells on the door, four young women glanced her way.

The floor was polished oak; the ceiling, high and decorated with pressed plates of tin. In between, from top to bottom: books, books, books. The walls *were* books. An old wooden table spanned the front of the shop. Farther down, the main space opened into smaller sections: HISTORY NOOK, BIOGRAPHY NOOK, COOKBOOK NOOK, TEEN NOOK.

By the door, an old-fashioned cash register sat on a tall counter. An employee perched on a stool there, legs crossed, a paperback splayed and propped up on her knee. She was around Maggie's age, Asian, and wore her black hair in two tight knobs, like gleaming horns. And she eyed Maggie with open interest. "You're new."

Maggie wasn't sure how to answer, so she just nodded and stuck her hands into her cardigan pockets. "Do you sell used books?"

"Basement." She tilted her head. "The stairs are way back there in the reading nook." She closed the paperback, half-stood, and asked hopefully, "Need help finding something?"

"Oh, no. No, thanks." Maggie slipped past the desk and the other customers, pretty sure they were watching her, and found the staircase.

The used section was darker than the upstairs. It was very quiet. Maggie looked around. There wasn't anyone else on the floor.

Her skin prickled with goose bumps. Her scalp tightened. A fast rattle stole the silence. It was the sound of her own breathing. She deliberately slowed her exhalation, tried to shrug off the panic, told herself, *This isn't the same. Stay calm.* She was alone, after all. She could hardly be any safer.

Until someone follows me down here. Until someone unsafe shows up.

She glanced uneasily over her shoulder. Instead of exploring the packed shelves along the walls, she stuck with the sales table at the foot of the stairs. The books were divided into sections, labeled CHEAP, CHEAPER, SUPER-CHEAP. She decided quickly, choosing a few classics she'd never read. The novels smelled musty, as if the previous owners had stored them for too long in damp basements, but they were only a couple of bucks each, so that settled it. Maggie didn't have much cash.

Upstairs, two of the customers Maggie recognized from earlier had made their way to the back. The girls sat cross-legged on either end of an overstuffed couch, unopened books in their laps and steaming mugs in their hands. They were talking about someone's Twitter addiction but fell silent when Maggie reached the top of the stairs.

She smiled stiffly and hurried out of the reading nook.

The person working at the desk looked like she was waiting for her. When Maggie set the books by the register, the clerk smiled and asked, "Find everything okay?"

"Yeah. Thanks."

The late-day sunlight spilled through the front windows and over the girl, teasing a blueness out of her black hair, and cast a shadow across the counter that (because of the buns) might have belonged to Mickey Mouse. The clerk drew the paperbacks closer to her and arranged them on the counter side by side.

Maggie found her change purse in her cardigan pocket and took out a wrinkled ten.

"Aha!" The girl brandished one of the paperbacks. "Good choice. Some French in the dialogue." Eagerly: "Do you speak French?"

"No."

"Not even a little?"

Maggie frowned. "No." *What the hell?*

"Oh." She sighed. "That's too bad. I thought maybe you would." She set down *Villette*. "You kind of look French."

"I do?" *Huh.*

"Well, I *think* so. I've never actually been to France." She clasped her hands under her chin and considered the other two books' covers. "*The Tenant of Wildfell Hall*." She hummed appreciatively. "One of the first feminist novels. Haven't read it. Not yet. And a third Victorian. *Middlemarch*." She twinkled a smile. "That'll keep you busy."

Maggie stared at the girl. Did she always comment on her customers' purchases? And appearances? How . . . rude. It was probably a good thing she didn't work in a grocery store. ("Oh, these are the overnight pads with wings. You must get heavy periods. And Little Debbie Star Crunches? Bad for you.") Maggie pointedly held out her money.

The smile widened. "I'm interested in what people read." She shrugged, as if her interest excused the nosiness, then rang up the books. "I'm going through a Russian phase, myself," she said airily. "Chekhov, of course. Some Tolstoy. A little Dostoyevsky." She handed Maggie her change and slipped the receipt and books into a brown bag. "And I'm finally getting around to Nabokov. I started *Lolita* last night. Ever read it?"

Maggie shook her head. She had zero interest in reading *Lolita*.

"Our book club just finished *Doctor Zhivago*, but we're shifting back to contemporary stuff and doing *My Name Is Lucy Barton* next."

"By Elizabeth Strout?" Maggie had been wanting to read that.

The girl nodded. "In a few weeks." She reached down and brought back up a flyer. "Here's our schedule." She leaned forward to hand it to Maggie, then stayed that way, hanging over the desk. "We need more members."

Directly behind Maggie, someone muttered, "Really bad."

Maggie whirled around.

This girl rubbed a tattoo of a feather by the base of her throat. "There are only four of us." She twisted one of the piercings along her ear. On the side of her neck was another tattoo, not a picture but a word and numbers. Maggie had just made it out—Romans 12:9—when the girl turned to glare out the window. "You should come." She said this fiercely, almost daring Maggie to disagree.

"Thanks." She swiftly collected her bag. The two book club members had her practically sandwiched. She sidestepped toward the door. "I'll, um, think about that."

"Great!" The clerk shared a victorious glance with the other girl, as if Maggie's involvement in the book club were a done deal, then added in a singsong manner, "See you soon."

"Good-bye!" the girls from the back of the bookstore called.

Disoriented by this show of excessive interest and warmth, Maggie mumbled a good-bye and backed out of the store, holding her bag against her chest like a shield.

3

THE WIND ROLLED off the lake, grabbed Maggie's hair, and flung it straight up. She held her cold forearms and hunched in her T-shirt. Mom and Aunt Wren were gone for the day. Maggie finally had the beach to herself.

Summer was over. On the trees edging the water, orange and scarlet streaked the foliage in narrow swaths. Even the September sky belonged to fall: fitful, moody. Silver-edged clouds, like dirty fingerprints, smudged the bluest blue.

She caught her hair and held it down. Aunt Wren's bit of shoreline was like a lopsided smile, quirking on the one end, a short bluff with a bent pine, and drooping into a marshland on the other. Maggie looked beyond the cattails. In that westward direction, the land formed a narrow peninsula, craggy with giant rocks and lush with maples, oaks, and locusts. The muck, tall grass, and vines made the place unapproachable. But even if she wanted to tackle the swamp to reach it, she shouldn't. It didn't belong to the aunt. Wren had said so herself. Isolated, severe, wild, it didn't seem like the kind of place *anyone* could own.

Maggie lowered her gaze to the sand and started walking.

The lake was inventive. Each lapping break delivered something new. Along the water-laced sheen where waves and land met, she looked for beach glass. Mixed with wet stones, the remnants of old bottles glinted. Frosted white, pale green, warm amber, deep blue, smooth and rounded—small treasures. Once she started, she couldn't stop. The search—the mindlessness of it—was addictive. As the morning wore on, beachcombing became brain-combing, a soothing repetition of walk, pause, bend, collect, white, green, amber, blue. Thoughts turned blunted like the glass, as if the waves had plucked the sharp things from her head, carried them to the lake on a retreating swell, and then tumbled them over and over, ground them into something bearable, before sweeping them back to her. *Here. They can't hurt you now.*

Nothing to wonder but the simplest question—pebble or glass? Nothing to feel but the lake circling her ankles and the sun threading warmth through her hair. Nothing to look out for but harmless things, half-buried in shifting sand, a coin among broken shells, a glimmer by a silver feather, a bright wink under sodden wood.

The simplicity of the exercise pleased her. After a couple of hours, it struck her as funny. Who needed college? What would she have done with an English degree anyway? Maybe she wouldn't bother reading those crazy-long Victorian novels she'd bought yesterday. Maybe she would give up words entirely. She'd just pick up glass from now on, day in and day out, this way and that, walk, pause, bend, collect, white, green, amber, blue. The pockets of her rolled-up pants sagged damply with chips of glass. Her feet were numb from the cold water; her nose, sunburned. She didn't care. She was going to tell her parents not to worry. They could stop freaking out about the scholarships, put away their fears for her health and happiness. They didn't need to stress about her lost year, this year, the leave of absence Carlton had readily granted. Just to get her the hell out of the way, Maggie suspected. Put an end to the ugly press. *Shoo, shoo. And take your bad business with you.*

This was her destiny. Clean Lake Ontario of all its glass. A good occupation. A safe one. Wasn't this safe? Just her and the churning body of water, dumb and constant. No designs, no lies.

She laughed, a high-pitched trill.

The sound jarred her. She was shaking, gasping. She squeezed her eyes shut, willfully slowed her breathing. She needed to stop thinking. *Stop thinking.*

Then she stopped altogether. Not to calm down or bend and collect, but to listen. Beyond the water's hollow roar, under the screech of gulls, along with the hum of wind—a human sound, a swelling holler. She turned, just as a shouting child reached her.

The girl stormed Maggie. Not a hug. A tackle. They staggered together into the water. She was barefooted, brown-skinned, black-haired, and small enough that her barreling, as measured on Maggie, was only a hip-high collision. She laughed and yelled, "Got you!"

Startled, Maggie grabbed the child's elbows to steady them both and scanned the shore.

Aunt Wren's assistant, Sam, was scowling at the rutted drive. He gripped his hair, then strode across the beach.

The girl bounded over to him. "Daddy!"

He caught and hugged the child without looking at her. Maggie raised a hand in a halfhearted wave and began to sidle out of the way, but his expression gave her pause. "Everything all right?"

He shook his head. "Where's Wren?"

"Out for lunch with my mom. I think they're going to the Memorial Art Gallery afterward."

"Fuck." He glared at the lake. When the girl squirmed, he set her down but took her hand. His troubled gaze focused on Maggie as if he were finally registering who she was. "I—I need some help." He plowed a hand through his hair. "Can you help me with Kate? For, like, just an hour?"

Kate slipped out of his hold and ran for the water.

"You want me to watch her?" Maggie asked.

He nodded impatiently.

She looked over her shoulder. Kate jumped into the swell of a wave, soaking herself to the waist. Five years old, Maggie guessed. She swallowed. "She doesn't know me." *I am not a good choice for a babysitter.* "Won't she be scared?"

He grunted. "She's not scared of anything." When Kate flew back to him, he sat on his haunches and loosely held her in place. "Hey, sweets, give me a kiss good-bye."

The child's smile disappeared. "You said you'd play with me."

"I said I'd take you outside. I have to go somewhere for a little while."

"Can I go, too?"

He shook his head. "I'll be back real soon. Want to play on the beach with Wren's niece? Want to play with—" He glanced up.

"Maggie."

"With Maggie here?"

Her expression said no. But she answered, "Okay."

"That's good. I'll pick you up in a bit." He kissed the top of her head, straightened, hesitated. To Maggie: "If Wren gets back, tell her . . ." His mouth closed, tightened. He briefly shut his eyes. "Tell her Linnie's missing."

"Want to make a sand castle with me?" Maggie asked, scanning the beach. With what? She didn't have a cup out here, let alone a pail and shovel.

Kate ignored her and watched her father walk away. When the screen door slapped shut, the child slunk toward the house. She kicked the base of the porch stairs, as if the bottom step, specifically, were to blame for separating her from her father. Arms folded and head lowered, she lingered there, kicking the rickety wood, climbing the stairs, stopping at the closed door, trudging back down, a deliberating little person, until the studio wing's back door slammed and the old pickup growled and shot out of the driveway. Then she ran after the truck, straight down Ash Drive.

"Oh shit." Maggie, who'd thought she'd give the kid a few minutes to adjust to the notion of a strange babysitter (and, okay, give *herself* a few minutes, too), raced after the girl, calling breathlessly, "Kate! Hey, Kate! Want to see what I've got? I've got . . ." What did she have? What did she have? "Beach glass!"

She caught up with her on the side of the parkway. Kate was stomping in an eastward direction, her expression scared and pissed.

The road stretched empty and gray. A loose piece of macadam gouged one of Maggie's bare feet. She winced and then arranged her features into what she hoped passed for cheerfulness. "Want to see my beach glass collection?"

Kate scowled.

Maggie reached down to collect the small hand, but the girl jerked away. "Please?" Maggie sighed. "I'm not sure where he's going. But he said he'd be back in an hour."

Silence. They continued walking. Finally, the child halted and released a frustrated sound that pitched into a sob.

She let Maggie take her hand and escort her back to Aunt Wren's place. On the beach, she let Maggie situate her on a warm patch of sand. And when Maggie sat across from her, she let her talk. All these allowances: bitter, condescending.

Maggie emptied her pockets and made up lame stories for the pieces of beach glass. ("This one must really be jade. I'm going to sell it. Think how rich I'll be." "Here's a little topaz. Pirate booty. Bet the rest of the treasure will ride in on a wave any minute now.") Inane chatter and an unspoken plea: *Don't run away again.* She thought about the tremble in the hand she'd held on the way back to the cabin. When was the last time Maggie had reached for a hand and held it? When was the last time she'd touched someone more scared than herself? Where her fingertips had grazed the fragile wrist, Kate's pulse had fluttered like a trapped winged creature.

Sam was wrong. His daughter was not fearless. It bothered

Maggie that he believed this. It worried her that his daughter pretended to be.

Kate watched and waited, eyeing Maggie suspiciously and then checking the driveway, back and forth, again and again. She didn't talk except twice, once to clarify, "You are not my mom or my teacher or Wren," a statement that Maggie interpreted to mean, *You are nobody important.*

And a second time: After Maggie finished a convoluted magical sapphire story for a blue chip, Kate turned to stare at the driveway and said, "Stupid. It's just glass. I've seen broken glass lots of times."

"It's too early to go to bed," Mom said, "and you haven't even had supper. Did you eat *anything* today? You've got to eat, Maggie."

"I did." Earlier. At some point. Didn't she? "I'm not hun—"

"Wren and I went out of our way to stop at a bookstore this morning, just so I could buy that book you wanted. Can't you do this little thing for me? And look. Look at all this stuff we brought back." Takeout containers covered the kitchen table. Maggie's mother seized one and cracked the lid. "Cashew chicken. You used to love cashew chick—"

"Okay, okay." *Jesus Christ.* Hot-faced, Maggie sat.

Sam, who'd been frowning at the floor, glanced at her. Kate was in his arms, sleeping against his chest. There was another visitor at the aunt's table: Thomas Blake, Sam's dad. His attention veered Maggie's way.

Maggie trained her gaze on the table. She wished her mother wouldn't talk so much, wished, too, she'd known these people would be staying so she could have complained of a headache beforehand and hidden in the loft.

After her day with Kate, Maggie just wanted to be alone.

Mom and Aunt Wren had gotten back a few minutes ago. Sam arrived hard on their heels; his father, not long after. An arranged gathering, Maggie figured. Sam must have phoned the others at some point during the afternoon.

Maggie's hour of babysitting had turned into four. The child spent the end of their time together sobbing and screeching for her dad, only quieting when the sisters returned. With relief, Maggie handed Kate over to the aunt. Sam's pickup appeared a moment later.

No one had said much since gathering at the table. Now Mom rose and went to the cupboards to collect dishware. When she began filling glasses with water, Maggie stood to help but got a "No, no, stay put."

Aunt Wren sat with her elbows on the table, her head in her hands, as if her thoughts were too heavy to mull without some scaffolding to prop them up. Thomas's folded hands on the table were white-knuckled. Sam, miserable-looking, shook his head at the floor. And Maggie—knowing she didn't have anything to do with whatever had happened to bring these people together and certain the situation wasn't any of her or Mom's business—was about to mumble about the make-believe headache and the possibility of taking her supper to her room, when Sam said, "Thanks for watching Kate, Megan."

"Maggie," Mom corrected, arranging plates around the table.

"Sorry. Maggie." He ran a hand down his daughter's hair. "Didn't realize it'd take me so long to accomplish nothing."

"That's all right," Maggie lied, and inched into a hover above her seat. "Think I'll—"

"Here you go." Mom forked a helping of chicken onto Maggie's plate. Then, just as if Maggie were Kate's age and needed mealtime modeling, her mother smacked her lips and said encouragingly, "Yum."

More heat flared under her skin. "Thanks." *Thanks for making me feel like an imbecile.*

The aunt, still holding her head, tilted up her chin and smiled across the table. "She forgot your bib."

Maggie sighed.

Wren leaned back in her chair. "The police have anything to say?"

Sam laughed shortly without smiling. "Oh, they know all about Linnie, but they haven't come across her recently. Officer McPherson was nice about it—asked if I wanted to fill out a report." He raised his hand, a helpless gesture. "I said I didn't think so. She's twenty-one. If an adult leaves willingly, she's not exactly missing."

"You checked with Jess?" Thomas asked.

"Yeah. No clue."

Mom stacked three spring rolls on her sister's plate and put a small, covered container next to the arrangement. "Hoisin sauce."

The aunt gave the plate a disbelieving look. "Now she's doing it to me."

"Eat." Mom slipped a folded napkin under her sister's fork. "Any other friends she might have said something to?"

"Friends. I wouldn't use that word to describe them." Grudgingly, Sam added, "Except Caleb."

Thomas smiled a little. "Caleb's cool."

"Caleb," Wren repeated hopefully. "Of course. You checked with him?"

Sam nodded.

"No word?"

He shook his head.

"What about Allie?" his dad asked, holding the rice container but doing nothing with it.

"Hasn't seen Linnie all week."

"Ashlyn?"

"Same."

The father set down the container and asked quietly, "Kyle?"

Sam made a face. "I even called him."

A silence fell. Maggie easily recognized its tone: awkward embarrassment. Seemed like she caused this feeling wherever she went last year. *Tell us what happened—tell us everything*, the people who were supposed to be helping her would say. Then afterward, in expression if not words, *Shit, did you have to tell us everything?*

She forked a piece of broccoli and dragged it across her plate. Adults raised kids to tell the truth, speak up, spill the beans. But they didn't mean it. Not always. A lot of times, people shied away from confessions—worked hard, in fact, to dismiss or ignore them. What they *really* wanted to hear was a confirmation of what they believed in or hoped for or needed. Maggie thought about Sam's assessment of his daughter: never afraid. How often had he reinforced that quality in his daughter? *You're a tough one, aren't you, Kate?* Maybe it was his way to make sure she'd be more like him and less like her mother. Whatever Linnie was or wasn't, Maggie couldn't say, but she guessed resilience wasn't her strong suit.

Mom broke the lull. "Want me to hold your daughter so you can eat?"

Her mother's offer made Maggie glance at the sleeping kid and inwardly shudder. *Better you than me.*

"Thanks," Sam said, "but I couldn't eat a thing."

Neither could anyone else by the looks of it. Aunt Wren gave his arm a pat. "Try not to stress. This isn't the first time she's . . . gone away for a while."

Sam ran a hand over his head, went back to his eyes, and rubbed them hard. "Never like this, though—packing first, and not just a comb and her toothbrush. A picture of Kate. It freaks me out."

Thomas put both hands flat on the table. "I think it's time you and Linnie called it quits."

Sam glared at his father. "How the hell can we? She's missing."

"You know what I mean. It's not working, buddy."

Sam squeezed his eyes shut, a person either closing down or taking a hit, absorbing it. Maggie couldn't tell which.

More gently, Thomas said, "You can't keep doing this."

"I owe it to her." Sam put his face in his daughter's hair. Softly, "You know how I feel about this one. She means everything to me. But look at what having her cost Linnie."

"We could say the same for you," Thomas said.

"Well, not exactly," Wren said slowly. "At least Sam was able to finish high school."

36

"Linnie could have gotten her GED," Thomas snapped.

The aunt raised an eyebrow. The two friends' expressions—one skeptical, one defensive—made Maggie think there was an old argument behind their exchange.

"You're handling your responsibilities," Thomas continued. "Linnie isn't."

"She just . . . can't," Sam said.

"She might be able to if she got the proper help. Not your kind. Professional help."

A short laugh. "With what money?"

"You know I'd chip in."

"Again? I don't want you to."

"This isn't about what you want. It's about Linnie and what she needs. You've set her up as a kind of mission, like if you're patient enough and supportive enough, you'll erase all those years she spent in foster care." Thomas dropped his gaze and traced a gouge in the table with his thumb. "Sometimes I think this has to do with your mom passing away."

Sam flared his eyes. "Thanks for the insight, Dr. Blake."

Aunt Wren, in an obvious effort to ease the tension, said lightly, "Technically, he is a doctor." To Maggie: "Thomas teaches at Allenport College."

"*History*," Sam said. "Not psychology. I don't need a therapy session."

"Everyone could benefit from therapy," Mom said.

Maggie felt her mother looking at her but pretended she didn't.

"Especially Linnie," Thomas muttered. "Therapy, rehab, *something*, for Pete's sake."

Sam shook his head, defeated. "Linnie's troubles are beside the point. I have to consider what Kate needs. She needs her parents. Both of them. A child deserves that. I'm just trying to make it happen."

Mom shrugged. "Well, that's true enough."

At the same time, Sam's father and Aunt Wren shook their heads. "Not in this case," Thomas said.

The aunt cut her sister a sardonic glance. "You don't really think that."

Mom straightened. "Believe in the benefits of a child having two loving parents? Absolutely, I do. And I'm sure I have the backing of countless studies."

"*Loving* is the operative word," Thomas said.

"Linnie loves Kate," Sam said sharply.

"Linnie's a poor wreck," Aunt Wren said. "Listen. More than anything, Kate needs stability. What she's got now is not stable." She threw up her hands. "Do you want to know how Kate will make out living in a precarious situation, living with constant trouble? She'll grow up scared and sad and angry. She'll grow up thinking about fighting or fleeing. She'll grow up trying to get away." She rapped the table with a knuckle. "She'll grow up like I did."

Mom's mouth dropped open.

Her color hectic, Aunt Wren glared at her sister. Then she looked away and pressed her lips together.

"But—but our parents, Wren, I mean . . . how they brought us up with church on Sundays and good food on the table and taught us to share and be honest and work hard." She searched her sister's face. "Dad was a little distant, but Mom—Mom couldn't have been gentler . . ."

Kate suddenly groaned. Flushed with sleep, hair sticking up on one side, she scrunched her face, raised her head, and squinted at the table gathering, all while voicing displeasure, a sound between a whine and a cry.

Sam smoothed her hair. "Boy, you wake up grumpy, don't you?"

She dropped back to his chest hard, a head-butt, and shut her eyes again.

Aunt Wren stood quickly. "I'll get you some milk, sweetie."

Mom pulled her anxious frown away from her sister and smiled halfheartedly at Sam. "Evening naps are the worst. When Maggie was that age, I could never keep her awake when she wanted to sleep, especially if we were in the car. No matter what time it was, if we started driving somewhere, she'd pass out in seconds. And if it happened on the way to a restaurant, she'd spend the whole meal just like that. Miserable." She turned a more genuine smile on Maggie. "Do you remember that, honey?"

"No." Not the crankiness or the napping, either. Sleep. It was hard to believe she'd once slept so easily.

Maggie curled onto her side and peered out the window overlooking the woods. A paleness sifted through the trees. Moonlight or dawn? She had no idea what time it was. In the morning, Aunt Wren would go back to work in the studio, and Mom would drive home, though Maggie would see her and Dad at Thanksgiving, and her mother had promised to return again at Christmastime.

Maggie would miss Mom. But she needed a break from her. A break from reporting on how much she'd eaten or how long she'd slept or how she was feeling. Maggie would finally have time alone.

Well, not *really* alone, of course. There was the aunt. And Sam. That guy was always around and obviously not just because he was the studio assistant. Maggie suspected he'd show up even if he didn't work for the aunt, on account of his dad's friendship with Wren. Sam was clearly comfortable hanging out at Wren's place, leaving his child in her care, sitting at her table, sharing food and conversation, listening to advice and criticism—at home here, regardless of whether or not the aunt was around.

This didn't bother Maggie too much. Sam worried about Linnie. He worried about Kate. He did not worry about Maggie. In fact, he hardly seemed to notice her. He called her Megan and Mindy and, once, inexplicably, Lisa.

For six months, Maggie had been the object of interest, speculation, hatred, accusations, and jokes. She was grateful for Sam Blake's lack of interest.

4

"I **WANT YOU** to take it."

Maggie closed her hands into fists, crossed her arms, and tucked those fists under her armpits for good measure. "I don't want it."

"But your *friends*, Mags." Mom presented the phone in a pleading way. "Don't you want to stay in touch with your friends?"

They stood by her mother's car. The morning sky, heavy with clouds, turned the lake into pewter. Maggie said to the hard gray, "It isn't just friends who write to me now." So did people who despised her. Who believed she'd lied, exaggerated, wanted precisely what Matt Dawson had arranged and helped deliver, who blamed her for his and his pals' expulsions, who thought she hadn't just gotten rid of Carlton's champion and ruined the football season but fucked up the team, tarnished the Tigers' reputation, stolen the whole town's—the whole *state's*—good fun.

Maggie stared blindly at the lake, remembering the posts she'd read on social media. *Another trashed bitch runs off at the mouth . . . Shit, girls exaggerate, lie, fuck around on their boyfriends, then pull a stunt like this to cover their tracks . . . Matt Dawson and five others are facing expulsion for what?! I can't believe it. Those boys could snap their fingers and make girls appear, just like that. This doesn't make sense. They don't need to break the law . . . Here's one nasty strategy to worm your way into the limelight: Find some decent guys, point your finger, and lie, lie, lie. Thanks a lot, bitch . . . We're behind you, Matt! One hundred percent! Vermont loves you! . . . Women who falsely accuse men should be locked up in prison . . . This sounds like a girl who couldn't get a date with The Dawson. This sounds like petty vengeance . . .*

"Maggie. *Maggie.*"

She blinked.

"We need to tell the police if you're getting mean messages."

"No." No way. Maggie was done with the justice system. "Please don't."

Mom shook her head, noncommittal, and thrust out the phone. "Take it. Delete whatever you're unsure about. Don't even read it. But I can't have you cutting yourself off. It's not healthy, honey. What about Shayna and Jen?"

Mom didn't mention Sara Wood. Maggie sighed, thinking about the girl she'd hung out with at Carlton last year—almost daily until March. Turned out, Sara hadn't been such a good friend, after all.

"You've known Shayna and Jen forever, long before all this happened."

Before. Was there such a time?

Her mother ducked her head.

Maggie looked up. And what she saw was an exhausted woman, helpless, hurting, a mom who couldn't change what had been done to her only child. No kiss could make everything better. There wasn't a simple solution or even a hard one, not for Mom, not for Maggie. Just addressing what had happened heaped trouble upon trouble.

Mom's sadness undid her. Maggie put out her hand and accepted the phone, accepted the tight hug, too, and let Mom tuck the charger in her hoodie pocket.

After her mother left, Maggie went up to the loft to charge the phone. When it was plugged in, she stayed crouched by the short wall, holding the phone and staring at its screen, before abruptly dropping it on the floor. Rising, she swiped her hands against her sweats, then hurried down the stairs.

Maggie had one objective for the foreseeable future: to work on keeping the worst parts of her mind from working. But she didn't want to just bum around, reading and beachcombing. Well, she kind of *did*, but that didn't seem very fair to her aunt—not that Wren had said anything about her earning her keep.

Since Maggie couldn't cook, she figured she'd clean. On Monday, the day after Mom left, she polished, swept, and scrubbed her way through the cabin.

At suppertime, clay-streaked and rubbing her neck, the aunt entered the kitchen and froze. "Wow." She took in the room with wide eyes. "Thanks, Margaret."

Tuesday passed. Then Wednesday. Maggie got into a solitary routine, eating suppers with Aunt Wren but otherwise idling along by herself. Their meals weren't major productions. Toast and more toast. Soup, then leftover soup. Maggie ate little and quickly, and whenever she took breaks from the beach and returned to the cabin, she washed any dishes she found in the sink.

Mostly, Maggie just read—primarily outside. The beach was preferable to the loft. She hadn't checked her phone yet. Still attached to the charger, it seemed to be waiting for her. *Do it. Get it over with*, she kept telling herself. But always, the thought of hundreds of unread emails and texts stopped her.

Hateful words were buried in the inbox. She was sure of this. And they were like land mines. She didn't want to risk being blasted. Or reeled back to the past.

So she stuck to the outside as much as she could. On an old quilt from the loft, spread across some sand by the cattails, where the shoreline began its curve toward the rugged peninsula, she plodded through *Villette*. Lucy Snowe's world distracted her—until Thursday rolled around. On Thursday, she read whole chapters without absorbing a word.

Her own story, the narrative that wouldn't leave her brain, took over. Her memory of what had happened last year . . . it was like a book, too; more like a *flipbook* with random pages torn out, a story she was forced to read.

She tried to whip through the details and finish, *just, please,*

God, let me get through this, but instead, she tripped over moments, got stuck on stark specifics—Sara Wood standing with Maggie in the frat house, a loud corner rank with beer and sweat; Sara laughing up at the guy who was backing her out of the room; Matthew Dawson smiling at Maggie and handing her a drink; the drink, itself, with its strange salty sweetness and potency; Maggie, uneasy, deciding she should leave, abandoning the half-finished drink on the filthy kitchen counter, looking for Sara, staggering dizzily into a room, "Have you seen Sara? Sara Wood, I mean," holding her stomach, palming her forehead, trying to focus; Matt exchanging a glance with a shorter guy, then suggesting she check in the basement; Maggie, gripping a bannister to keep herself upright, panicking at the odd weakness in her legs, calling for Sara from the top of the staircase, making her way down, down, down into a cellar, empty, musty, dim, and then not empty because someone, Matt Dawson, was shadowing her and then another guy, too, and then another and another and another and another; and Matt glancing toward the top of the stairs and ordering, "Shut the door."

Maggie curled up tightly on the old quilt spread across the sand and buried her face in the novel she was reading and not reading.

Its pages smelled like mold. She choked out a sound.

Help.

Friday was better.

For the most part, Maggie was able to concentrate on *Villette*.

Toward the end of the novel, a great V of geese crossed the

sky. The cattails wavered woodenly, except for their shriveled tips, which trembled violently in the wind that swept off the lake.

By late afternoon, she finished the novel and went inside to swap it for another. *Middlemarch* sat on top of her stack of new books. The novel was huge. That nosy girl at the bookstore was right: This one would keep Maggie busy for a while.

When she flipped through it, something fell out of its pages—a small rectangle of paper that swooped to her feet. It was a payroll check made out to a Carina Applegate. A check for two hundred and thirty dollars.

Maggie picked it up. That was a lot of money. Whoever she was, Carina Applegate was probably missing it. Maggie would have to drop off the check at the bookstore. It was dated the first of August. Would a bank cash a seven-week-old check? Maybe it was too late—and Maggie would be off the hook. Automatically, she picked up her phone to call her dad. He'd know.

As soon as she thumbed her password, she came out of her distraction and realized her mistake. "Shit," she said, absorbing the daunting numbers bubbled over the icons. "Oh *shit*."

Forgetting all about the check, she stared at the illuminated screen. Then abruptly, before she could change her mind, she tapped it.

Texts first. There were fewer of these than emails. Plus, they seemed safer, since the only people who had her cell number were friends, family, and acquaintances—in other words, no one who wanted her jailed or humiliated.

The messages came from familiar people who were checking in. That's what most of them actually wrote, a nervous "just checking in," as if Maggie were a creepy motel in a horror flick, the kind of place where a guest had to glance continually over her shoulder, shower with the curtain parted, and sleep lightly, if at all. *I've become the setting of a scary movie. Great.*

She didn't answer the texts. Mom was right. Maggie *did* want to cut herself off. What happened hadn't just ruined her freshman year of college; it had sabotaged everything that came before it. It was like a black sweater shoved into the washing machine with the whites. The innocuous, happy, sweet memories were now tainted, sullied, grayed.

Shayna, her friend since kindergarten, and Jen, her high school pal—Maggie was close to these two . . . or had been, at one time. She'd never collected a ton of friends. But there were also texts from Rhea, the girl she'd worked on her Greek civilization project with last year; and Kim, Doreen, and Tara, college freshmen she'd been getting to know. And, of course, Mom and Dad. Maybe a dozen people total, just checking in. Nothing from Sara Wood.

Maggie got out of her messages and frowned absently at the blue sky framed by the windows. *I'll write back to them later. Eventually.*

She dried her sweating palms on her hoodie and then, holding her breath, checked her emails . . . hundreds and hundreds of unread emails. After scrolling all the way down to the oldest ones, she began deleting. The majority she deleted without reading, but some she read. There was a nice email from Dr. Warner, her Chaucer professor, another sweet one from Kendra, the girl she'd sat next to in statistics. Maggie would have to write back to them, too. At some point.

Again, nothing from Sara Wood. But business advertisements,

47

college reminders, and absolutely anything from a stranger with a male name—automatically deemed unreadable. *Delete, delete, delete.*

She opened a few from women and then wished she hadn't. The fourth one left her trembling and clenching her jaw. After that, she erred on the side of caution and deleted anything from a stranger. *I know better,* she thought, angry and impatient with herself. Women didn't always have other women's backs. Sara Wood had been the first to teach her that. Maggie should have learned by now.

The light faded in the loft. Shadows lengthened. Maggie lost track of time. The personal emails dwindled the closer she got to the present—went from a glut to a scattering to, by July, practically none at all.

Maggie exhaled. Maybe the haters had spent their hatred—or simply found someone new to hate. Or maybe they'd heard that Maggie had left Carlton. She pictured them cheering, *She's gone! We won! Go Tigers!*

She waded through one advertisement after another—Amazon, Forever 21, *Prairie Schooner,* H&M, *Kenyon Review,* Zara—and deleted them swiftly. Once, she paused to lower her tense shoulders, roll her neck, and look around dazedly. *One more month to go.*

She nearly had her phone back now—*really* back, as in something she could actually use. She'd excised the hatred, cut out the malignant parts. She could move forward. Hit reset. Everything that had happened before—deleted. She was determined to forget. *I'm giving myself a do-over.* She felt a little spark of something good. Something like hope.

And then . . . another message from a stranger.

It was a relatively recent email, from someone named Jane Cannon. Still riding that wave of relief, Maggie hesitated only for a second, long enough to reason away the possibility that someone would be trolling her six months after the incident, and then she opened it.

Jane Cannon

To: Margaret Arioli

Hello

September 15 at 1:33 AM

Hi. My name is Jane Cannon, and I'm a freshman at Carlton College. We've never met, so I hope this email doesn't annoy you, but I don't have anyone else I feel like I can talk to, not when it comes to what happened. Actually, I don't even think I can write about it. But I know something similar happened to you. I guess I'm just looking for someone to talk to and maybe give me advice. If you're willing to talk, please let me know. Thanks.

Maggie reread it. She shook her head, swallowed hard, and re-reread it. *Oh no.*

A quiver traveled through her body. The phone fell to the floor. *No, no, no.*

She tucked her hands under her chin and tore her gaze off the phone. Bleakly, she focused on her shadow, a black puddle spilled across the floor.

I know something similar happened to you.

Maggie drew in her legs and wrapped her arms around them.

Oh God, she was sorry for this Jane Cannon; she truly was, but . . . no. *No way.* The girl had asked the wrong person for advice, any kind of advice, but especially advice on *this.* Maggie wasn't the right person to reach out to—wasn't reachable, period. She shook her head again, thought wildly, *I can't help anyone. I can barely help myself.* She didn't want to reflect on what had happened or offer guidance to someone else. She *couldn't.* Going back mentally would totally ruin starting over.

"Margaret?"

She started with a gasp.

"Margaret, honey?" the aunt said louder from the foot of the stairs. "You all right?"

"I'm okay." Her answer came out wispy. *I am not okay. I am not all right. I am not the right one to ask for help.* Queasy, clammy, she cupped her damp forehead and scooted back toward the stairs. Her butt hit something. *Middlemarch.* The check to Carina Applegate was on the floor, too. She grabbed it and scrambled to her feet.

"Well, you've been up there frickin' forever," the aunt said, her teasing a thin veneer over worry. "Want to come down and have some supper?"

"No. No, thanks." She glared at the phone from across the room. All she wanted was to be left alone. Why couldn't she be? Was that asking too much? Just to be left the fuck alone?

She'd scrunched the check. Smoothing it against her stomach with a shaky hand, she turned her back on her cell. "I—I have to run out real quick," she said from the top of the stairs.

The aunt didn't say anything for a few seconds. "Where?"

"To the bookstore in Kesley." She'd go for a drive, a fast drive. Get away. Forget. *Delete, delete, delete.* "Can I borrow your truck?"

"Well, you can, but . . . are you sure you don't want me to drive you?"

"That's okay. I just have to drop something off. I'll be back in under an hour."

Maggie stood in the doorway and looked around, disoriented. The bookstore was packed.

"Excuse us," a gangly man said. He was herding a small boy in front of him so they could depart single file.

"Oh. Sorry." She shuffled to the side.

Adults milled around, nodding at one another, smiling politely. Their expressions matched: the cautious friendliness that people wore around others they'd met before but still didn't know. Children outnumbered the adults and traipsed around the long table, sometimes under it, too.

Maggie was in the way. She hurried toward the magazines and dug the wrinkled check out of her cardigan pocket.

The nosy girl was working again. Standing beside the antique cash register, she handed a customer a bag, then leaned forward so that her hair, this time worn in sleek braids, dangled over the counter. She grinned at the two girls hugging the customer's legs. "Bye, bye. Be good to your mom."

"Watch what I can do," the smaller child said. She stuck out her tongue and touched her chin with it.

"Cool. Can you do this?" The clerk rolled her tongue.

The girls proved they could.

"Excellent. Now, for *next* Friday, I want you to practice bringing your tongue to your nose."

The children started practicing right away.

"Try harder," the clerk murmured.

The mother laughed, raised her bag in a clumsy wave—"See you, Ran"—and nudged the girls toward the door.

Maggie watched them leave. She was sorry to see them go. An absurd reaction, she realized. She didn't know these people. But for a minute, they'd distracted her from Jane Cannon's email. *I know something similar happened to you, I know something similar happened to you, I know something similar happened to you . . .*

"Hey!"

Maggie jerked around.

The young woman behind the counter was beaming at her. "It's you."

Maggie headed in her direction and bumped into another customer. She mumbled an apology and sidestepped past two women talking by the table. Books, cookies, and pretzels were everywhere.

When Maggie reached the desk, she shook her hair away from her face and held out the wrinkled check.

"How's it going?"

Maggie nodded.

The girl laughed. "Me too," she said, imitating Maggie with a frown and a bob of her head.

A customer brushed against Maggie's shoulder. She flinched. "You're busy."

"Because it's Fun Fiction Friday," the clerk explained. She took hold of her braids and tied them under her chin. With a covert scan of the crowd, she slouched sideways and said softly, "This is the weekly gig that keeps my family's shop going. We try to make it entertaining—story time, snacks, author signings, giveaways, costume parties, discounts—and it's become a Friday tradition for a lot of locals. Sometimes I think they show up and shop just because they're worried we'll tank." She sighed. "Like tons of other Kesley businesses have." With a slap on the counter, she straightened. "What's that?"

"Hmm? Oh." Maggie frowned at the wrinkled check in her hand and thrust it toward the girl. "I found this in one of the used books I bought from you."

"Carina." She accepted it with a cluck. "Not surprised. She works for us part-time. Smart woman but a total flake." She slipped the check under the counter. "I'll give her a call. Thanks for bringing it by, ah . . ."

Maggie stared at her dumbly.

The girl laughed again. "I'm Ran Kita. And you are . . . ?"

Maggie opened her mouth, then closed it. Margaret Arioli, Maggie Arioli—both had been in the news and not only in Carlton. She didn't want to ring a bell. "Marge," she blurted.

"Marge. You don't hear that one very often."

Maggie shrugged. *Unless you're hanging out in a nursing home.*

"Just Marge?"

She nodded and took a step toward the door.

"Like Rihanna. Or Madonna. Cool. Well, don't forget Saturday, Marge. Not tomorrow Saturday, but two weeks from tomorrow. Here. Seven o'clock. Bring your questions. Bring your epiphanies."

She stared at her, confused.

"Our book club meeting?" the clerk prodded. "Bring the novel, too. You need a copy?"

Maggie shook her head. She honestly didn't. Mom had bought her the book in Allenport—not that Maggie had any intention of reading it for this girl's club. She'd just been wanting to read it, period. *For myself, by myself, without anyone bothering me.* And then with a pang: *So I'm sorry, Jane Cannon. But no.*

A silver-haired gentleman creaked up to the counter. Ran grinned at him. "Hello, Mr. Holley. Be with you in a second." To Maggie, she said, "Thanks for dropping off Carina's check, Marge." She dismissed her with a waggle of fingers. "See you in a couple of weeks."

Maggie murmured something vague and hurried for the door. Behind her, she heard the older man say, "Marge. Now *that's* a pretty name."

"Are you saying *Ran* isn't pretty, Mr. Holley?" the clerk teased.

"Oh, heavens, no. *Ran's* very nice. A good name for a quick girl like you."

5

MAGGIE FELL ASLEEP late Friday night, slept poorly, and woke to the sound of rain and the agonizing thought, *Why the hell did Jane Cannon have to contact me?*

She rolled onto her back and rubbed her eyes. If only that girl had reached out to a friend, family member, professor . . . *I'm a perfect stranger, for Christ's sake.*

She crawled out of bed, went downstairs, and slogged into the kitchen. Aunt Wren was there, pouring a cup of coffee. She must have been up for a while. Clay streaked her clothes.

"Morning, Margaret." She took a hasty sip and smiled apologetically. "I'll be MIA today. Have to catch up on an order, then head out for a one o'clock guild meeting." She patted Maggie's arm and crossed the kitchen, taking her coffee with her. "Just pop in the studio if you need me."

"Okay." After her aunt left, Maggie drank her coffee in front of the rain-smeared window and worried about the email. It was two weeks old. Probably by now, Jane had gone to someone else for help, like her RA. *Yeah, her RA. That makes much better sense. I'm getting myself worked up over nothing.* Maggie set down the mug and looked around the empty kitchen. A distraction. She needed a distraction. Maybe the aunt had something in the studio she could do, a chore to keep her busy. She almost went to ask Wren but decided against it. The studio was the aunt's workplace. She didn't need her niece hanging out in there.

After eating some toast, Maggie trudged upstairs. *Besides, it's not like I'm a social worker or a counselor. Jane needs a professional. I can't help her. I wouldn't even know how to help her. Christ!*

Before slipping back into bed, she shed her cardigan and strategically tossed it. It landed directly on top of her phone. She stayed in the loft for most of the sodden Saturday and Sunday. While the rain pinged overhead, she frowned at the first page of *Middlemarch* and tried not to think about Jane Cannon's email.

Monday brought back the sunshine. Relieved, Maggie escaped the cabin. *And who knows if the email's legit?* she thought as she crossed the beach. She kicked at a clump of seaweed. *It's probably from some jerky Tigers fan out to trick me into responding, so she can use my words against me, like a—a sting operation!*

The cool wind felt bracing. She walked up and down and up and down the shore until she realized she was ambling to the rhythm of *I know something similar happened to you, I know something similar happened to you, I know something similar happened to you.* She halted and scowled at her feet, then turned on her heel and stomped inside.

While she was pouring a glass of iced tea, Thomas Blake showed up at the back door with Kate. Sam strode into the kitchen to greet them.

"I have a department meeting," Thomas explained quickly. "Forgot all about it. Sorry, buddy. Got to go." He kissed the top of his granddaughter's head, nudged her into the house, and waved good-bye as he jogged to his car.

Aunt Wren was in Rochester for the afternoon, and Sam, coated in clay, was obviously in the middle of a job. He stood in the kitchen, filthy hands raised, probably to remind himself not to touch anything, and frowned at his daughter as if he didn't know what to do with her.

Uh-oh. Maggie inched toward the back door.

Sam turned.

She froze.

"Do you mind keeping an eye on Kate?" he asked. Begged.

His daughter stamped her foot.

Maggie *did* mind. So did his kid.

"Please?" he added.

He looked desperate, and Maggie didn't have a good excuse (or even a bad one) to avoid helping out. "Sure." She sighed.

Kate wrinkled her nose.

"Great." Sam strode out of the kitchen and called from the hallway, "Be good!"

Kate fell into a chair and folded her arms. "You are not my mother. And I don't like you."

"Gee. Thanks." Where *was* this kid's mother, anyway?

There was no television in the cabin—or toys or coloring books or crayons. No tablet. No 3DS. Maggie found a deck of cards in a drawer by the fridge, but Kate couldn't stand War and thought Old Maid was stupid and Go Fish "stupider." Shuffling the cards at the table, Maggie said, mostly to herself, "I wonder if I remember how to play rummy."

"I know how," Kate said, "and I hate that game, too." Then she shot out of the kitchen.

Maggie caught up with her in the studio. Sam looked up from the slab roller, where he was flattening a great ball of clay into a slender brown sheet. "Just a few more minutes," he promised impatiently, "and I'll be done."

The few minutes stretched into more than an hour, sixty-plus minutes of Kate disdaining tic-tac-toe and hangman. When Maggie went back to the drawer where she'd found the cards to search for something else to do with the kid (or *the little shit*, as she was starting to think of her), Kate scrambled out of her chair and raced into the hallway.

Not again. Maggie briefly closed her eyes in exasperation, then wearily followed her, calling, "How about my beach glass? Want to see my beach glass collection?"

"I hate your beach glass!" Kate screeched. "I want to stomp on it! I want to throw it in the lake! Take your beach glass and stick it up your—"

"Whoa." Sam opened the studio door and caught his daughter. "That's not nice. Say you're sorry."

"I'm *not* sorry."

"You are sorry. Because if you aren't, there's no way I'm taking you to the movies tomorrow."

She spat an apology and ran back to the kitchen.

"Sorry about that." Sam shook his head. "One of her friends is having a rough time because her dad got remarried. Kate comes home from school with stories about Kennedy's evil stepmother. I think the situation has her freaking out, wondering if, well, with Linnie gone . . . if you might—that is, if you and I . . . ." Embarrassed, he shrugged.

"Oh no," Maggie said, her eyes wide. *Oh my God, no.* She wasn't interested in Sam. In *any* guy. For the rest of her life. That sort of thing was impossible—*inconceivable*—now.

He smiled ruefully and pulled the studio door shut behind him. "I won't dump on you again," he murmured, digging his keys out of his pocket.

Maggie nodded. She didn't dredge up an "I don't mind" or a "That's okay." It *wasn't* okay. Maggie wasn't up for handling Kate's misery, fear, issues. She couldn't even handle her own.

Sam turned onto Redman Road. "Want to listen to anything?" He reached for the radio.

Maggie pressed her back against the seat. "That's okay."

He let his hand fall, palm down, on his thigh. "All right."

"I mean"—she turned to stare out the window, caught her expression in the side-view mirror, and ironed her features— "unless you want to."

"Nah."

They passed a thin woods, a hunting shack, an orchard. The yellow foliage held a dull shine in the October haze. The orchard gave way to a plowed field, then a farmhouse with a long porch, then a barn, big enough to house the house. Up ahead was a stop sign. On either side of the road stretched fields of cabbage. Inside Sam's truck stretched silence.

She should have said yes to music. This silence was like another presence in the truck, a goading one that pointed out Maggie's discomfort.

What the hell was she thinking? First it was Kesley with its Tree Hollow Books and that prying clerk, and now there was *this*, a drive to Allenport to help Sam pack up his apartment. Maggie was supposed to stay at the aunt's—the end of the earth, hidden, not interesting to outsiders, a nowhere place for someone with no plans for an impossible future.

She'd mapped a tiny world for herself, but between Kesley and Allenport and the email from Jane (dragging Maggie's mind back to Carlton, to pain and fear, and burdening her with an unbearable sense of responsibility), her new world was expanding to include the foreign and the old, losing its manageable perimeters, growing unwieldy, dangerous . . .

She scowled at the field they were passing and, to drown her thoughts, searched for something to say, finally coming up with, "Cabbage plants are cute." Her face burned. Well, that was stupid.

Sam grunted a laugh. "Kate said the same thing last week." He sighed. "Strange to think we won't be going this way anymore." He sped through an intersection and cleared his throat. "Tons of cabbage grown in these parts. The fields will stink to high heaven after harvest."

"Yeah." Rotting cabbage reeked. Maggie knew that from the farms around Carlton.

They continued for some minutes without talking, but when

he turned onto Ridge Road, he said, "Almost there." And then abruptly: "Thanks for offering to help. It shouldn't be that bad. We don't have a lot."

"Sure." Helping him clear out his apartment beat the alternative—watching Kate.

According to Wren, Sam's landlord had called him first thing that morning, complaining about the "characters hanging around the place" and how Sam was late on the rent again. In short, he wanted Sam out, preferably immediately.

This wouldn't leave Sam homeless. Twice, just in Maggie's hearing, Thomas had brought up Sam and Kate's moving in with him. Wren told Maggie that Thomas had even offered to lend a hand with the move. But the local elementary was holding an in-service Friday, which meant the kids were off, and since the aunt had to work in Buffalo for the day, there was no one to watch Kate.

Wren had mentioned this dilemma to Maggie over their morning coffee. "Told Thomas I'd call him back if I came up with a solution," she said. "Wish I could help, but I can't miss the gallery opening. Otherwise, I'd babysit Kate. Do you think maybe you could . . . ?"

Maggie set down her mug with a thud. "Just because I have a uterus doesn't mean I like watching kids." Especially *that* kid.

The aunt's mouth quivered, then she burst out laughing.

Maggie frowned. *I am dead serious.*

"Point taken," Wren finally said, then started laughing again, brokenly acknowledging through her mirth, "Kate's a handful, isn't she?"

"That's putting it mildly," she muttered. Then, in a kinder tone: "But I'm happy to help Sam with the move."

Well, maybe not *happy*, but she'd much rather heave furniture than play nanny. Thomas could watch Kate. Maggie was done babysitting that kid.

Still, this going-somewhere business left Maggie feeling discombobulated, misplaced. She frowned at the passing houses. The whole week had sucked, and not just because Jane's email kept needling Maggie, making her feel miserable and guilty.

First, she'd faced the Tortured-by-Kate Monday.

Then a weird Tuesday. She'd spent it polishing and scrubbing everything in the cabin, whether it needed it or not. But when she'd entered the hallway and crouched to gather the cleaning supplies, she'd heard her aunt talking on the phone: "Well, duh, Adam. Of course I'd like to finish it by December. It's not like I'm trying to go slow, and I need the money. Fuck it then. We'll do the show without it. Okay. Fine." And Maggie had hurried past the doorway, wondering who Adam was and what project had him harping on her aunt.

Then Wednesday and Thursday, though moderately encouraging on the reading front (she'd managed to finish *My Name Is Lucy Barton* but gave up on *Middlemarch*) and brilliant with sunshine, had suffered from squalls of a different kind. Almost all the rumblings related to Linnie. On Wednesday, after a nearly two-week absence, Linnie suddenly reappeared, not at her and Sam's place but at Kate's elementary school. Without warning anyone, she picked up her daughter, took her on a trip—to Darien Lake Theme Park, Sam discovered from Linnie's breezy text—and dropped her off at Thomas's house the next day. For those twenty-four hours, the aunt's house teemed with angry calls and worry.

And the returned Kate, exuberant about her mother's brief

reappearance, soon after plunged into the dismals. She answered Sam's questions in a sullen way: No, it wasn't just her and Mom. Kyle came, too. He went on some of the rides but got sick. Maybe from the rides—how was she supposed to know? Then he took his medicine and went to the motel. Mom got her cotton candy for supper. And pop. *Mom* lets her drink pop. A cab to the motel? What's a cab? Oh. No. A man gave them a ride. She didn't know who. He was nice. He shared his fried dough.

Sam took this in with astonishment. Only when she finished had he closed his eyes for a spell and exhaled. Then he'd met his father's somber gaze and, with a shake of his head, said, "That's it. I'm done."

Now Sam turned right at an intersection. On either side of the street stood rambling mansions with fancy brickwork and old maples. The traffic increased, and the estates gave way to modest houses, then gas stations and plazas. "Our place is just off Main," he said. A minute later, they crossed the lift-bridge, the truck sounding a clanking strum over the Erie Canal, drove slowly past shops and cafés, and turned left at an old movie theater.

Sam inhaled sharply. He tapped the brakes hard. "You have *got* to be kidding me."

Bewildered, Maggie sat up from her slouch and followed his gaze to a faded grayish-green house. On a front porch step sat a young woman, blond and voluptuous, pale hands folded in her lap—obviously waiting. When Sam parked on the side of the road, she smiled wryly and, without unlinking her thumbs, raised both hands for a wave before tucking them against her chest. Her expression turned inquisitive when she switched her attention to Maggie.

Sam stared. "Linnie."

Hard to believe this was the infamous Linnie. She looked angelic. Had the landlord gotten in touch with her as well? "I'll just stay in the truck for a bit. Give you guys time to talk." Maggie didn't want to get involved. Twisting the curling ends of her ponytail, she added, "I don't mind hanging out here."

He cracked the door. "Come on. She won't stick around. Kyle's waiting for her." With a jerk of his chin, he indicated a blue Saab in the driveway.

A man was sitting in there, sleeping perhaps. His head was tilted, propped up by the car window. Maggie was surprised Linnie would bring a new boyfriend to an old boyfriend's place. Would Sam confront him? Would they fight? She bit her lip. "I think I'd better . . . stay out of it. She doesn't know me."

"Actually, she does. Well . . ." He widened the door. "She knows about you."

Maggie absorbed this.

He shut the door and strode around the truck to the sidewalk. Linnie had gotten to her feet. She murmured a few words in response to something Sam said, but she was still mostly focused on Maggie. She beckoned with a wave. Alarmed, Maggie pretended she hadn't noticed and slid lower in the seat.

A moment passed, and then her door was opening.

"Hey, hi, come on out."

"Oh! That—that's okay. I'm fine in—"

"Seriously. Join us." Linnie crossed her arms—blond-haired, brown-eyed implacability. "I've wanted to meet you."

With a sinking sensation, Maggie unfastened the seat belt and slid out of the truck. Linnie backed up toward the house. Maggie trudged onto the grassy strip by the curb.

Without warning, Linnie grabbed her hand, pulled her along to the sidewalk, and after Maggie stumbled forward, seized her other hand, too. Her smile widened to a grin. "You're gawking."

She closed her mouth.

"Margaret Arioli. I have heard all about you."

That didn't bode well, and the teasing quality in the young woman's tone was provoking. Maggie straightened. "And I've heard all about you."

Linnie breathed a laugh and released her. "I bet you have." To Sam: "Kate's off today. You didn't bring her?"

"To clear out the apartment? No."

"That's too bad. I was thinking Kyle and I would take her out to eat."

"You could always swing by Dad's place and just kidnap her."

Her laugh was sharp this time. "Can a mom picking up her kid from school *be* a kidnapper?"

"Kind of, when you don't tell anyone beforehand that's what you're going to do, when you involve that"—he indicated the man in the Saab with a flick of a hand—"person and take her away without warning, without thinking about things like homework and a healthy supper and the next day of school and—"

"What you're saying is, I'm a shitty mother. You don't need to tell me that."

He immediately looked chagrined. "I know you love Kate."

"I'm awful for her." Her smile had turned brittle. "That's why I'm keeping my distance as much as I can bear." Her voice cracked

65

on the last word. She tossed her head and continued tersely, "I am who I am. You used to like me this way." To Maggie, she explained, "I was the genuine dragon, but he didn't mind clinging to my tail and going along for the ride. We practiced being angry together in high school. Then he turned nice." She glanced at Sam and shrugged. "You should know by now scolds won't change me."

"You don't want to change." Glumly, almost sheepishly, he said to the sidewalk, "Dad was telling me about a new program through the college, a theater therapy—"

She hooted, grabbed his arm, and swung her laugh against his shoulder. "Theater therapy! What's next? Come on, Sammy. Please. Don't start on that again. Just don't start. Let's not talk about it." Clutching her forehead, she turned fast, as if she couldn't stand looking at him any longer, and settled a fierce gaze on Maggie. "So. No more Carlton College?"

Uneasiness rippled down her spine. "Not for now."

"Hmm."

Maggie stepped back toward the truck.

"Can I ask you a question?"

No. Maggie knew from experience what it would be. "Did they really do that to you?" or "Did that actually happen?" What people meant was "Are you a liar?" Variations on the same question—all painful. Sort of like asking a discharged veteran, "Did you kill anyone over there?" Maggie had mastered the blank face, had learned to ignore the questions.

But she was out of practice. She took another backward step toward the truck.

Sam put a hand on Linnie's arm.

She shook him off. "I just want to know why she left." To Maggie: "That's the only part I didn't like. Everything else . . ." She splayed and closed her hand in a conjuror's way. "Perfect. Those boys"—she shook her head—"they didn't see you coming, did they? I mean, look at you. A skinny thing." She smirked. "They probably thought, this is going to be so easy. But you called them out. Every fucking one of them. I read about it, how the police blew you off and the prosecutors didn't want to file charges, so you reported it to the university. Then the assholes, one after the other, punted out of college." She whistled. "You were so strong. Determined, you know? I can't imagine having the guts to do that. I just can't imagine." She shook her head again, bemused.

Maggie stared. She wasn't used to hearing support. "They should have gone to prison."

Linnie nodded. "They should have. But *you*. You should have stayed right where you were. Why did you leave?"

Because she hated being hated. And recognized by everyone. A notorious spectacle. "Enough people wanted me to."

"Fuck them. You shouldn't have run away."

"You're one to talk," Sam muttered. "You run away all the time."

She glanced at him coolly. "Away? Away from what? A home I've never had? I just run."

"You had Kate and me."

Linnie swallowed and ground the toe of her sneaker into a crack in the pavement. "You're better off without me."

He shook his head but didn't argue. He looked defeated. Stuffing his hands into his pockets, he frowned over his shoulder. "I've got to pack up the place."

"Moving in with your dad?"

"Yeah. Want to get your things?"

She peered up at the ugly house, distantly, as if she hardly recognized it. "No. Toss it if you don't want it."

"You sure?"

She folded her arms and nodded. The small smile she gave Maggie was wistful. "I'm glad I got to meet you. You make me think of that poem. Remember the one by Hopkins, Sam? The one Mrs. Michaels had us memorize junior year? 'It is the blight man was born for, it is Margaret you mourn for.' I loved that poem."

"And Mrs. Michaels," Sam said. "You liked her a lot."

"Oh, I *did*. She taught twelfth-grade English, too. I might have gotten her again if I hadn't dropped out." She drifted toward the car in the driveway, raised a hand, and said without turning, "Good-bye."

Sam and Maggie drove back to Wren's a couple of hours later. Between the two of them, there had been a lot of heaving, hauling, and packing but little conversation. Now, though, Sam burst out with, "Linnie says and does plenty that pisses me off." He glared at the road. "But some of what she told you wasn't true. Like how I wanted her for how she used to be—angry and nuts. *Not* true." He gave his head a furious shake and slapped the steering wheel. "She's hell on my feelings."

Maggie caught her lower lip in her teeth. She didn't know what to say. No doubt Sam liked Linnie for all sorts of reasons, good and bad. The woman was smart, beautiful . . . and what else?

Unreliable, unpredictable, unchecked.

She mumbled a sympathetic, "I'm sorry, Sam," and turned to gaze out the window. The truck whipped past maples. She absently noted the colors in the foliage: yellow, orange, red. The hues of a blaze.

Linnie. Not what she expected.

6

MAGGIE STUDIED THE shifting darkness in the loft. She was sore. Sam's furniture had weighed a ton. Her arms hurt. Her back hurt. Some of her thoughts hurt, too.

Linnie had called her strong, determined. Gutsy. Maggie exhaled a short laugh. She wasn't. She couldn't even face her own phone.

She squeezed her eyes shut. *I know something similar happened to you, I know something similar happened to—*

"Fine," she growled, kicking down the blankets. She felt around for the switch on the bedside lamp.

The cardigan was still on the floor. She shoved it aside and picked up her phone. Before she could lose her nerve, she unplugged it, thumbed the password, and began to mentally compose a response to Jane, strumming up suggestions for responsible people the girl could go to for help. *Anyone but me.*

Sitting cross-legged on the bed, she scrolled down through the unread emails to find the old one from Jane but spied something in passing, backed up, and gasped.

There was *another* email from Jane. A new one! Maggie hadn't expected this—had never guessed Jane would write again when her first message had gone unanswered.

"Shit." With a horrible sense of foreboding, she opened the email.

Jane Cannon

To: Margaret Arioli

Hi

October 2 at 11:02 PM

Hi, Margaret. I've been worrying I pissed you off with my last email, since you don't know me and since I'm bringing up something you most likely (if you're anything like me) are trying hard to forget, but today I heard you left school on a leave of absence. I don't know if you got my last message. Maybe CC suspended your email account. Anyway, if you are receiving this, I just wanted to tell you I don't blame you for going away. I want to go away, too. I hate it here. I can't concentrate, and I'm already failing half my classes, even conservation bio, and that's for my major. I avoid everyone. I'm scared all the time. How did you make it through last year? I don't think I'm going to last a month. And I still don't know if I should tell anyone about what happened. I heard you were put through the wringer, and not just by the police, but the college, too. Was it even worth it?

Was it?

Maggie let go of the phone. It landed in her lap. She dropped her head in her hands. Her skin was damp with sweat. *Is it worth it?* How many times had she asked herself that question? She dried her face with the bottom of her shirt.

Jane was right: Even the college disciplinary proceeding had been a nightmare.

She drew the covers over her head and tried not to think about it. Breathing fast, she scrambled out of bed and paced around the loft. *Don't think about it.*

But it rushed back to her.

"Where's the evidence?" The college's chief legal officer threw up his hands. "Until the police release their statements—"

"Mr. Rhine, you know full well Dean McGrath has a duty to investigate this independently," the court chair said. "The Police Department can pursue its own investigation. It doesn't have any bearing on this occasion."

He slapped the table. "Well, that's just stupid. We're pushing this off. We need to. We're talking about expulsion here, Sue; we're talking about something pretty damn big. We have an obligation to consider anything in the police statements that might influence the final decision."

Susan Brown gave Maggie an uneasy glance, then scowled at Ted Rhine. "Margaret wouldn't be here today if the police had handled her situation in an appropriate manner."

He dismissed this with a wave. "It's my job to guarantee that all parties comply with the law, and I'm telling you, we need to hold off until we get those statements."

The court chair pointed her pen at him. "And I'm telling you, Ted, to stop talking. Your job, in this context, according to the rules of the university court, is to silently observe the hearing. Legal counsel are allowed to confer with their respective parties. What they can't do is address us."

"Can we just wait until—"

Dean McGrath ran a palm over his bald head. "We are not pushing this off."

Susan Brown nodded. "We're taking care of it today."

"With one shitty-ass afternoon hearing? That's not fair." Ted Rhine folded his arms and settled a glare on Maggie. "This girl gets the better bargain. She's holding all the aces."

Maggie glared back. She wanted to cry out, "Better bargain? This hell isn't a good deal for me. And I don't hold all the aces." Or any aces. She was only trying to do the right thing. Outside of finding a shred of justice, what did she hope to win by retelling the most painful and humiliating thing that had ever happened to her?

She took a deep breath and looked away—and then realized she didn't know where to look. There were too many people in the room. People who hated her and who'd hurt her. People she'd never wanted *to see again. She settled on staring out the window and wished her-self out there, anywhere that wasn't here. Just . . . gone.*

Perched on the edge of the counter and twirling the ends of her ponytails, Ran Kita glanced toward the door when Maggie entered the bookshop and grinned. "Yay!" Her hands, still holding the ponytails' ends, flew up over her head. Then she flung back the hair and shouted toward the back of the store, "She came! Marge is here!"

Marge. Maggie winced.

"Ye gads, Ran," a low voice scolded.

Maggie whirled around.

A trim man with silver threading the hair at his temples stood by a front window, arranging the novels on display. Smiling apologetically at Maggie, he straightened, then nudged his glasses up the bridge of his nose and collected a stack of books. "You're hurting the poor girl's ears," he told Ran, and brought his armful to the counter.

"Sorry, Dad," she said cheerfully, and slipped to the floor, "but I was excited. I'm so glad you're here, Marge. I was waiting to see if you'd come. This way!" She hooked an arm through Maggie's and steered her through the bookshop. "You're all out of breath. Did you run here?" She nodded at a customer flipping through an enormous cookbook.

"Oh, no. Just from the parking lot to the store." She hadn't thought about how dark it would be at seven o'clock in the middle of October. Or how silent and empty she'd find the streets. Truthfully, for a week, she hadn't thought about much of anything. After that sleepless night eight days ago, she'd somehow tamped down the memories Jane's second email had stirred, but just barely. It was as if she'd chinked her mind with feathers, newspaper, and glue. That barrier had fallen apart this morning. She'd woken up from a nightmare and immediately suffered a panic attack. That was why she was here. She needed a distraction. A place to go.

Ran looked at her funny and steered her toward the reading nook. "Here we are!"

Three girls sat in a row on the overstuffed couch. Maggie recognized them from her first visit to the shop.

Ran presented a chair with a wave, waited until Maggie sat, then threw herself into the last available seat: a rocker. It pitched back quickly and alarmingly, then creaked forward. She planted her feet on the floor to brake the motion. "Five of us," she said with satisfaction. "Five! Now *this* is a book club." She kicked back the chair again.

"You're going to tip over that rocker and crack your head open," the girl with the many piercings said gloomily. She ran a hand over her shaved head, rubbed the tattoo on the side of her neck, and slumped into the corner of the couch.

"You sound like my mother." Like a ballerina, Ran stretched out a leg and indicated with the toe of her shoe the friend who'd just spoken. "Hope." The foot swung to the girl with the bob— "Colleen"—then toward the last one on the couch, a pretty girl hugging her legs to her chest and smiling shyly. "Julia."

Maggie didn't think Ran would manage the foot-pointing feat with her, but she did, executing a half split. "Marge."

Hope laughed grimly. "You're crazy."

"That's why you love me. Now say hello to Marge."

Greetings were exchanged, then Maggie looked around the reading nook, uncomfortable with the curiosity in the other girls' faces. "So do you all go to the same college?"

"Yeah," Hope said. "Kesley Community College."

"We didn't go to the same high school, though," Colleen said.

Julia lifted her chin up from her knees. "We're from all over the county."

"But *you* don't go to the community college," Ran observed.

Maggie treated it like a question and shook her head.

Ran smoothed the arms of the rocking chair. "Didn't think so. I never see you around. You must go to Allenport then."

"No . . ." She gave the book in her lap a fluttery tap. "I'm taking a year off."

"A gap year," Julia said reverently.

"Awesome," Colleen breathed.

"You are so *lucky*," Ran said. "I wanted to do that, but my dad wouldn't let me—said I could figure out what I wanted to do with my life while I was taking care of the basic coursework at the community college." She scowled toward the front of the store.

Maggie wasn't exactly taking a gap year. She chewed on her lower lip, thought about correcting the girls' assumption, but decided against it.

"Did you go to school around here?" Hope asked.

She shook her head. "Vermont." Then, quickly, to change the subject: "I'm staying with my aunt. She has a place by the lake." She breathed a bit easier. At least that was true.

Ran looked even more aggrieved. Leaning back in the rocking chair, she muttered, "Traveling is what *I* wanted to do, too."

Hope grunted. "Your parents must be cool, Marge."

A librarian and an accountant? Maggie didn't correct that assumption, either.

Ran sat up and nodded at the book in Maggie's lap. "What did you think about *My Name Is Lucy Barton*?"

"It was good." At least she thought it was. Honestly, she wasn't sure. She'd been so distracted while she read it. She shrugged. "I liked it."

The girls gazed at her expectantly. Kindly. Without judgment or suspicion or—worse—titillation.

And suddenly, Maggie felt intensely, almost *limply* relieved. She was doing what she'd set out to do: start over from a point of anonymity. She didn't know these girls. More important, they didn't know her.

This book club was just what she needed.

Pressing the novel against her chest, she racked her brain to think of something to say about the book and settled on the one thing she'd noticed: "Lucy's relationship with her mother was interesting, how the two are close without being . . ." She glanced around, searching for the word, and finished, "Open."

Ran hummed a note of agreement. "There was something really tender about that mother-daughter relationship . . ." She kept talking, going on about the ways the characters showed their love, and Maggie half-listened.

But the other half of her was replaying her own words: *how the two are close without being open.* Maybe that could happen in her relationships, too. Close but closed. Friendly but private. She felt a tiny thrill at the possibility and thought, *That's how I'll operate. I can be interesting Marge, enjoying a gap year, traveling, visiting my cool aunt. I can be whoever I want!*

She realized this probably wasn't the point of Strout's book—realized, too, some self-serving self-justification was going on with her interpretation.

She didn't care.

7

MAGGIE HOVERED IN the studio doorway, took a step forward, changed her mind, and stepped back. She should have waited until lunchtime to pass along the information. Her aunt was busy, working at the potter's wheel.

"Hey." Wren looked up from the pot she was making. "What's going on?"

"Thomas stopped by. He left a bag of butternut squash for you on the counter."

"That was nice. Guess what we're having for supper?"

Maggie smiled weakly. Mom wouldn't be happy if she knew the kinds of dishes her daughter and sister were calling meals, most of which came down to a single thing in a bowl. "Want me to put one in the oven?"

"In a bit. Come check out what I'm making first."

Maggie stuck her hands into her cardigan pockets and shuffled in. The aunt had never said the studio was off-limits, but until now, neither had she asked Maggie to hang out with her in here and chat. Hanging out and chatting just weren't Wren's thing, not even during mealtimes. They exchanged a few words, ate, and parted. This didn't bother Maggie. The quiet held a comfortable quality. But Maggie would have liked to have spent more time in the studio as well.

It was a cozy place, dusty and redolent with something earthy, probably the clay. Though the downcast morning grayed the windows, the room was well-lit, and the metal equipment shone cheerfully. On the worktable, the aunt had three rows going, a series of roundish white pots, then a line of knobbed lids, and finally a row of what looked like miniature cooling towers. Spouts. "Teapots?"

"Yep. In porcelain."

Maggie walked by the table. "Why don't you do all of one thing at a time?"

"I probably could for the spouts, but you've got to measure the mouth of the body to get the right size for the lid. With these." She picked up a long, two-legged tool. "Calipers." The aunt returned the tool to the work stand. "No beachcombing today?"

Maggie bent to better examine an oddly shaped knob. "Too gloomy out."

"You look good."

She glanced up, smiled. "Thanks."

Aunt Wren nodded slowly. "Rested for a change. A hell of a

lot better than you looked last week. Did you have a nice time at the book club?"

"I did," she said, and heard the surprise in her own voice. The meeting would have been worthwhile, even if it had just served as a diversion and kept her from remembering last year—and from thinking about Jane Cannon. But between that discussion about love and how funny Ran was, it had turned out better than she'd expected. The girls had even invited Maggie to go out with them afterward—to check out a friend's new apartment.

She'd mumbled an excuse. She wasn't ready for anything like that. But the meeting had been nice.

"Excellent," Wren said. "Good to make some friends around here. You must be missing your old ones."

Sara Wood immediately came to Maggie's mind. This annoyed her. She should have thought about Shayna and Jen instead. Sara wasn't a friend. She'd abandoned Maggie—and not only at that disastrous party. After the party, too. When the police had questioned Sara and the college had gotten involved and the battle had started, every person in Carlton, including Sara Wood, had taken a side.

And she didn't take mine. Maggie shook her head. She still couldn't believe it—couldn't get *why*.

Don't think about it. Hugging herself, she turned quickly and crossed the room to a shelf of finished vases. She forced herself to focus on them. "Your supply's dwindling."

"Sam's been busy shipping and delivering."

She nodded. She hadn't seen Sam since she'd helped him clear out the apartment . . . on the day she'd met Linnie. Maggie frowned out the window at the gray lake.

"What are you thinking about?" the aunt asked.

"Linnie."

"Hmm." She slipped her hands into a bucket of water and began to rub off the porcelain. Around her wrists, the clay made her skin look like the cracked surface of a dry riverbed. "That girl had a rough start, saw some bad things happen to her mom." She dried her hands on the towel hanging off the work stand and added quietly, "And experienced some ugly shit herself." She wagged her head. "To know love and safety early on? I don't think we can overestimate the power of that, how it gives a person a steady foundation and the means to handle trials later." Her smile was sad. "You had that. That's partly why you pulled through last year like you did—with moxie. It was kind of remarkable, that strength."

Maggie didn't know what to say. She was astonished. First Linnie, and now Wren—another person pointing out her strength. How ironic that that was their impression—the opposite of her own. By the end of the school year, she'd felt utterly flattened, sapped, wrecked. Scared and scarred.

The aunt was saying, ". . . and that business with her mom went on for eight years. By the time social services got involved, Linnie was too troubled to last in any one foster home. She got shuffled from place to place."

"Four in all," Sam said.

Maggie jumped.

He was standing in the doorway to the mixing room.

"You startled me," Maggie said, her hand pressed to her chest.

"Sorry, Meg."

"Maggie." Wren rolled her eyes. "For the love of God, Sam, learn my niece's name."

He smiled sheepishly and palmed a plastic bag of blue powder, as if he were weighing it. His smile wilted. Eyeing the chemical, he murmured, "Poor Linnie. Two of the foster placements were shitholes. They came with their own unique crappiness." He blew a sigh and tossed his head. Briskly, to Maggie: "Didn't think you'd find me here, working on a Sunday, did you? Your aunt's a tyrant."

Wren smirked. "Sam's helping me catch up."

"I didn't see your truck out back," Maggie said to him.

"Pickup's in the shop. I walked." She must have continued to look surprised, because he smiled. "I'm not *that* out of shape. It only takes ten minutes."

"Didn't you know Thomas is my neighbor?" the aunt asked. "That's how we got to know each other. When I bought this place—back in the good old days when my sculptures were raking in cash—the Blakes were relieved. There had been some talk in town about using this property for a casino, of all things. Sam's folks were glad I purchased it."

"Grateful," he said.

She smiled. "We became fast friends. Muriel and I used to take yoga together. She was an artist, too. We even collaborated on some projects." The aunt gazed distractedly at the teapot body on the wheel and then, with a little shake of her head, picked up the wire tool and ran it under the pot.

"They liked to co-mother," Sam said with a lopsided smile, "the two taking turns telling me what to do."

Aunt Wren sniffed. "You were a handful."

"I kept you busy." He raised the small bag. "We're low on cobalt carbonate. Want me to add it to the order?"

She nodded. "And chromium oxide. I need to marble some clay."

Maggie wandered to the windows. She considered both ends of the stretch of beach, the short bluff and the long. "Which side is yours?"

Sam went to stand beside her. "We've got a little beach west of here. Nothing like Wren's. Mostly what we have is that." He pointed to the long end, where the low cliff jutted over the water. "Devil's Tongue, it's called. Dad has an awesome old map from the early nineteenth century, with that name scrawled across the bluff, along with 'Vile Graveyard of Many Ships.' The reefs go for almost a mile into the lake. They fucked up the barges and boats coming in."

"Sank them?"

"Or trapped them. The visible part of the bluff's scary enough, rocky and steep. Not worth investigating—believe me, I've tried—and no point, really. The fishing there sucks."

"So the bluff is yours?"

He shrugged. "As much as something like that can belong to anyone."

Maggie studied the peninsula. Devil's Tongue. A good name for a dangerous place.

Later, Maggie drifted outside. The sun, which hadn't bothered to show up all day, made a belated appearance in the evening—a beautiful entrance, swollen and sinking in a pool of pink and violet. Now it rested, like a golden fruit, on the end of the rocky bluff.

A wind unfurled off the lake and made her shiver. Drawing the cardigan more tightly across her chest, she considered what Sam had mentioned about Devil's Tongue and then thought about what her aunt had said before that—about Linnie, about Maggie . . .

Strong. It was nice that anyone would see her in that way.

She just didn't think it was true. How could it be? Her mind was falling apart. Falling *back* . . . whenever and wherever. She couldn't keep her head on straight.

Plus, if Maggie were *really* strong, she wouldn't leave Jane Cannon hanging. She'd write back and help her. Even if the helping hurt.

But she didn't.

Dread kept her away from her phone. It kept her up most of the night, too.

On Monday morning, she ignored her exhaustion and threw herself into another cleaning frenzy. Starting at the top of the cabin, she scrubbed the windows; took down light fixtures, giving them a good washing before refastening them to the sockets; and did *not* think about Jane Cannon. She wasn't up to worrying about the girl. *I just can't get into that shit right now.* Maybe she'd be ready eventually. At some point. But not today. *Sorry, Jane.*

She reached her last room, the kitchen, by midafternoon, and got to work, just as Sam's truck roared out of the driveway.

The aunt was in there, sipping a cup of coffee. "He's picking up Kate from school," she explained.

"His truck's fixed?" Maggie had spotted it first thing this morning, parked in its usual location behind the cabin.

Wren nodded, smiling wryly at the bucket of cleaning supplies and rags. "I can always tell when you're trying to avoid something. You start cleaning like crazy." Her smile widened when she took in Maggie's expression. "Am I right?"

She answered with a noncommittal sniff and stepped onto a chair to reach the pendant light over the table.

"Thought so," the aunt murmured.

"I didn't confirm your theory."

"No need." Wren sauntered out of the room.

She made a face and began to loosen the little screws. A layer of furry grime covered the glass shade. "Your fixtures are disgustingly dirty," she said loudly.

The aunt's laugh drifted in from the hallway.

Later in the day, while Maggie and Wren were finishing supper, Sam returned to the cabin, Kate in tow. "She said she missed you," he told Wren.

"But not her." His daughter pointed at Maggie.

"*Kate*," Sam scolded. "Be nice. She's nice to *you*."

The girl shrugged. "But she's not my mother," she declared warningly.

Maggie flared her eyes at her plate of buttered noodles. *Thank God.*

The aunt chuckled, sat back in her chair, and hoisted Kate onto her lap. She gave her a bear hug, then bounced her on her knees. "Want to play with the clay? Want to make something?"

"A piggy bank."

"A *piggy bank*? That might be tricky. How about a bowl? For your Froot Loops? Would you like that?"

"Yes!" Kate clapped, then pitched forward and squealed when Wren tickled her.

Maggie poked at her pasta with her fork and took in the laughing exchange with a bitter sensation. "Can I make something, too?" she blurted.

Wren, Sam, and Kate turned to stare at her blankly.

"Well, sure," the aunt said. "I mean, yeah. Why not? If you want to."

Maggie was miffed. *Jeez. Rein in the enthusiasm, why don't you?* Swallowing her irritation, she got to her feet. "I'll go change."

"Put on something you don't mind getting stained," the aunt suggested. "Red iron oxide is murder on clothes."

"Mine are bigger than yours," Kate said.

The little girl was standing by the wheel and coolly eyeing Maggie's . . . bowl? Cup? Hollowed-out blob? Maggie slouched over the wheel, raised a limp hand to shove away a curl that had escaped her braid, and then, remembering the current state of that hand, dropped it to her lap instead. It didn't matter if she left a splat on her jeans. They were filthy.

The pot, big enough to hold a strawberry, three blueberries, max, was the single outcome of two hours of repeated failures. This one would have gone the mushy way of the others if the aunt hadn't taken pity on her and provided some hands-on assistance.

Maggie couldn't believe how horrible she was at this. "I suck."

"That's not a nice word," Kate said, circling the table where she'd put her finished creations: three—*three!*—pots.

"Sorry. Awful. I'm awful."

Sam shrugged. "Why do you think I never wheedle wheel time out of Wren?"

"You're not a potter?" Maggie asked.

"I like to think of myself as a sculptor. This though . . ." He flapped a hand over the wheel and shook his head.

"It gets easier with practice," Wren said, "just like everything else."

"I thought it'd be relaxing," Maggie said, arching her sore back.

"Ha. Not at first." The aunt scraped a pile of mangled clay off Maggie's work stand. "Later, like years later, when you're really good"—she spread the wet clay on a wedging board—"you might begin to feel all Zen and meditative and one with the world, but early on, you're mostly—"

"Frustrated," Sam suggested.

"Humbled," Maggie said.

Kate grimaced at Maggie's pot. "Bad."

With a laugh, Sam rose. "Come on, Kate. We need to get you washed up. It's a school night."

After the two left, Maggie carried the tools to the sink, turned on the faucet, and rubbed the clay off a pin tool.

The aunt was reshelving some of her pieces in a plastic-lined cabinet to make room for Kate's and Maggie's pots. She had two of these cabinets—damp boxes, she'd called them. Wren smiled over her shoulder. "Did you have fun?"

"Let's just say I don't foresee a future as a wealthy potter."

"There's no such thing as a wealthy potter."

"You're doing okay, aren't you?"

"I'm staying afloat. But even in this poor part of New York, lakefront property costs a ton in taxes. My real bread and butter are the sculptures."

Maggie glanced at the larger damp box. It was closed, but behind the front curtain of heavy plastic, there was a murky shadow. She'd noticed it before. A sculpture, it looked like. Why wasn't it finished yet? Was Aunt Wren even working on it? Maggie never saw it out of the cabinet. She turned back to the sink to rinse the sponge and chamois. After squeezing them dry, she reached for the soiled bucket.

What a huge mess for one ridiculous little pot. "I didn't think throwing on the wheel would be so hard." In fact, when the arrangements for this visit had been made, she'd figured pottery was exactly what she'd be doing. No doubt her mother had expected that, too: Maggie would heal, strengthen, and move forward with the help of clay projects (and quiet and solitude). Granted, Maggie hadn't thought about the assault—or Jane Cannon, for that matter—while the clay had wobbled and flailed, but that was only because keeping every lump from flying off the wheel had demanded so much concentration. "This isn't exactly art therapy," she muttered, shutting off the water.

The aunt grinned. "Is that what you thought you'd be getting here?"

Maggie gave her a dark look.

Wren sputtered a laugh. She finished shelving the pots, then carefully brought down the folds of heavy plastic.

"You know, Maggie, I didn't invite you here just for your sake. I was thinking about myself, too." She clipped the sides shut.

Maggie waited for an explanation.

But Wren only nodded and left.

She stared at the empty place where the aunt had stood, while the washed bucket dripped, sending water along her arm to her elbow and down to the concrete floor.

Later, in the quiet of the loft, Maggie sat on the floor and picked up her phone.

She shoved a curl out of her face. Her hair was still wet from her shower. Through her mouth, she inhaled and exhaled slowly. *I can do this. I only have to write back, give her a little advice, tell her who to contact. I'm making this harder than it has to be.* Quickly, before she could change her mind, she scrolled through her messages. She'd skip over the new ones and just take care of Jane's.

But one of the new emails *was* Jane's.

Maggie stared at it, her thumb poised over the girl's name. "Not *again*."

With a groan, she tapped open the email.

Jane Cannon

To: Margaret Arioli

Me again

October 20 at 2:14 AM

I'm exhausted and depressed and will probably regret sending you another email when I get out of bed tomorrow. I don't even know if you're receiving these, but if you are, I wish you would write. You'd understand what I'm going through. I keep thinking about what happened, what happened at first and then what happened afterward, like how when I went to the police station to press charges, they put me in a room with two men for questioning. Couldn't they have found a woman detective to hear me out? It was humiliating. It felt like an interrogation. The one guy wondered if I had a boyfriend, and when I asked him what that had to do with anything, he shrugged and told me that a lot of girls go to parties, drink too much, and make bad decisions. He said, "Then they panic because they don't want to get in trouble with their boyfriends." That made me so mad, I just left. Can you believe he said that to me? Can you believe what he was implying? After what I went through 48 hours beforehand? I couldn't believe it. I still can't.

Maggie put down the phone with a trembling hand, rose, and crossed to the window overlooking the woods. Her heart was pounding. She could almost *hear* it pounding.

Stars shone in the trees, like strings of lights. The naked branches formed a frayed canopy that was one shade darker than the sky—a ragged blackness beneath indigo blue. The world from here looked like a far-reaching bruise. She put her hands to her cheeks. They were wet.

When she returned to the floor, she reentered her password, hit REPLY, and wrote:

I'm sorry I didn't write back sooner, Jane.

She put down the phone and scrubbed her damp palms on her thighs. She picked up the phone again.

I've been in rough shape. But I know what you're going through, and I feel sad for you.

She went back to Jane's email, reread it, and then, just briefly, squeezed her eyes shut. Gritting her teeth, she made herself continue.

I had a bad experience with the police, too. They weren't helpful. They

The phone slipped out of her trembling hand. She curled up on the floor and tucked in her head.

"What do you hope to get out of reporting this?" the officer asked. The station door swung open, and he looked away from Maggie to smile at the uniformed man trudging in. "What? No supper for us tonight, Gary?" he teased.

The other officer shrugged and stomped the snow from his boots. "No money." He gave Maggie a curious look as he walked past where she sat on the bench.

"Did you hear me?"

Disoriented and in shock, she looked up at the officer. He was frowning down at her again. "I—I don't know what you mean."

"Listen." He rolled back on his heels and scrubbed his face with a hand before sighing, "These situations . . . they're hard to prove. People are going to wonder if you were drinking at that party, if you were making out with the guys beforehand—"

"With all of them?"

"Sure. This was a Tigers party. You didn't think you were attending a Baptist youth group meeting, right?" Impatiently, he shook his head. "Did you try to get away? Did you tell them to stop? Okay, okay. But did you scream it—loud enough for someone to hear you?"

"I—I don't know. I guess I didn't. I was afraid people would walk downstairs and—and see me like . . . that."

"Now, come on, don't cry. I'll grab Gary, and we'll take care of the interview and try to clear up this mess. We'll have to record it, just so you know. Hey, now. Stop crying, okay? I'm only trying to help."

8

THE AUNT HEFTED a mound of clay onto the scale, scooped off a chunk, eyed the weight, and removed a bit more. "When's your next book club meeting?" she asked abruptly.

"Hmm?" Maggie raised her chin from her palm. Her head seemed to weigh a ton.

"The book club?" the aunt repeated slowly, as if Maggie had a shaky grasp of English. "When is the next meeting?" She strode over to her wheel.

Maggie peered around blearily. When was she supposed to go back to the bookstore? "Soon," she said. "On a Saturday." Hard to picture herself going. She wasn't up for it.

"As in this Saturday? Some Saturday next month? A Saturday in a year from now?"

"The last Saturday of the month, I think." Maggie squinted out the window. "What's today?"

"Thursday."

So nine days from now. It wasn't an actual meeting, but Ran had asked the members to meet at the shop so they could check out the latest releases and brainstorm ideas for their next read.

They can do that without me.

"I'm worried about you. Three days now you've gone around looking not so good." She blindly patted the chunk of clay into a ball, her stern gaze on Maggie. "Flat-out bad, actually." She fell into her seat, slapped the clay onto the wheel, and planted her hands on her knees. "I think I'd better call your mom."

"Oh no." She straightened, alarmed. "Don't call Mom."

The aunt answered with a disapproving hum and plunged her hands into the bucket of water. After stepping on the pedal and shooting the wheel-head into a whirring spin, she began centering. "Do you want to talk about it?"

Maggie shook her head. She did not want to talk about it, about *any* of it: Jane's situation or Jane's emails or how Maggie couldn't pull her shit together long enough to manage a reply. Talking about Jane was too much like talking about herself.

And that was the whole problem.

"You're a mess. Either jumpy or comatose, but continuously morose. Here we have a stretch of warm October weather, and you don't spend a single hour outside beachcombing." Without smiling, she quipped, "And everyone knows how much Margaret loves her beach glass. What's going on?"

"Nothing."

Wren jerked up her chin, like a header, shooting Maggie's lie somewhere else, then she just waited, eyebrows raised.

Maggie hunched lower in the clay-smeared chair.

"Come on. Tell me. Maybe I can—"

A thud resounded from the mixing room, followed by an explosive "Shit!"

"Eek." Wren leaned back from the spinning wheel and called, "What happened?"

Sam appeared in the backroom doorway. "My *project*." He clutched his head. "I dropped the base of it!"

The aunt returned to the wheel, her expression decidedly unsympathetic. "I warned you, and after all this time, you ought to know better. You can't transport unfired sculptures." To Maggie: "Until it comes out of a kiln, clay's basically mud. Wet mud, dry mud"—she shrugged—"doesn't take anything to bend or crack or chip it." She opened the centered mound. "Sam, Sam, Sam . . ." Her head wagged. "You need to finish that project here."

"How can I?" He stomped into the studio. "I watch Kate every evening now. That's my only time to work on the stupid thing, so I *have* to get it home. It's not smart, bringing her over to the studio and letting her run around and play, just so I can sculpt. Too many things in here could hurt a little girl."

Maggie grunted. *Or vice versa.*

The aunt ran the wire under the bowl. "I can help watch her."

"You've got a deadline on that thing." He swatted the air in the direction of the closed damp box. "I can't ask you to babysit." His exhalation carried a sound that was like a whimper. "You're way too busy."

The aunt murmured something about making time and chipping in.

Maggie dipped even lower in the chair and avoided Sam's gaze, half-wishing she wore a sign that read, DON'T ASK ME, a generic notification to ward off anyone asking for anything or anyone asking *about* anything: Jane, the aunt, Sam, her mother, Linnie, Ran, *everyone*. A big PLEASE LEAVE ME ALONE.

"I need to get going. Dad's teaching tonight." Glancing over his shoulder, Sam growled in disgust. "I'll have to start over on the damn base now." He rubbed his forehead with both hands, smearing a powdery white over his brown skin. "If I can just get the other half home without breaking it . . ."

He looked so defeated and miserable that Maggie couldn't help it—she felt bad for him. "Is it something I can hold on my lap?" she asked reluctantly. Holding she could do. Babysitting Kate—not so much. "I'll just walk home afterward." She perked up a little. Exercise would probably be good for her—fresh air to clear her thoughts. Plus, if she left with Sam, she could avoid the aunt who was now frowning at her, as if she'd suddenly remembered the interrupted heart-to-heart.

His face brightened. "That would be awesome. Thank you, Meg—um, Maggie."

"If you wreck your piece, don't say I didn't warn you." Wren dropped the wire by her bucket and sighed. On a kinder note: "Why don't you take off tomorrow morning? That'll give you a few hours to sculpt while Kate's at school. You can come back after lunch."

"You sure?"

She nodded and cast the closed damp box a glum glance.

"Not much for you to do here anyway while I work on that thing." Wren waved away Sam's thanks and watched Maggie drag herself to her feet. "Catch you later." She widened her eyes meaningfully, a we-have-unfinished-business look.

Maggie frowned. *Not if I can help it.*

The aunt smiled. "And thanks for helping Sam, Megummaggie."

The ride to the house next door seemed to take a long time. Sam's project was big and busy, a conglomeration of jagged corners and voluptuous folds, and it was slightly malleable, too. ("Not quite leather-hard," he'd said, situating it carefully on her lap.) Maggie was afraid to move.

As close as her face was to the groggy clay, she couldn't get a good idea of what the sculpture was supposed to be but didn't dare maneuver it. When Sam turned off the rutted Ash Drive and onto the slightly smoother length of the parkway, she finally blurted, "What is this?"

"A brain"—Sam gave his sculpture a pained look—"under duress. Not literally, of course. Like a metaphor for an internal geography, filled with bad shit."

Huh. Maggie frowned at the piece.

He smiled wryly. "At least that's what it's meant to be. Not one of my subtler creations, but at least it showcases technique. I'm working on my portfolio for college." At Maggie's interested glance, he continued, "My top choice is south of here—Alfred University. It has one of the best ceramic-art departments in the country. Your aunt went there. I'd like to go at least part-time, if

I can figure out how to manage the commute and the financial aid and my work schedule. And Kate."

"That's a lot to figure out." Crazy to think he'd been juggling Kate and work and everything else since he was seventeen. Talk about pressure. Maggie frowned at the rough clay. Was that why Linnie had left? Did everything just get too . . . hard?

He sighed. "Yeah."

They turned right onto Wayside Lane, a dead end that ran parallel to the aunt's drive. It was so thick with foliage that Maggie couldn't make out the lake through the flickering orange. Along the short passage, the mesh of branches and leaves formed a shadowy tunnel, but it ended brilliantly, opening to a sun-filled property and a jewel of a house, a good-sized place, not a rickety cabin like Wren's, and modern. Its many windows gave the impression that it was comprised entirely of glass. It reflected the molten glow of the evening sun and the light-shattered gold of the maples and the sky and the lake—blue on fire to the west and rumpled water twinkling along the north. The lake wore a gently curving sheen until it met the base of Devil's Tongue, where it broke apart in shimmering explosions.

The beauty was arresting. For the first time in days, Maggie's spirits lifted. "Wow . . . how beautiful."

"Thanks." He opened his door. "Don't move. I'll come around."

Taking her directions from Sam, who trudged behind her lugging his sculpture, Maggie hurried ahead to open a side door that led into a dim garage, shut the door after him, and trotted up three steps to do the same with another door. She followed him into a mudroom, lined with shoe cubbies, coat hooks, and two more doors.

The mudroom opened to a tall-ceilinged great room. The sweeping area encompassed the living and dining spaces, as well as the kitchen. Maggie hardly spared it a glance. The world through the windows demanded her attention. Sun, sky, lake, and trees—the landscape made the inside, however awesome, undeniably inferior.

Maggie whistled softly. "This place is all about out there, isn't it?"

"My mom's plan. Dad used to tease her about it, how they could have saved a ton of money and just camped out under the stars." He headed for a door off the dining area, and Maggie hurried to catch up with him and open it. "Thanks." He trudged into a room—a combined office and workshop—and gently perched the sculpture on a butcher-block counter.

A voice from overhead called sharply, "Sam?"

"Down here."

Maggie heard footsteps on the stairs and a fast stride across the great room. Thomas Blake appeared. He gave Maggie a distracted nod, then scowled at his son. "I'm late for work."

"Sorry, I was—"

His father, already half-jogging toward the mudroom, held up a hand without turning. "We'll talk about it later." The door to the garage slammed shut.

Sam winced. "Great. He's pissed." Then he hollered, "Kate?" When no one answered, he strode out of the workshop toward the foot of the stairs, beckoning Maggie along with a hauling motion of his arm. "Daddy's home!" When silence greeted this announcement, he called even louder, "Kate?"

"I'm *busy*," his daughter said.

"Doing what?"

"Writing a book. Jeez!"

He smiled at Maggie and started climbing the stairs. "Come on up."

She followed slowly. Kate wasn't going to be thrilled to see her, but this house was cool. Maggie wanted to check out the second floor. To her left, framed maps, brown with age and ragged-edged, decorated the staircase wall. She paused to examine one that she recognized by the label on a bluff: *Devil's Tongue*. The elegant script curved across the protrusion. No lanes or drives bisected this portion of Lake Ontario's shoreline. No parkway ran parallel to the water. Except for a thin horizontal road marked *The Ridge* at the very bottom of the map, everything south of the water, for what must have been miles and miles, was dense forest. Across the sketched canopy flowed two words, and Maggie read them aloud: "Black North."

"That's what the settlers called this area. It was a wilderness for a long time, decades after the Holland Land Company sold off its parcels southwest of here."

"How come?"

"Probably because of the quality of the land. Swampy." He stuffed his hands into his jacket pockets and trudged up the rest of the stairs.

The landing opened directly to a den, its couches and chairs upholstered in oatmeal chenille, the wood of its tables and bookshelves painted white. The second-story rooms shot off from this neat space. Sam headed for a light-filled doorway, but Maggie lagged behind to peer into another room, most likely, given its size, Thomas's. Windows made up two of the walls, and one side overlooked the water. From the doorway, she could just make out the bluff below and a stretch of sand to its right. The sun had set, and the swelling darkness blurred the terrain's edges. In the bedroom, the elegant furniture looked colorless in the muted light.

She backed away, then walked through the den in the direction of Sam's voice.

"What are you working on?" he was saying.

Just shy of the room, she paused. Sam was crouched by Kate, who sat cross-legged on the floor by a frilly canopy bed, its pink and yellow blankets and pillows scrunched and askew. Tons of toys filled the room. *Spoiled*, Maggie concluded.

Red crayon poised over a drawing, Kate grinned up at her dad. "A book about poisonous kitties."

"Cool."

He turned to smile at Maggie.

When Kate followed his gaze, her smile collapsed, and her eyes narrowed. "What's *she* doing here?"

"Use your manners," her father chided. "Say hello." He started picking up toys and tossing them into a corner basket.

"Hi." Profound unfriendliness weighted the syllable.

Maggie responded with what she hoped passed for a genuine smile. "How's it going?" After sidling into the room, she gingerly patted the girl's head.

Kate jerked back and glared.

102

Yikes. Maggie crossed her arms, tucked her hands into her armpits, and glanced down at the splayed book. Across an unlined page, Kate had drawn a few cats, stick figures except for their faces. Three huge heads sported angry feline eyes, bristling whiskers, and giant ears. "Writing a book?"

"It's a diary." She slapped the book shut and planted a fist on the cover. "Private."

Maggie smiled tightly. *Oh, good, because I didn't want to read it anyway.*

Sam was making the bed, pulling up the sheet and smoothing it flat. He frowned over his shoulder. "Jeez, Kate. Be nice."

The girl kept scowling.

"Diary," Maggie repeated with a nod. She stepped back but couldn't resist murmuring, "I thought you said it was a story about poisonous kitties . . ."

"It is. I *am* a poisonous kitty."

"Ah. That makes sense."

"My name is Splash. And this is *my* diary. No one can read it unless I say so. My dad can read it. My mom can read it. (And you are *not* my mom.) Grandpa can read it." She paused, as if deliberating, then added, "Wren can read it, too. That's all."

"Except for you," Maggie said lightly. "You forgot yourself."

"Well, duh. It's mine. *My* diary."

Maggie turned and rolled her eyes at a bookcase. *I don't want to steal a peek at your stupid diary.*

Sam flung the edge of a pink quilt across the bed and straightened it. "There's a nice way to talk to company, Kate, and how you're talking isn't it. Why don't you show Maggie your new American Girl—" His phone chimed. He dug it out of his jacket pocket, checked the screen, and briefly closed his eyes. On his way out of the room, he answered tersely, "What's up, Linnie?"

Maggie and Kate stared after him.

"Right now?" he demanded, gripping the back of the couch. "Can't Kyle go get you?" After a moment of listening, he breathed a humorless laugh. "So why don't you just crash there?" He began to pace, head lowered, his free hand tugging at the hair by his nape. Halting, he squawked, "*What?* You can't do that. We're not paying rent anymore. Shit, we haven't even paid up on the rent we owe." He fell silent for a few seconds, then snapped, "Well, no wonder. I don't blame him. He probably figured you'd pull a stunt like this." He blew a loud sigh. "Listen. I'm beat, Dad's teaching, and I've got Kate."

As if the sound of her name was her cue, Kate sprang up and bounded into the den. "I'll go! We can both go! Let's go get her!"

Dread filled Maggie. She should have left when Thomas had. She did not belong in this drama. She didn't *want* to belong.

Kate kept begging her dad.

Sam gave Maggie a pleading glance.

Note to self: Avoid Kate at all costs. Maggie edged closer to the girl, mentally scrambling for a way to tempt her back into the room. "Hey, Kate. What's that thing? You know . . . the new thing your dad mentioned?"

The girl didn't even look at her. "Let's get Mom! Let's go!"

"Sh." He put a hand on his daughter's shoulder. "Sorry, Kate, but we can't do that." To Linnie, he said in a bitter rush, "I'm not dragging my daughter out that way, and I seriously wish you'd start making some better decisions. You're—you're—" He breathed quickly, almost a pant, and finished, "*Impossible.*"

Maggie, standing outside the doorway to Kate's room, could hear Linnie's answer: a trill of laughter.

Sam growled. "Fuck you." He ended the call, threw the phone on the couch, then fell beside his cell, the top of his head landing in his palms.

Kate slipped to his side.

"Sorry I swore," he said gruffly.

"Where's Mom? Is she okay? Are we going to get her?"

"She's fine." He cleared his throat, straightened, and tried for an assertive tone: "I'm sure she'll be fine." He glanced at Maggie and said wearily, "She's stuck in the old neighborhood—went there to hang out at this total loser's place. I guess things got crazy fast. Neighbor came over, complained about the noise, threatened to call the cops. Linnie tries to avoid the police"—his glower briefly made room for a bitter smile—"for good reason. So she left, figured she'd just stroll down the street, over to the apartment we used to rent, and pass out there." With sudden fierceness, he flung his head back against the couch and glared at the ceiling. "Unbelievable." He rubbed his eyes. "Anyway, the landlord changed the locks, and now she's stranded. She does this to me. This . . . *shit*"— he backhanded the air—"all the time. It's like a test. 'If I hang off this branch, if I cling to the cliff's edge, will someone save me? Am I worth saving?'" He groaned. "I don't know if it's a conscious thing, but that's her routine. It sucks. And I am *so sick of it*."

Maggie nodded. She wasn't sure what to say or even if she should say anything. His little kid, perfectly still and wide-eyed, was staring straight at him.

He glanced at her, too, and regret crossed his face. He slumped on the couch, head in his hands again.

"I'm scared." Kate began to cry. "I want Mom. I want her right now."

He drew her close and wrapped her in his arms, while murmuring soothing shushes and "She's fine . . . don't worry . . . nothing to worry about."

Maggie sighed. Doomed. "Go ahead and get her, if you want. I'll watch Kate."

Sam glanced up hopefully.

But Kate-the-sad-stray disappeared. "No way!" she shouted.

Maggie flinched. It was embarrassing how much this kid loathed her.

Kate flew off the couch. "I want to go with you! I'm not staying with her! I *hate* her! She is not my mom!" She stomped around the den, fists flailing, tears flying.

Sam stood. "That's enough!"

Kate stormed into her room, slammed the door, then opened it again to deliver some encore door-slamming.

He shot after her and grabbed the knob. "Cut it out."

"I won't stay with her. She is *not* my mother. You can't make her be my mother!"

Maggie shuffled toward the staircase.

At last, the door was shut, and it stayed shut, but sobbing persisted on the other side. Sam gave Maggie a mortified glance. "Aren't we one big happy family?" He ran a hand down his face. "I'm sorry."

Maggie shook her head. "I'll go."

"I don't blame you. I'd go, too. But it's getting dark. Sure you don't want to wait until Dad's back? Then I can drop—"

"No. I mean I'll go get Linnie, see if I can find her"—she shrugged—"if you want to lend me your truck."

He stared. "Do you remember how to get there?"

She nodded.

His features sagged in relief. "Thank you. I wouldn't be surprised if she heads to Caleb's. He lives down the street from the old place. You'll know which house is his. He and his housemates always have friends over Thursday nights. I'll give Wren the heads-up, let her know I'll be getting you home after Dad's back from his class." He rubbed his nape. "You sure you're okay with this?"

"Yeah." No. Not really. But she'd rather look for Linnie than stay here with Kate.

9

MAGGIE LIKED DRIVING Sam's truck—or more specifically, she liked driving it *fast*. Through the open window, the cold air, smelling like leaves, blew across her warm face. She sank into an electric mindlessness, a state she recognized as both an achievement and, aided by how fast she flew down Redman, the start of a good emotion. A rare one. Freedom.

She was getting away.

There was a clean emptiness to this place, a smoothness that made speeding easy. The cloudless sky poured stars all the way down to the flat fields. Without mountains or even hills to embellish the horizon, the lake country was like a hand splayed to palm the night.

When she neared Allenport, however, she lost the happy rush.

Her heart thudded faster; her skin prickled. Main Street was busy.

Stopped at a light, she glanced over at a busy café. Its windows framed a space filled with diners. On either side of the café stood bars, their windows inky except for the neon beer signs. Most of the shops were closed for the night. Outside Tin Tavern, a few people talked, and on the steps leading up to a tattoo parlor, four lanky guys sat and smoked—college students starting their weekend early, Maggie guessed. She wondered if Ran and the book club girls were out tonight. And she wondered about Jane Cannon. *What's she doing right now?* How *is she doing?*

Maggie gripped the wheel tighter. She wished she could shake the guilt. The light changed, and she drove on, only to brake a few seconds later at the sight of a figure waiting on a corner. The woman hurried across the street, raising her hand in thanks. A streetlight illuminated her, the high cheekbones, the flash of red hair. She was young, younger than Maggie had first thought. Young and alone.

She drove on but glanced in the rearview mirror. When the girl got into the passenger side of an idling sedan, Maggie started breathing again.

At the corner of Main and Lincoln, Sam's old street, she stopped at another light. In front of the movie theater, a couple argued. Opposite the theater, a few girls laughed their way out of The Mason Jar. Two guys, wearing short sleeves despite the evening chill, crossed the street, the shorter of them calling toward the giggling girls, "Time for McGregor's?" Both men's gazes veered

Maggie's way when they passed the front of the truck. She pretended she didn't notice.

Rolling up her window, she had the grim thought, *Everyone here . . . hunters or prey.* Then she gave her head a toss and flexed her hands against the wheel, distractedly noting her body's rigidness, the dampness of her skin. When the light turned green, she waited for a car to pass, then turned left and took a deep breath. *Just find Linnie.*

House lights brightened Lincoln Street. People were outside, but there was no traffic, so Maggie was able to investigate at a snail's pace. She leaned forward to peer at the duplexes and small apartment buildings (shabby places, student housing probably) and looked for Linnie's blond hair and full figure. When her search caught pedestrians' attention, they stared back, annoyed or pleased, depending—well, depending on a lot of things.

At the end of the street, she pulled the truck into a crumbling driveway to turn around and scan the other side of the road. No one looked like Linnie. With a sting of unease, she slowed when she passed the dark-windowed place Sam and Linnie used to rent and then rolled her shoulders to try to unknot them.

Near the movie theater, she turned around and repeated the search, all the way to the block's end. One house there was a possibility. She parked to consider it.

Lights shone in the smudged windows. No curtains concealed the inside, and people appeared in passing. On the front porch, a few more drank and smoked, leaning against the posts and railings.

She got out of the pickup, shut the door, and stuffed Sam's keys into her cardigan pocket. Her phone was in there, too, and her mind grazed the matter of Jane Cannon before settling on the situation ahead of her, the house of strangers.

It's just a party. Jesus, Maggie. It's supposed to be fun. Sara Wood's words. Maggie stumbled on the sidewalk.

Approaching the porch, she blotted her forehead with her arm. She felt . . . muddled. As if conch shells were pressed to her ears, muting other sounds with their waves. As if she'd fallen into those waves. Her hand trembled. She wrapped it around Sam's keys.

The people on the porch eyed her with unmasked curiosity.

She focused on the person closest to the door, a woman with dark hair in a high ponytail and a hand clutching her coat at the throat.

"I'm looking for Linnie . . ." Linnie who? What was Linnie's last name? Why hadn't she asked Sam this beforehand? Lamely, she started again. "I'm looking for someone named Linnie. Do you know her?"

The woman with the ponytail and someone across from her shared a wry glance. She raised her Labatt Blue to indicate the door. "In there." She took a sip. "Somewhere."

Maggie exhaled. "Thanks." She trudged up the stairs and slipped inside.

The place was crowded. Talk and laughter mixed with music, and it took her a moment to recognize an Ariana Grande song. To her left, smoke clouded the living room. People lounged on three couches, mismatched and ratty, around a table cluttered with drinks. Somewhere in the house, a dog barked. The dining room to her right had a table that was missing its chairs. Four men were talking and drinking by the table.

No one in the living room seemed to register her arrival, but the tallest guy in the dining room huddle did. His eyebrows shot up. He smiled. "How's it going?" He drank what was left of his beer.

Maggie just nodded and folded her arms. "Do you know where I can find Linnie?"

"Not sure." He raised his hand, an apologetic gesture. "Can I get you a drink?"

"No. No, thanks. I just need to find Linnie." *I need to find Sara. Sara Wood. Do you know her?*

"Hey, Tim." He tapped the guy next to him with his bottle.

Tim turned in a staggering way.

"Where's Linnie?"

"Basement, maybe."

"They still playing beer pong?"

"As long as there be beer, young Caleb, there be pong."

Caleb. While Tim snorted a laugh at his own comment, Maggie wondered if this was the guy that Sam had mentioned. Caleb rolled his eyes at Tim and said something about dumb jokes.

She retreated a few steps. The door to the basement was probably in the kitchen. Should she ask to make sure or just find her own way?

"Who are you with?" Caleb asked.

She took another step back. Waves slammed in her ears. *I was with my friend, but I can't find her.* "My boyfriend . . ." *Jesus, too loud, shut up.* In a higher pitch, she added quickly, "He's a cop."

"Oh." He looked at her funny. "Okay?" His wide shoulders came up. "I'll show you the basement."

Maggie followed him through the dining room. She stared

straight ahead. She didn't want to know if anyone was studying her. She didn't want to make eye contact. *Yeah, you. Come over here. Free shots for Matt's special guests. Now don't say that. If you're pretty, you're automatically Matt's special guest.*

Caleb led her into the kitchen. Its counters and stovetop were littered with empty bottles, plastic cups, and the remains of a huge birthday cake decorated with a unicorn and frosted in purples and pinks. The horn, swirling forelock, and blue eyes remained.

Caleb smiled sheepishly. "It was on sale. Help yourself." With a tilt of his head, he indicated the door between the microwave and fridge. "I think she's down there." He looked at her questioningly. "Let me know if you need anything." He nodded once and went back to the dining room.

Maggie stared after him blankly, then took a step down. At once, mustiness and shadows enveloped her. Laughter drifted up.

Her stomach roiled. She reached sideways, found the thin bannister, and held it tightly. This place was familiar. The dankness. The darkness.

She knew where she was. She'd never left it.

At the foot of the stairs, she closed her eyes and shuddered. "Sara?"

"Who?"

She blinked.

Three women, sitting cross-legged on the concrete floor and harboring two stacks of cards and a few bottles between them, stared up at her. More cards were fanned in their hands. One player with gleaming hair falling in a tawny sheet over her shoulder repeated, "Who?"

Maggie shook her head. Smoke curled throughout the room

113

and seemed to enter her head like a thick miasma, wafting around and clouding her perceptions. *Yeah, in there. Kill the light. You have her? Let me see. Hey, now, there's nothing to get bitchy about. This will be fun. Just calm—fuck. That hurt.* "I'm looking for . . ." She swayed and grabbed hold of the railing again.

A skinny guy, leaning over a stack of boxes a few feet away, smirked. "I want what she's on." He rolled a blunt and crossed to the card players to pass it to the woman who'd spoken.

Holding her splayed cards against her chest, she flicked her curtain of hair over her shoulder before accepting it.

Maggie sidestepped past them into a sprawling cinder block space of boxes and chairs and free weights and a treadmill and music and smoke and then the broad backs of men, *one, two, three, four, five, six,* strong and laughing, *come on, now, you're only hurting yourself,* grouped around something, someone, spectators to an activity.

Maggie swerved closer, arms outstretched.

One muttered, "Good form," and another said, "Too easy. Tack on another fifty."

Linnie. The name came to her, a submerged body at last breaking the surface. "Linnie!" she cried and shot forward, making an arrow of her body that parted the men who'd turned at the sound of her shout.

She froze.

They were not circling Linnie.

It was a sweaty man on a bench. A weight bench. With a surprised laugh, he rested two dumbbells on his damp stomach. "Seriously?" he asked her. *"Linnie?"* He let his head fall back and moaned.

Everyone laughed, a response that simultaneously mortified and grounded her.

One of the guys snickered, "Better keep lifting, buddy."

Another said, "You're really, really close, Jack, on the brink of passing for a man."

The brunt of the jokes released the weights to the floor on either side of him. He drew up his T-shirt and mopped his face. "I could do a decent Linnie impression." He sat up, widened his eyes, and asked in a soft lilt, "Mind if I crash here for a week?"

"Or a year?" another asked in a falsetto.

When the laughter died, Jack finished, "And smoke all your weed?" His smile slipped. He slumped on the bench. "Fucking Caleb."

The others nodded. One of them muttered, "First Mark, then Tatum, then Fluffster—"

Jack glanced at Maggie and, with a weary wave, explained, "A mutt. Absolutely infested with fleas."

"Caleb's a sucker."

"He kind of reminds me of Santa Claus," a scrawny guy said.

"Well, I'm sick of it. He can get his own place and run it as a free boardinghouse." Jack grunted. "Let *him* feed them."

"And weed them."

The laughter started up again, but Jack shook his head and swatted the air to his left. "Linnie's in there." He smiled sourly. "Do us a favor. Take her with you."

Maggie secured her seat belt with a trembling hand, started Sam's pickup, and pulled away from the curb. She sighed. Even her breath shook. She shot her passenger a sidelong glare.

Linnie slouched against the door. Her smile was sweet. If she was drunk and high, she hid it well. "Thanks for getting me."

Maggie barely nodded. She was pissed.

Linnie swept a knuckle against the fog blooming on the window. In a musing way, she murmured, "Don't know why I went to Jimmy's in the first place. He's an idiot, and so are his friends. Everyone got plastered, then someone broke a window. I took off. Kind of thought I'd be hanging out at Caleb's for the night. I'm glad I didn't have to do that. Caleb's cool, but . . ." She drew a circle on the window. "I've asked him for favors before. I hated to ask him for another."

Maggie flicked on the defroster. Warmth sprang into her eyes and grazed her forehead. She adjusted the air to a cooler temperature. She was hot enough.

Linnie dragged herself upright, raised a limp hand. "Don't head down Redman. Kyle lives a bit farther off the Ridge." The hand fell to her lap. "His car was impounded." Her mouth curled. "Hopefully, Kyle wasn't, too."

Maggie shook her head.

"What?"

She managed a tight shrug.

Linnie turned to gaze out the passenger window. She folded her hands against her stomach.

They drove in silence for a while. Streetlights swept into the truck, a silvered caress over Linnie's fair hair, a stroke down her arm. Maggie wrapped her fingers more tightly around the steering wheel and tried to concentrate on the empty black road, but she kept thinking about where she'd found Linnie in the basement, lounging between two guys in a half-finished room, doing shots and laughing, the door closed, not a single other girl present.

How little Linnie cared for her safety. How little she seemed to care for Sam and Kate and Thomas and Wren, the people who loved her, who wanted to help her. How freely she dumped on other people.

"You don't take good care of yourself." She pressed her lips together, surprised she'd said that aloud.

Linnie didn't respond immediately. When she did, her tone had lost its lightness. "I take care of myself just how I want to."

"Hanging out wherever, getting trashed with whoever." Frustration edged Maggie's exhalation, revved it to a growl. "You make yourself vulnerable. You could get hurt."

Linnie laughed once. "You could get hurt, you could get molested, you could get raped." She clucked. To her window, she continued softly, "Passive voice, Mrs. Michaels called it. It's a problem. Don't you hear how it's a problem, Margaret? You, of all people? Dropping the subject? Erasing the *perpetrator*? Acting like it's up to you to be on your toes, practicing the buddy system, looking over your shoulder, mastering kung fu in your free time, dressing right, smiling"—she thrust out a warning hand—"but not too much, having fun"—she held out the other hand, doubling the halt—"but not too much, and running your mixed drinks to the lab to have them tested for drug contamination. One false move, and boom, you get nailed"—she shook her head—"but by *whom*? Fucking passive voice. *Somebody's* doing this shit."

Maggie pressed two fingers to her temple. "That's just how it is." Not fair. But true.

"Well, I'm sick of it. It's creepy, acting like a girl drinking too much is setting herself up to be raped. What does that have to do with anything? Maybe she shouldn't drink so much because booze is bad for her. Maybe she shouldn't drink so much because she could get addicted." She tapped the window with a knuckle, then admitted quietly, "Maybe she shouldn't drink so much because drinking's a stupid way to escape what's wrong with her life." She gave her head another shake and sat up, rallying. "But to say, 'Don't drink too much, or you'll get raped'? She doesn't *get raped* because she overindulged or underdressed or forgot to bring along a bodyguard. She gets raped because some asshole raped her."

Maggie licked her lips. They were dry. Linnie wasn't saying anything she hadn't thought about a thousand times before. But it was disconcerting, hearing someone else speak her thoughts. No, *not* just that. Also hearing someone talk openly about . . . rape.

I know something similar happened to you, I know something similar happened to you, I know something similar happened to you. Rape was the something-similar-that-happened-to-you. Unutterable. Taboo. Secrecy hid rape, and it wasn't right, just as it wasn't right that people didn't mention the aggressor when they talked about sexual assault. So, yeah, Maggie understood what Linnie was saying. And Maggie understood that her own silence and shame were problematic. She hadn't earned the shame. She didn't deserve it. It was the reaction that played into the hands of people who wanted to spread the blame around, who wanted to know what the victim wore and how much she drank. It made her angry with herself—ashamed of her shame. She thought about this and swallowed a perverse impulse to laugh. *Oh God, too many layers of shame.*

". . . sexist bullshit," Linnie was saying. "I wouldn't warn Sam, 'Button up your shirt, buddy, and stop pounding the shots, before you get raped.'" She harrumphed, crossed her arms, and fell silent.

Maggie braked at the Redman and Ridge intersection and struggled to organize her chaotic thoughts. When the light changed, she stepped hard on the gas. After a moment, she felt calmer, more clearheaded. "It's not like I disagree," she said quietly. "I don't at all. But hating the double standard doesn't make it disappear."

"Ha." Linnie sagged and closed her eyes. She looked abruptly deflated. Defeated. "You'll never make it disappear," she said. "The world has stupid rules."

"We need to change them."

"Good luck with that."

"Well, *I* want to change them." She did. Or at least, she had. Coming forward last spring was proof of that.

Linnie grunted a laugh.

Maggie frowned. "Anyway, ignoring reality isn't a smart way to go about changing it. You shouldn't ignore it, either. Someone could have hurt you tonight."

Linnie opened her eyes. "At *Caleb's*? Not at Caleb's. Those guys are decent."

Maggie gave her a skeptical glance. "You sure about that?"

"I refuse to believe every guy is just waiting for a chance to pounce. That's a myth, too."

A myth. But then, Maggie had never expected Matt Dawson to do what he had done.

"Your head's stuck in Carlton."

She flared her hands against the wheel. What Linnie said was true. That didn't mean Maggie liked hearing it.

"Those guys are friends. And that was hardly some frat party. They served a *unicorn* cake." She smiled a little. "I mean, come on. A unicorn."

Still. "You should . . ." *Act more responsible.* "Be careful. What happened to me could happen to you."

"It wouldn't."

"It could."

"No, Maggie. It really couldn't." She drew up her knees and hugged them to her chest. "I'm not you. I spent the second half of my childhood in foster homes, the first half with a really bad mom and a really mean dad. You don't think I know how you feel? The difference is how your story unfolds. You're a familiar character, the protagonist we can all pity and like. You were drinking but not drunk. You fought and left marks. You had sufficient medical proof. And no history of partying or reckless behavior. I bet you didn't sleep around." She searched Maggie's face. Her mouth quirked. "See? A good student, a good girl, a hometown girl. Check, check, check. And afterward, so obviously hurt, so outraged." She shrugged. "I'm not trying to minimize what happened. It was terrible. And it's awesome how you tackled it head-on. But for a lot of girls, it's not like that. It wasn't for me. A bipolar dropout with an ugly history, an addiction or two, and a record, for good measure? I don't qualify for justice. You, though . . ." She breathed a thin laugh. "Shy of those assholes jumping out from behind bushes and wearing ski masks, you painted a convincing picture, a classic picture. Nearly a dictionary example."

The steering wheel was slick under her hands. "Not for everyone."

"The cops, you mean?"

"And others. People convinced the whole thing was a lie. Maybe a misunderstanding."

"Or an accident. 'Whoops. Didn't mean to put that there.'" She shook her head, disgusted. "Well, at least the college handled it." She sighed. After a lull: "No one ever handled anything for me."

Not true. Every single day Maggie saw people handling Linnie's problems. "Sam tries."

"Sam wishes I were someone I'm not, someone like his mom. He wants to save me."

"What do you expect when you call him for help?"

She conceded with a throaty sound. "But for the record, I only called him after trying Ashlyn, Jess, and Allie."

"He thinks you *want* him to save you—that you're testing him, putting yourself in dangerous situations, then waiting to see if he'll rescue you."

She smiled. "My whole life is dangerous."

"You upset him. That upset Kate."

Linnie looked away sharply. "I'm sorry about that, but why did he get worked up with Kate standing right there? He could have taken my call in a separate room. He could have just said, 'Not available. Got to go,' and hung up instead of lecturing me. I didn't ask him to rail in front of Kate. He should have known better."

He should have. Maggie had listened to his side of the conversation and thought the same. But why was Sam stuck parenting Kate alone? If there was ever a kid who could use two parents, it was Kate. That little kid could use, like, a *dozen* parents. "I don't get how you can criticize Sam's parenting. At least he's . . ."

"Parenting?"

"All I'm saying is, there's such a thing as personal responsibility. Why don't you—"

"Go get a job? Pursue a career? With my nonexistent college diploma? With my nonexistent high school diploma? With my nonexistent car and money? With the nonexistent support of a nonexistent family?"

"Now who's the dictionary example? I'd look for you under *E* for excuses. You have support. If you don't want it from Sam, you could get it from his dad or even my aunt. Why don't you see a therapist?"

"Please. Their drugs aren't any different from mine." She made a face. "And look who's talking. Why don't *you*?"

"I'm trying to . . ." What was she trying to do? Hide? Disappear? Erase what had happened? Erase herself? She cleared her throat. "I'm trying to get better on my own."

"And how's that working out for you?"

Maggie bristled. "At least I'm *trying*. You don't look like you're trying." *Don't you want to be a better person? Don't you want to get your GED, find a job, fight your addictions, whatever they are, and overcome your past? Don't you want to be a good parent, instead of a crappy one like your own apparently were? Don't you care about your daughter, how you're scaring and neglecting her?* Maggie struggled to contain these questions, all of them judgments. Linnie wasn't easy to like. But she wasn't easy to hate, either. And Linnie was dealing with years of troubles, probably with the kinds of abuse Maggie couldn't even begin to fathom. What right did she have to judge? She finally just asked, "Don't you want to get a life?"

"That's it. That is it precisely." Linnie fell back against the seat and closed her eyes again. "I'm not sure."

10

THE NEXT MORNING, when Wren asked what happened the previous night, Maggie just said, "Linnie was stranded. I tracked her down and gave her a lift to her boyfriend's." She didn't want to get into her conversation with Linnie. And she *really* didn't want to discuss her near-breakdown.

"That girl . . ." Wren picked up her coffee cup. "She's heading straight for disaster."

"Yeah, well, I think that's her plan."

"Oh, man, I could tell you some Linnie stories. Like when she got pregnant . . . it couldn't have happened at a worse time."

"She was a junior in high school, right?" Maggie winced at the thought. Weird that Linnie was only a few years older than her.

"Not only that. Muriel—Sam's mom—had just died." The

aunt set her mug on the table, arranged it, as if she were positioning it for a photograph. "Linnie was in rough shape." She smiled grimly. "Rougher than usual. Drugs, depression, alcohol, cutting. In no position to become a mother. And she knew it. But Sam—he cried and begged . . ." She shrugged. "Thomas sided with Sam. He didn't come right out and admit it, but it was pretty obvious, the way he was offering tons of support to help them raise the child."

Wren sat up and took a sip of her coffee before continuing, "Linnie pulled her shit together as well as she could during the pregnancy, then fell apart again afterward." She heaved a sigh. "So they kept Kate. And we all love her, including Linnie." The aunt must have seen some doubt in Maggie's face, because she said curtly, "I'm telling you, Margaret, Linnie *loves* that little girl. Taking off is just her messed-up way of protecting her kid, shielding Kate from herself, from the sight of her problems." She ran her hands over the surface of the table. "I'm not dredging up this drama to gossip. And I'm not giving Linnie a free pass. But I—I guess I want you to understand her a bit better. It's not like she dropped the ball after Kate was born. The ball was already dropped. Sam and Thomas knew this, but they bullied and guilted her into doing what they wanted. I get that they were grieving and hurting and missing Muriel. I *get* that. But still. What they did . . . frankly, it pisses me off."

The end of October passed quietly, the days drifting by like the leaves sashaying to the ground, silent and slow.

Even Maggie's brain—usually so quick to find triggers that could hurl her back to last spring—gave her a freaking break. If there were Linnie crises or Kate tantrums, Maggie didn't hear about them. In fact, she didn't hear much of anything from anyone. One Sunday morning, without coming right out and disinviting Maggie from the studio, the aunt made it clear she needed her workplace to herself. "Hope you're okay with pizza and subs this week. And you'll probably be eating them by yourself. I have *got* to finish my last piece. The show's in the beginning of December." She looked harried and gloomy but pinned on a weak smile to tease, "We'll get you in the studio for your next therapy session as soon as I wrap up the firings."

So Maggie was on her own. She read. She cleaned. She walked along the beach. She poked around the strip of woods and stood for a long time staring at a single oak in a stand of maples, wondering why the tree kept its copper leaves. And for some reason—maybe because of the episode at the party, which, however scary, she'd managed to survive, or maybe because of Linnie, who lingered in Maggie's thoughts (sometimes like a sad cautionary tale and sometimes like a frank feminist)—by Friday night, she felt steady enough to tackle the Jane Cannon situation.

It'd been days since she even picked up her phone. In the loft, she checked her missed calls first. Almost all of them were from her parents. Maggie grimaced, remembering her most recent conversation with her mother. "It doesn't make sense that I can only reach you on Wren's landline, Mags," her mom had said. "You *do* have a cell, you know." Maggie had mumbled something about forgetting to turn it on, an excuse Mom had rejected with a sigh.

Maggie checked her texts to procrastinate a little longer. She had only a few of those. Mail, however: a ton. Feeling shaky but determined, she began to work her way through the emails, not opening them, but registering the subject headings and deleting as she went. Almost right away, however, she found a message from Jane Cannon—a new one.

This time, Maggie wasn't surprised.

She took a deep breath and exhaled slowly through her mouth. In the windows over the bed, the night sky bloomed. The moon was the thinnest crescent, as slight as a nail clipping. The loft was dark, except for the glow from the phone.

She tapped the screen.

Jane Cannon

To: Margaret Arioli

Just me

October 28 at 10:53 PM

I hate it here. I'm frightened all the time. I wake up from nightmares every night. I want to believe it wasn't a big deal, and I tell myself to get over it, but I can't. I just can't. And if I can't forget it, how do I live with it?

"Oh, Jane," Maggie whispered. She didn't know how a person lived with it. She couldn't figure that out for anyone, least of all herself.

She reread the message and, with a trembling hand, put down her phone. Then, swearing under her breath, she immediately picked it up again. Heart pounding, she hit REPLY.

> Hi, Jane. I apologize for not writing back sooner.
> I've been avoiding my phone.
>
> I'm really sorry about what happened to you. It's
> good that you contacted me.

She stalled, suddenly overwhelmed, stuck in sadness, sympathy, futility, dread. How to proceed? How to *help*?

She wrote back haltingly, composing a paragraph, then changing her mind and getting rid of the whole thing, adding some more words, and deleting half of them. In the end, she invited Jane to email again or call, gave her the cell's number, and urged her to contact the Title IX officer. She told her there were good people at CC who'd support her (and thought about Dean McGrath and Susan Brown, who'd been at least a little more helpful and sensitive to Maggie than the police had been). She also encouraged her to make an appointment with one of the therapists and advocates at Safest Place, Carlton's crisis center.

Maggie scanned what she'd written, then added the half truth,

> I wish I would have used the center last year and
> talked with a counselor instead of trying to handle
> the situation without professional support.

Finally, at the end of the message, she wrote,

> You're not alone, Jane.

Maggie's first thought Saturday morning: *I did it!*

She rolled toward the edge of the bed and snatched her phone off the floor. Jane hadn't replied yet, but that was okay. The worst part—for Maggie—was over. She'd finally written back to someone who needed her and hadn't once broken down while doing it.

Proud of herself, she got dressed, made a fresh pot of coffee, found some leftover Boston cream doughnuts in the fridge, and ate two of them. After bundling up in her winter coat, she headed outside. The wind was fierce and cold, but the sun shone brightly. It glittered across the choppy waves and warmed the top of her head as she searched for beach glass. She carried her palmful of smooth pieces and high spirits up to the loft and checked her phone.

The girl hadn't written back yet, but Maggie was (guiltily) kind of relieved. The correspondence ball was in Jane's court. Maggie had finished her part, at least for now.

Then she called home.

"You remembered you had a phone," her mother said by way of hello.

The surprise and happiness in her mother's voice made Maggie smile. "Hi, Mom."

"How's it going?"

"Good. Just beachcombing."

Her mother laughed. "Got any other plans for the day?"

Did she? It was the last Saturday of October . . . oh! "I do. I'm meeting my book club friends in Kesley. We're going to decide on our next read."

Ran led the way into the back room and brandished a hand to present a few books in the middle of the floor. "Ta-da!" She knelt by the stack and began humming along to the music playing in the background, a song from *Rent*.

Maggie looked around, confused. On top of the filing cabinet, in two corners, on the desk, on the table, *under* the table—books, books, books, hundreds of books, new and old, peeking out of boxes, loosely piled, and forming book versions of the Leaning Tower of Pisa. But where Ran sat, there were only four hardcover selections.

"That's *it*?" Hope stood over the short stack, hands on her hips.

"Yeah, well, to save time, I thought I'd give you options." Ran patted the floor on either side of her. While Maggie and the other girls joined her, she continued, "It's not like we have forever to make a decision. These are the ones I figured we'd like the best."

Under her breath, Hope muttered, "*Options.*"

Ran arranged her crossed legs into a lotus pose and drew the stack closer to her.

Hope, hunching over her own loosely crossed legs, rolled her eyes. "We know, we know. You're super flexible."

Ran drummed the cover of a book. "What's that supposed to mean?"

Hope thumbed the frayed end of a black bootlace and shrugged. "You're competitive."

"Nonsense." Ran sniffed.

Maggie and Julia, sitting next to each other, shared a smile.

Colleen suggested diplomatically, "She's just a perfectionist."

Hope blew a raspberry. "She wants to win. At everything."

"What a flattering observation." Ran glared at her. "Since you're done pointing out my failings, why don't we—"

130

"Who says I'm done?" Hope held up a finger. "*And* you're controlling." Then she knitted her hands in her lap and grinned. "Okay. Now I'm done."

"How about *you* pick our next read?" Ran said through her teeth.

"Sure." Hope leaned forward and raked the books her way. "Then I'll check the time"—she held up her wrist, where what looked like a genuine army multifunction watch hid part of a tattoo—"and we'll see how many minutes pass before you tell me why I made the wrong choice."

Ran and Hope continued to bicker. Maggie would have found this exchange worrisome if Colleen and Julia (chatting and laughing about something Samantha Bee had said) didn't look completely unfazed. Since Hope wasn't paying any attention to the books, Maggie drew the stack her way.

The first novel was by Jodi Picoult, *Small Great Things*. Maggie read the description. It sounded interesting. And the next one, *News of the World* by Paulette Jiles, sounded great, too. She picked up Jennifer Niven's *Holding Up the Universe*, but as she opened it to check the synopsis, the bottommost book caught her attention—*Something Else* by Trinity Haskins.

With a bittersweet pang, Maggie admired the cover's stark illustration of two women's silhouettes. Haskins wasn't just her favorite contemporary writer; she was a professor and one of the reasons Maggie had decided to stay in her hometown after high school. While so many other kids had sought the escape that distant colleges promised, Maggie had chosen Carlton College partly because Trinity Haskins taught English literature there. She was a popular professor, her classes filled up quickly, and Maggie had known she'd have to wait until her junior or senior year to win a seat in the writer's classroom. She hadn't minded. Haskins was worth waiting for . . .

"Then how about we let Marge decide? Marge. *Marge*." Ran poked Maggie in the knee.

Maggie looked up, disoriented.

The girls were smiling at her expectantly.

"*Sheesh*," Ran said. "I was practically screaming your name."

"Sorry."

"Is that the one we should read?" Julia asked, nodding at the Haskins novel in Maggie's lap.

"Well . . ." She covered the book with her hands, suddenly feeling fiercely (if absurdly) territorial about it. She would answer "Absolutely," if she could brag about kind of knowing Haskins personally, having seen her on campus many times and attended three of her readings, and maybe boasting a little, too, about Carlton College's great reputation, its kick-ass English department, especially.

But she couldn't, not if she was sticking to her plan: to wipe away her past, surge ahead, stay focused on the future, and become more of a Marge and less of a Maggie.

She pushed the other three novels across the floor. "Let's do one of these."

11

A RACKET WOKE Maggie. With a gasp, she jerked up and pushed out her hands, instinctively preparing to ward off an attacker. Heart pounding, scalp tight, she listened hard for a moment, then collapsed back onto the bed with a moan. The noise was coming from outside, a sound like a bucketful of gravel hurled at the windows. There was a clatter across the roof, too, heavier than the usual pings of rain. The wind roared, and the panes shook and strummed. The loft was under some strange climatic siege.

She rolled over, got to her knees, and squinted out at the white and silver of the sky, wind, and lake. Winter had shown up early and was transforming Wren's corner of the world. Leaning to the side, Maggie managed to get a view of the Blakes' property. The air, thick with driving ice and snow, blurred Devil's Tongue.

She thought about the previous night, Hope and Ran's arguing, the Haskins novel, Maggie's initial thrill and pride when she'd spotted the book . . . and how, for the sake of anonymity, she'd kept her reaction to herself. Though not without a pang.

Staying silent on her past—her master plan—came with costs. Hid the bad parts, yes, but it also meant giving up the good. And that sucked.

What had Linnie said that first time they met? "You should have stayed right where you were. Why did you leave?" If Linnie found out what Maggie was up to in the book club, she'd accuse her of running scared—and doing just what the Carlton haters wanted her to do: making herself vanish.

"*She's* one to talk," Maggie said under her breath, frowning at the weather. She scrambled out of bed, wishing she could leave the uncomfortable thoughts under the rumpled sheets. Her phone was on the floor. With a heavy sigh, she checked her emails. No reply from Jane yet.

The storm lasted all day. While the snow flew around the cabin, Maggie marked the passing hours by visiting her email and trying to concentrate on *News of the World* for the book club. Why wasn't Jane writing back? The girl's silence made Maggie nervous.

After the first week of November, the weather improved, but still there was nothing from Jane. Maggie was exasperated. For the longest time, this person had written without any encouragement at all. And now—after Maggie had finally replied—the girl couldn't even muster a *hey*? A *thanks-for-the-advice*? A *don't-worry-I'm-fine*? Like, what the hell? It was aggravating. Maggie checked her junk mail. She also went into her sent mail and reread her own message. Had she mentioned something that could have pissed off Jane? That might have hurt her feelings?

By the following week, Maggie's irritation had disappeared. Now she was plain scared. She sent another email, a brief just-seeing-if-you're-okay message. That went unanswered, too.

On Thursday, almost two weeks after she'd written her first message to Jane, Maggie reread the girl's last email and swore. The more Maggie thought about it, the more the short paragraph sounded like a suicide note. Rattled, she stared at her phone until the screen grayed and turned black. What if Jane wasn't writing back because she'd harmed herself . . . or worse?

Maggie tossed aside her phone. She had to tell Wren.

She found her aunt in the hallway, about to enter her studio. Before Maggie could mention the situation and ask for advice, Wren greeted her with a vague nod and said, "Oh, good, you're up. Can you do me a favor and head over to Thomas's to tell Sam he has the day off? He's not answering his phone, and I—I need . . ." She ran a hand over her red eyes and then curled her fingers around her throat. Flatly, she finished, "I can't have him around."

"Sure . . ." Maggie frowned. Her aunt looked sick. "Are you all right?"

Wren shook her head. "Fine." She must have registered the contradiction in her answer, because she smiled dimly and added, "I just need to be alone today—wrap up things in the studio without interruptions."

Maggie swallowed her disappointment. She couldn't ask her

aunt to help her with Jane's situation, at least not immediately. "Finishing the sculpture?"

Wren gazed at her bleakly. "And calling your mom." She took a step into the studio. "My truck keys are on the kitchen counter. Thanks for telling Sam." She shut the door behind her.

Calling my mom? Maggie stared at the closed door.

Frustrated and confused, she trudged into the kitchen. Maybe she should talk to Sam about Jane. He was smart. He'd probably have some good advice.

But he didn't. Or rather, he *might* have, but Maggie decided not to ask for it. He looked about as approachable as Wren had.

The Blakes' garage door was up. Sam stood outside, but he was facing the house and shouting something—at Kate, Maggie realized. The girl stood in the garage. Maggie rolled down the truck window and heard him say, ". . . and catch a cold? Jeez. Get back inside. Right now!"

His daughter ignored him. Maggie's arrival had caught Kate's unhappy attention. She crossed her arms and stuck out her tongue at Maggie. Then she bared her teeth. Then she stuck out her tongue again.

"Yikes." Warily eyeing the girl, Maggie stayed in the aunt's truck and waited for Sam to walk over.

After she passed along Wren's message, he nodded. "Dad will be relieved. I can drive Kate for a change." He turned and shouted, "Go get your coat and backpack! I'm taking you to school."

"No!" Kate flew to the outer edge of the concrete floor, punched the air, and stamped her foot. "It's a snow day."

"No, it's *not*," Sam growled. "Hurry up."

"Mom said."

"Your mother doesn't decide if it's a snow day. The superintendent does."

"Mom *is* super. She said we could make a snowman today. I am *not* going to school. And I hate you!"

He turned slowly, hissing an exhalation. "Linnie decided Kate needs a mental-health day," he told Maggie in a low mutter. "Jesus Christ, that woman's making my life difficult." He flared his eyes at the sky. "Thanks for driving over, Megan. Catch you later."

She didn't bother correcting her name. Making his way toward the house, he looked defeated, his head lowered and back bent. In the garage, he tried to take Kate's arm. She shook him off, her glare on Maggie. Sam waved a hand over his head, an explosive I-give-up motion, and stomped into the house. Kate stayed where she was, a belligerent sentinel.

"I'm not trying to breach the castle walls, little girl," Maggie said under her breath, and put the truck in reverse.

The snowball hit the passenger window just as Maggie finished the K-turn. Alarmed, she rolled up the window on her side and stepped on the gas. In the rearview mirror, she saw the girl kick at some snow, shake her fist, and holler something after the truck. Maggie couldn't hear what she said, but if she had to guess, it was probably something like, "You're not my mom!"

Friday wasn't an improvement over Thursday. Jane didn't write. Wren must have given Sam another day off, because he never showed up for work. The aunt, herself, was still holed up in the studio. And here Maggie was facing a crisis—without the least bit of help from anyone! By the end of the day, she decided to send a third message to Jane:

> I'm worried that something has happened to you and wondering if I should try to find your home phone number and contact your family. Your silence is troubling. Please write back.

First thing Saturday morning, she checked her phone. Nothing.

Discouraged, she slunk back into bed with the book by Jiles. By suppertime, she'd finished it. She wasn't hungry, so she stayed in the loft and got dressed for book club, strongly tempted not to go. It wasn't as if she'd have anything to say about the novel. She had barely absorbed a word. Plus, she knew she was going to be lousy company.

A familiar song jingled from under a pile of strewn clothes.

With a jolt of hope, she flung aside a flannel shirt and seized her phone.

Just Mom. Drooping to the edge of the bed, she answered the call with a cheerless "Hey."

"Oh, honey."

Her mother sounded weird. "Are you okay?"

"I—I've been thinking about things a—a lot lately, and I've decided you should"—her mother drew a tremulous breath—"come home. I need to—to see you."

Maggie shook her head, bewildered. "But you will, like in a

week and a half. Remember? You and Dad are coming for Thanksgiving."

"No. I need you back here."

"*What?*"

"You would be better off with me . . ." Her voice trailed into a sob.

Maggie cupped her forehead. "What's going on?"

In a trembling rush, her mother said, "I made a mistake sending you there. I don't . . . I just don't trust her."

"Who?"

"My sister."

Huh? "Mom." Maggie frowned out the window at the woods. The sun had turned the upper branches into a golden filigree. "Please tell me what happened."

Her mother choked out, ". . . can't talk about . . . I'll tell you when . . . after I get paid Friday, I can send you money for . . . love you, sweetheart." Then she ended the call.

Maggie stared at the screen. "Holy shit."

She tossed the phone onto the bed and hurried downstairs. Mom and Wren must have had a fight. Could it have been on Thursday? The aunt had mentioned needing to call Maggie's mother and wanting privacy for the conversation . . .

The hallway door to the studio was closed. Wren had made it clear she couldn't be interrupted, but Maggie entered anyway. This was an emergency.

Just past the threshold, however, she froze. *Another* person, somewhere deeper in the studio, was crying.

Wren was not a crier, but who else could this sadness belong to? Maggie hesitated, torn between checking on her aunt and leaving her in peace and disturbed that the two women she was closest to were falling apart at the same time.

Finally, she stepped back and softly closed the door. She'd leave the aunt alone for now and try talking to her later.

Dissatisfied with this compromise, she wandered aimlessly and ended up in the kitchen.

On the counter, a note was next to Wren's keys. Recognizing the aunt's handwriting, she picked up the square of paper. *Soup's in the fridge. Take the truck tonight. Have fun at your book club meeting. The sculpture is all but done. The hardest part's over. I'll see you in the morning.*

Maggie looked around the kitchen. "What the hell is going on?" she asked. Again. The question had become her mantra. It covered all the bases—Jane, Mom, Wren, Linnie.

Nothing and no one were making sense.

"I hoped it would turn out differently." Julia drew her feet up to the reading-nook couch and hugged her knees to her chest. "Kept wishing Johanna would get to go back to the tribe."

Hope nodded, glum. "The Kiowas were her family."

"They didn't want her back," Ran pointed out.

"You're right." Julia sighed. "And isn't that heartbreaking?"

Ran tapped the cover of the book in her lap and murmured the title aloud: "*News of the World*." She kicked back the rocker. "It's pretty damn bleak." Her chair filled the lull with a *creak, crick, creak, crick* . . .

"What was the name the tribe gave her?" Hope asked, thumbing through the novel.

"Oh—oh, I know this," Julia said, and lifted her chin off her knee, her forehead wrinkled in concentration. "Let me think. It's on the tip of my tongue . . ."

"Colleen?" Ran raised an eyebrow. "Do you remember?"

She shook her head and slipped lower into her corner of the couch.

"Cicada!" Julia declared. Her smile wilted. She rubbed her cheek against her knee and added gloomily, "Then all those annoying white people tried to make her answer to Johanna. The poor girl didn't even get to keep her name."

"Yeah. Hmm." Hope, in the middle of the couch, leaned back and exchanged a speaking glance with Ran. Then she considered Colleen in a sidelong way. "You didn't read the book, did you?"

"Yes, I did."

"I don't think so."

Colleen scowled and sat up straighter on the couch. "I *did*."

"You skimmed." Hope shrugged. "I can tell. You usually have all sorts of things to say."

Ran peeled back in the rocker and mused to the ceiling in a singsong fashion, "Someone didn't do her homework."

"Why are you picking on me?" Colleen pointed at Maggie, sitting in the old wingback chair. "Marge isn't exactly talking up a storm, either."

"Good point." Ran slapped her foot on the floor to halt the motion of the rocker. "Marge?"

Maggie smiled wanly. "I did read it but not closely. I'm sorry. The last couple of weeks have been stressful." Suddenly silent Jane. Now Mom and Wren at war. November was getting rougher by the minute.

Julia tutted. "That sucks."

"Last week was bad for me, too," Colleen said peevishly. "It was, like, crazy busy."

"So many *Game of Thrones* episodes to catch up on," Hope said drily, "and so little time."

Colleen made a face.

"How has it been stressful, Marge?" Ran folded her hands against her stomach. "Tell Cousin Ran all about it."

Maggie plucked at the loose threads on her cardigan's hem. "You know . . . mostly family stuff."

Ran grimaced. "*Blech*. Family. They're the *worst*." Then she muttered about how her mom had cleaned her room and thrown out the concert ticket stubs that Ran had been saving for her college scrapbook, "not to mention a bunch of other things Mom shouldn't have been touching in the first place."

Maggie nodded but only half-listened. She was struggling . . . fighting a temptation . . . to tell. To share Jane's situation and the other crises simmering in and around Aunt Wren's cabin. These girls—funny and smart and quirky and kind—would almost certainly listen and sympathize, and maybe even offer good advice.

But how could she unburden herself without *revealing* herself, without becoming again that-girl-who-was-raped? Blowing a sigh, she smoothed the threads along the cardigan's hem. Better if she just stuck with Marge.

"Margaret Arioli!"

Maggie jerked upright in her chair.

Sam Blake grinned down at her. "Why, if it isn't Margaret Arioli." Holding a huge hardcover book at his side, he rocked back on his heels. "Are you proud of me? Margaret. Arioli. I remembered the first *and* the last."

Maggie opened her mouth. Closed it.

Of all the times for him to remember her name! Heart pounding, she licked her dry lips and asked faintly, "What are you doing here?"

"What do you think I'm doing?" He smiled cheekily. "Book shopping, of course. Dad offered to hang out with Kate today so I could go to the Drexler exhibition at the Albright-Knox. I noticed this place coming back. Thought I'd stop in and check it out." He looked around admiringly. "It's cool." He raised a hand, then strolled out of the reading nook.

Full of dread, Maggie slowly turned to face the girls.

Except for Julia, who was focused on a page in her copy of *News of the World*, they were gazing at her in amazement.

Shit. Maggie held her breath and waited to get peppered with questions—waited to be outed.

Ran, poised on the very edge of the rocker and gripping the chair's arms, broke the silence with a whispered, "Oh my God. That is—*by far*—the most *gorgeous* man I have *ever* seen."

Maggie blinked.

Colleen murmured dreamily, "He's like a . . . a . . ."—her head lolled back—"a model or something." She collapsed sideways, over Hope's legs. "A *super*model." She reached past Hope to poke Julia in the thigh. "Don't you think so?"

"I guess," Julia said impatiently. Irritation sharpened her features. "Why are you asking me? Ask them."

"Julia's gay," Ran explained to Maggie.

"She's got eyes, doesn't she?" Colleen insisted from Hope's lap.

"Get off," Hope ordered. "You're squashing me." After

Colleen sat up, Hope confirmed matter-of-factly, "But yes. Supermodel hot."

The gushing over Sam made Maggie anxious. Uncomfortable. She didn't like thinking of him in this way. Of *any* guy in this way.

Ran smiled. "How do you know him, Marge? You and he aren't . . . ?" She wiggled her eyebrows.

"No!" she shouted, and pressed the book against her pounding heart. *Can we change the subject? Please?*

The girls gaped at her.

Ran gave her head a shake. "Are you okay—"

"Oh, hey," Sam said.

There was a trio of screeches from Ran, Colleen, and Hope.

Sam sauntered into the reading nook again. He still carried the hardcover book, but this time, he held it in both hands so that the cover was visible. *Masters of Earth and Fire* the book was called. "Forgot to show you this. It's your aunt! On the *cover.* Isn't that amazing?"

She swallowed a moan. *First* he spilled the beans with her name, and *now* he was revealing her relationship to Wren Heed, an artist clearly famous enough to make the cover of a book? For the love of God, what was next? A copy of Maggie's birth certificate? Christ! She glared at him. *Shut up.*

But he was busy admiring the cover. "I think I'm going to buy this." He opened the book and cringed. "Though it costs a fortune . . ."

"It's half off," Ran said quickly.

"Wow, really?" His smile widened.

Julia rolled her eyes and mouthed, *No. Not really.*

"Just let me know when you're ready, and I'll check you out," Ran said, nervously glancing toward the front of the store, probably plotting how to finagle Sam's discount without her dad's noticing.

"That means I have enough to buy Kate a book, too." He looked over his shoulder. "Where's the children's—"

Colleen bounded off the couch. "I'll show you!"

"Oh, just point me in the right direction. Or I can ask the man working up front. I hate to break up your meeting."

Colleen dismissed this with an airy wave, then dabbed at her bob and peered up at him through her lashes. "I'd better show you. This place is like a maze. You could get lost. I don't mind. This way." She fluttered her fingers to steer him out of the reading nook and, as soon as his back was turned to the book club members, gave the girls a victorious smile and preened, kicking up a heel and flaring her hands. She sidled ahead of Sam and murmured, "I know this place from top to bottom."

Ran glowered after them. "No, Colleen," she grumbled softly, "*I* know this place from top to bottom. Because this place happens to be *mine.*"

Maggie shoved her hair out of her face. Her hand trembled. Her skin was damp. Maybe Sam's effect on the girls was a good thing. They'd paid a lot more attention to how he looked than to what he'd said. "I'm sorry, but I need to go."

"Already?" Julia asked.

Maggie nodded and grabbed her things off the floor: coat, book, keys. She had to get out of there.

"That's too bad," Hope said.

"I'll text you," Ran said, "and let you know when we're meeting next."

Maggie mumbled a thank-you.

Ran was eyeing her with a frown. Slowly, she added, "See you soon, Margaret Arioli."

The keys slipped out of Maggie's hand. She snatched them off the floor. *Damn.*

12

MAGGIE PRACTICALLY RAN out of the bookstore. A thin snow fell. In the glow of the streetlamp, the flakes swirled like a cloud of gnats. She hurried down the sidewalk. The cold felt good on her face.

Bells jingled. "Maggie!" Sam called. "Wait up!" He strode out of the store, and the door swung shut with another peal of bells.

She waited for him by the curb. Snow settled on his dark hair and glistened on his high cheekbones. She looked away.

"Left my books on the counter. I'll have to go back and buy them, but I thought I'd walk you to your car first."

"Thanks." She tried to smile. "That was nice."

"You parked over there?" He jerked up his chin to indicate the municipal lot.

"Yeah."

They crossed the street side by side. There was no traffic, but Maggie strode quickly anyway. She was anxious to get back to the cabin.

"So that's your book club?" Sam asked when they reached the sidewalk.

She nodded.

"Your friends seem sweet. Colleen was sad you were leaving—said she thought you'd be going to see *The Girl on the Train* with them tonight."

"Yeah. No." Maggie clumsily shuffled her book and phone to her side so she could don the half of the coat she hadn't put on yet.

"She invited me to go, too." His smile was rueful. "I'm kind of sorry I showed up. Feel like I crashed your meeting and ruined your discussion."

Just Marge. You just crashed and ruined Marge. She mumbled a nah-don't-worry-about-it and dug the aunt's keys out of her pocket, mentally listing the things she had to do: Get the hell out of here, talk to Wren, deal with Mom, figure out how to help Jane . . .

"Hey." He ducked his head. "What's wrong?"

She clutched the keys. Everything. Everything was wrong. Western New York was supposed to be her safe retreat—where she'd forget, hide, start over. It wasn't supposed to be a fucking zoo. "Wren and my mom." The words burst out of her, fast and loud. "They must have had a fight. Mom wants me to come home. She said something about . . ." Maggie shrugged, bewildered by her mother's sobbed words, and finished questioningly, "About not trusting Wren?"

There. She sighed, relieved—no, *intensely* relieved. It had felt great to tell Sam, to share at least one of the messes in her life. The ache in her chest eased.

"Oh boy." Sam turned a shuttered face toward the bookshop. Without glancing at Maggie, he asked, "She didn't say why?"

Maggie frowned at his careful tone. "No."

"And you haven't"—he tugged at the cuff on one of his coat sleeves—"seen Wren's sculpture?"

"Not yet."

He ran his thumb over his jaw. "It's not my place to talk about this." His gaze, when he glanced at her again, was sad. "You need to discuss it with Wren." He opened the truck door for her.

Confused, she automatically climbed in.

He took a step away from the truck but kept his hand on the door. After a moment of hesitation, he said with conviction, "But I can tell you one thing. Your mom's wrong. You can trust Wren. I trust her. I would trust her with my life. She's one of the best people I know."

Wren had left on the porch light, as well as the pendant over the table. But the kitchen was empty. Blindly reaching behind her to lock the back door, Maggie checked her phone. Nothing from Jane Cannon. She quickly toed off her snowy shoes and shrugged out of her coat. She had to find her aunt.

And you haven't . . . seen Wren's sculpture? The vagueness of Sam's question frustrated her. Or maybe she was perturbed by the fact that she *hadn't* seen the sculpture. The aunt had let him see it. Why not Maggie?

The hallway was dark; the door to the studio, closed. She cracked it open. The studio was dark, too. The aunt must have gone to bed.

And Maggie seriously wished she hadn't. She didn't relish the prospect of hauling her worry about Wren and Mom up to the loft, along with so many other unanswered questions. Obsessing about this latest situation would probably kill what little sleep she managed these days, between nightmares and spiraling thoughts.

Frankly, she'd had it with unanswered questions.

She flicked on the studio lights. Then, before she could change her mind, she shuffled over the threshold. It wasn't as if the aunt had forbidden her to see the sculpture.

Well, not explicitly, anyway, Maggie thought guiltily.

A few steps brought her fully into the studio. And face-to-face with a sculpture. With *the* sculpture. "Holy . . ." She covered her mouth with a fist. *Explicitly* echoed in her head, as she absorbed the sight.

Her calves hit Wren's wheel. Maggie had staggered back from the sculpture without even realizing it. She swallowed hard and stared.

The sculpture wasn't coy. In its details, she saw her aunt's history. Most obvious was how the work implicated Maggie's grandfather. Her naked grandfather. She flinched away from that telling state and dizzily took in the rest of the sculpture. It featured *everyone* in the aunt's immediate family, including Wren. Maggie's mom, too. Hollowed heads, groggy folds of clay, thick and frail slab elements, two emaciated subjects, one underfoot, one raised in a delicate suspension, and two giant shapes, the largest figure in a threatening stance, the other turned away, either indifferent or oblivious; it was hard to tell which.

No one came out looking pretty or normal.

"Margaret."

Startled, Maggie whirled around.

The aunt trudged in, head lowered, as if she were avoiding the sight of her own work of art.

"Oh, Wren," Maggie said, her voice cracking. She cleared her throat. "Why—why didn't you tell me?" *Why didn't I guess? Me, of all people? I should have guessed.*

Her aunt rubbed her eyes with the heels of her hands. "It's hard to talk about."

"I'm so sorry," Maggie said, and heard the futility in her own words. Sympathy—what difference did it make? It couldn't undo the past. Her gaze swung back to the sculpture. *Oh my God, that's Gramps . . .*

A wave of revulsion ran through her. Maggie looked away fast. "Are you okay?"

Wren's arms fell to her sides. "Not really." She dropped onto a stool. "Your mom and I . . . well. Let's just say, that"—she waved a hand in the direction of the sculpture without glancing at it— "has become an issue." She slumped against the worktable, letting her forehead land in a palm, and continued grimly, "It's the last one in the series. The others are already in New York"—Wren made a sound that barely qualified as a laugh—"the city, I mean. The show's coming up at the beginning of next month. I promised my agent this piece would be finished in time, but I'm cutting it so close I'll have to transport it myself just to get it there by the opening. And I can't even finish it yet."

"Why not?"

"I don't have an ingredient I need for the main glaze. Gerstley borate. It's hard to come by these days, but I think my pal Mark has a stash. He's in Avon but out of town this weekend. I'll have to head to his studio on Tuesday or Wednesday. Can't go Monday. I'm directing the first day of the Memorial Art Gallery's ceramics symposium." Her gaze flitted over the sculpture. "This thing isn't even bisqued yet. It's barely bone-dry." She dropped her head in her hand again. "I've been putting off finishing it for weeks."

Maggie considered the sculpture, this time out of the corners of her eyes, as if she were passing an accident. A safer angle—it made looking away that much quicker. "Because it's . . . painful?"

"Yes, and because I haven't known how to talk to your mother about it. Honestly, Margaret, if there had been a reasonable way for me to avoid telling Min, I would have. I didn't want to trash her happy childhood memories. Truly, I didn't. With the folks gone, memories are all she has left. That's the reason I'd never talked about what . . . well, what used to happen to me. I let her believe what she wanted to believe. And I still would have, except this show's going to get back to her. You *know* she'll hear about it. She searches for news about me."

Maggie nodded. Even when Mom and the aunt were at their most distant, going months without shooting an email the other's way, once letting an entire year slip by without talking on the phone, Maggie's mom was still fiercely proud of her twin's accomplishments. In fact she subscribed to art magazines for no other reason than Wren. Any word of praise for her sister thrilled her. So yes, she'd learn of this latest series.

Maggie winced, imagining her mother seeing this sculpture. It would devastate her. Maggie didn't doubt that for a second.

"I just tried to throw out a warning," the aunt said, "like 'heads up, sis; stay away from *ARTnews* for a few months.'"

Avoidance didn't seem likely. Somehow Mom would come across this work. What about the other pieces? Were they just as graphic?

"I'm sorry." The aunt touched her arm. "This can't be easy for you, either."

"This isn't . . ." She shook her head and finished in a whisper, "Easy." Her thoughts tumbled over memories, recasting holidays, birthdays, Sunday afternoon gatherings in uglier lights—remembering, dissembling, revising. *Holy shit.* "You don't have anything to apologize for. *I'm* sorry." Her eyes burned. "I'm sorry for you. This must have been painful to create."

"But necessary. Actually, it helped me." Elbows on the table, she folded her hands and tapped her knuckles against her mouth, like a prayer knocking for words. "It might help others, too."

Maggie kneaded her temples. "I'll talk to Mom."

Wren's head came up. "Would you? Oh, that would be really good of you, honey."

The hope in the aunt's face made Maggie sad. Wren didn't want to lose her sister. She wanted only to be free of a horrible secret—and relieved of the pain she'd kept hidden. *Mom shouldn't punish her for that*, Maggie thought with a flash of anger. *Mom should know better.*

"I—I'm afraid our Thanksgiving with your folks is off."

She nodded, soberly wondering if Wren knew Mom wanted *this* off—this whole extended visit. Mom wanted her to move back home.

"I'd appreciate it if you called her."

"I will." *Or I'll go see her.* Maggie wasn't sure how to accomplish it. She couldn't borrow the truck, not when the aunt had such a busy week ahead of her. And though Mom, during her emotional call, had choked out something about sending money, Maggie didn't want to wait for the cash to buy a bus ticket. Waiting suddenly seemed even more intolerable than the inevitable confrontations looming in Carlton. Just driving into that town was going to be tough. Carlton had become the crime scene, the indifferent judge, the suspicious jury, the enemy, all wrapped up into one. She hadn't expected to return so soon, if at all.

But she would. In fact, if she could, she'd leave right then. Not only because of Mom and Wren. Jane Cannon, too. Why wasn't the girl writing back? Maggie couldn't help but think that silence spelled trouble. Until she knew for sure that Jane was okay, she wouldn't stop worrying.

Maggie saw no other option. She had to go home.

13

THE NEXT MORNING, the decision to return to Carlton was Maggie's first thought. Out of the murk of her dreams, she woke to it, faced it, like one drifting through a sludgy water but in close proximity to the shore—there, just waiting for her.

Carlton was full of dark reminders. She didn't know how well she'd deal with them or how much she'd be able to help her mom or if she'd manage to track down Jane Cannon. But the trip itself seemed straightforward enough. Get into a car and go.

Maggie only needed the car.

After telling her aunt she was taking a walk and would be back in an hour or so, she headed for Sam's. She didn't have his number to call him beforehand but wasn't about to ask her aunt for it. Wren might get the wrong idea. Maggie and Sam's relationship wasn't romantic. There was only a friendship, and a new one at that. As much as Sam might complain about Linnie, he still painfully and obviously belonged to her, whether she wanted him or not.

Besides, Maggie wasn't interested in Sam.

Snow crusted the sides of the parkway. She hunched in her coat and shoved her hands into her pockets. *I will never be interested in any guy ever, ever, ever again . . .*

She shivered. The sun was out, but the air felt bitter cold. She should have worn her scarf and gloves. The wind blew from the north, rolling across the lake and shore, collecting the previous night's snow, and sending the white across the road in sinuous rivulets, like snakes.

Sam seemed like the best person to help Maggie figure out the car situation. She raised her face to the sun and exhaled a cloud. Okay, the only person. The aunt had enough on her mind— Maggie's mom, a week of obligations, firing the sculpture.

That sculpture . . . Maggie's stomach turned queasily. Poor Wren didn't need Maggie's worries in addition to her own.

The most pressing worry: finding a vehicle to use for a few days. Maggie didn't have enough money to pay for a rental and wasn't old enough anyway. But maybe Sam knew of someone who would lend her a car for a couple hundred.

She reached Wayside, where the woods muffled the sun. The leafless branches cast dark webs on the snowy ground.

The shadows made her uneasy. She walked faster. Her footsteps and breathing sounded loud to her own ears, and the stillness felt like a waiting thing. Heart thudding, she kept her eyes on the bright opening at the end of the tree-lined drive. A creature, maybe a squirrel or bird, created a flurry of movement in a maple's lower branches. The racket startled her. She broke into a run.

The tunnel of trees ended. The sun shone unimpeded, and a brilliance danced across the lake. She slowed to a slog to catch her breath and glanced around self-consciously, feeling stupid and frazzled and hoping no one had seen her running like a maniac.

Sam's pickup was in the driveway, and so was a sedan, not Thomas's but a shabby Corolla, tan and trimmed with rust and bumper stickers supporting the World Wildlife Fund, Planned Parenthood, Greenpeace, and Bernie Sanders.

She smiled faintly. Vermont would like this New Yorker.

She walked past the cars and peered up at the house, its windows bright mirrors reflecting the sky and water. Should she come back later? Since it was Sunday, she'd figured she would find Sam at home but thought he'd be working on the sculpture, not entertaining a guest.

A knock jarred the quiet. It was coming from inside. Maggie followed the noise toward the front and raised her hand to protect her eyes from the sun's glare. She could just make out a slight movement behind the glass. Then no movement. The knocking stopped.

Suddenly, a door opened. "Margaret."

Still shielding her eyes, she smiled, surprised. "Linnie."

"Are you here to rescue me again?"

"Do you need rescuing?"

"Not yet." She stepped down to the landing.

A paved path curved to the front of the house, its thin layer of snow trampled. Maggie followed the footprints.

"Did you run into Caleb?"

"Who?"

"Caleb. You know. From a few weeks ago. When you gave me a ride? He drove me over this morning, then went off with his dog for a walk. I'm waiting for Kate to get back. Thomas took her to Allenport to pick up McDonald's." She smiled a little. "Which was what Caleb and I were going to do, but whatever." She shrugged.

Maggie glanced over her shoulder. From a distance, the drive's opening into the woods looked like a gaping mouth. She turned quickly and walked the rest of the way up the path. "No. I didn't see him." Whoever he was. That night was a blur.

Linnie stepped past Maggie and called, "Caleb!" She shook her head and muttered to herself, "Where the hell did he go?" Louder, she hollered, "Caleb!"

"Jesus. Do you have to scream?" Appearing in the doorway, Sam nodded once at Maggie. "Hey." He raked back his hair, and his frown grew into a scowl when Linnie shouted for Caleb a third time.

Maggie's stomach sank. This was probably a bad time to ask for help. Sam looked pissed.

A dog barked. There was a whoop of laughter.

Linnie waved. A big blond guy with a dog bounded toward the house. Along the way, a stick got thrown, chased, retrieved, and then wrangled over.

Maggie did recognize him. It was the guy who'd pointed her in Linnie's direction the night of the party.

He whistled, called, "Fluffster! Come on, boy," and strode to the door.

"*Fluffster.*" Sam made a face, impatiently waved everyone

inside, panting dog included, then closed the door. "Couldn't you have come up with a better name?"

He grinned. "He likes it." His gaze fell on Maggie, and his face beamed happy surprise. "Oh, hey, I remember you. How's it going?"

Sam's eyebrows shot up. "You know each other?"

"Not exactly," Linnie said. "They met once, but I don't think I introduced them."

"Ah." Sam indicated Maggie with a wave. "So this is Wren Heed's niece, Margaret." He tilted his head. "Caleb Whitney."

He must have heard about her before. A flash of comprehension showed in his face, followed immediately by *apprehension*. Then sympathy. But he just said, "Nice to meet you."

Maggie mumbled a hello.

There was an awkward shuffling by the door.

With a cough, Caleb knelt by his dog—a German shepherd mix, not at all a furry Fluffster kind of creature—and gave his sleek head and back a brisk rubbing. The dog smiled around his pants, and his tail thumped the floor.

Brushing his hands together, Caleb straightened. "No Kate?"

"Not yet," Sam said. He pulled out his phone and checked the time.

"Just out for a walk, Margaret?" Linnie gave Maggie a nudge with her elbow. "What's up?"

"Not much." She dropped her gaze to the polished floor and stared hard at the pine knots among the swirling grain, as if they might give her a clue for how to bring up a difficult topic. Finally, she said, "I'm in a bind. I was hoping Sam might help me. I—I need to take care of a situation." Actually, more than one. But she didn't want to get into Mom and Wren's troubles—not with Caleb and Linnie around. Jane's situation however . . . "It can't wait. That is, *I* shouldn't wait." *Any longer than I already have.* Maggie pressed her fingers to her throat, then pushed back her curls.

"What happened?" Linnie asked.

"A girl from Carlton emailed me in September." Maggie let go of her hair. "Then a few more times in October. I didn't realize she'd been writing." *At first, anyway.* Heat climbed her neck. "I hadn't been checking my phone. From what I can gather, she was at a party and . . . and . . ." She hugged her sides, felt her ribs all the way through her coat. *And what? Say it. Name it.* "And someone raped her."

She released a long breath. She'd said it. Not an accident or a misunderstanding or a someone-just-got-carried-away or a disaster the victim brought upon herself or a shameful secret. Raped.

"*Holy shit,*" Linnie breathed.

"Is she a friend of yours?" Caleb asked quietly.

"I've never even met her, though she knows me, I mean"—Maggie pulled at the tab on her zipper—"heard about me."

"How'd she get your email address?" Linnie asked.

"College ones are easy to figure out. They follow the same format."

Linnie absently patted the dog's head. "She probably thought you'd understand."

Maggie nodded. "The police blew her off." *Like they did me.* "Now she's second-guessing herself, trying to get a handle on what happened, and not doing a very good job of it. She sounds pretty messed up."

"Did you write back?" Linnie asked.

She nodded. *Eventually.* "I asked her to email or call me and told her to contact the dean and visit the crisis center. The problem is . . . I don't think she has."

"Told the administration?" Caleb asked.

"Told anyone, that I know of."

Sam plowed a hand through his hair. "You haven't heard from her."

"At all. Not once. I sent her a couple more messages but haven't gotten a single reply."

"That's . . . really bad," Caleb said.

"You think she's done something to herself?" Sam asked.

Maggie pulled out her phone and found Jane's last email. She handed him the phone.

"Fuck," he muttered after reading it.

"Let me see." Palming the phone, Linnie read the email and touched her upper lip with her tongue. She passed the phone to Caleb, then threw an arm over Maggie's shoulders and gave her a squeeze. "Try not to freak. If the girl's missing, enough time has passed for someone to notice."

"Definitely," Sam said. "A roommate, RA, parent, professor. A ton of people, most likely."

"But I still feel responsible. She reached out to me, and I, well . . . blew her off."

"Not intentionally," Linnie said gently.

Maggie fidgeted with her hair, smoothed it. "I think I need to go there."

Caleb handed her the phone. "To the college?"

"Yeah. I feel bad that she was trying to contact me and I wasn't answering. I also need to see my mom."

"How come?" Linnie asked.

"Well . . . she and Aunt Wren talked on the phone recently. They . . ." She wrapped a curl around her finger. "They had a bad fight." She and Sam shared a glance.

Linnie and Caleb looked confused, but Sam just swiped the air and said, "Long story."

It *was* a long story. And in a couple of weeks, when the show opened, it would become a public story.

Sam rubbed his forehead. "I'll loan you my truck if I can figure out how to get Kate back and forth from school on the days Dad can't take her. Oh, wait . . . *crap*. Kate's got ballet Tuesday night."

"Ballet?" Linnie said. "Did she just start that?"

"Three weeks ago."

Pain flitted across Linnie's face. She lowered her gaze to the floor.

Sam didn't seem to notice. He was frowning at Maggie. "Dad needs his car on Tuesday. Still, maybe I can borrow Wren's—"

Maggie shook her head. "I appreciate that, but I'm not leaving you and Kate stranded without a car. And Wren's not going to be able to help. She has to get herself all over the place this week."

Sam nodded, resigned. "She's scrambling."

"If I could find someone willing to let me borrow a car just for a few days, I could give them what I have, a couple hundred."

Caleb, who'd knelt by the dog to rub his belly, rose. "Hell, take mine for free."

"Oh, no, I couldn't do that." She barely knew him.

"Sure you can. Half of my classes are online this semester

162

anyway. I'm doing independent studies in the other two, easy enough to work around. Seriously. Take it."

"Hold on," Linnie said. "Ever drive a stick shift, Margaret?"

"Oh." Her half smile died. "No."

"I could give you a lesson," Caleb said. "It's not too hard. You just don't want to stall the engine, but as long as you properly engage the clutch, you'll do fine. Only take care when you get close to Vermont. Hills can be tricky with this kind of car."

"And you don't want to select the wrong gear by mistake," Sam added.

"You could damage the mechanical components," Caleb explained.

Sam grimaced. "Or lose control of the car."

Maggie gazed at them, dismayed, and Linnie sputtered a short laugh.

Caleb flapped a hand. "But that's super unlikely."

"This isn't good," Maggie said.

"Want me to go with?" Linnie asked.

"You know how to drive a stick shift?"

"Um . . ." Linnie shook her head. "Not really."

Sam's expression turned intent. "You should go. You could stop and see Mary Tate."

"Mary who?" Caleb asked.

"Tate. Linnie's neighbor from a long time ago. She still lives in Baldwinsville."

"Outside of Syracuse?"

He nodded. To Linnie: "Would you go by there?"

Linnie avoided his gaze. She raised a hand to her ear. "Sam, please—"

"I think you should see her and pick up that letter. She went through a lot of trouble last August tracking down Dad's number, and you won't even call her back. Stop by. Find out what this letter's all about."

Maggie and Caleb glanced at each other, bewildered.

But Sam only said, "On your way back, do you mind swinging by Linnie's old neighborhood?"

"Sure," Maggie said. "I mean, I'd be happy to once I figure out the transportation. But I'm not driving Caleb's car"—she smiled a little at Sam and Linnie's friend—"though I appreciate the offer. I'm afraid I'd do something wrong, like break the, you know, those mechanical things." *Or our bodies. I might break those, too.* She pictured herself shifting gears incorrectly, losing control of the car, and shooting her and Linnie off a cliff, Thelma and Louise–style. Except accidentally.

Caleb shrugged. "I've got an idea."

14

"**THIS IS SO** nice of you." Maggie peered around the muzzle panting in her face. A long tongue swiped her. She dried her cheek with her shoulder and jerked back to dodge another lick. "Really nice."

"Oh, it's nothing. Fluffster, settle down. Down, boy." Keeping one hand on the steering wheel, Caleb reached to the side, found the dog's collar, and tugged him to the floor.

Fluffster sat at Maggie's feet for about ten seconds, then slunk up to her lap again.

"Sorry about that," Caleb said. "I usually make him stay in the back."

Linnie laughed. "You can't 'make' him do anything. That's the problem. Train your dog, man." She scooted to the edge of the backseat. "But Margaret's right. This *is* really nice." In a stage whisper by Maggie's ear, she added, "That's Caleb's thing: being really nice."

When Maggie turned to smile, the dog washed her neck. She grimaced.

Caleb glanced in the rearview mirror. "Why is it when you say that, it doesn't sound flattering?"

Linnie snickered, and they started exchanging verbal jabs. The banter was friendly. Earlier in the morning, Maggie had learned that the two had known each other for a few years. They'd met even before they had lived in the same neighborhood, when Sam's father had taught Caleb ("Thomas's favorite geek of all time," according to Linnie) four years ago. He'd been mentoring him ever since. "Sam's dad is why I'm a history major," Caleb had admitted. "He's awesome." The major had surprised Maggie. She'd pegged him as a future social worker.

Ostensibly petting the dog's face while really shifting him away from her, Maggie gazed out the window. They were close to I-90. It was Monday, just past eight o'clock. The worst of the morning rush hour traffic was behind them. And Aunt Wren's cabin was *far* behind them.

Maggie felt like she was abandoning a safe place, leaving her second home. The previous day, after she'd returned to the cabin, Maggie told the aunt about her travel plans, without mentioning the Jane Cannon part of her agenda. Wren nodded decisively and said, "I'm glad. Min needs you. I hope . . . well, I don't want to dump on you, honey, but maybe you can smooth things over for your mom and me." With a heavy sigh, she started slicing the loaf of bread on the counter, then looked up with a startled, "Oh! I almost forgot. Your book club friends were here looking for you." A bemused smile lifted the frown off her face. "Interesting bunch."

Maggie, when she'd recovered from this news, had said, "I'll get in touch with them." *Later*, she'd added silently. Then: *So much for Marge.*

Now Maggie frowned at the traffic whizzing by. Caleb drove much slower than she did. Still, if delays and stops could be avoided, they would make it to Carlton by midafternoon.

Then it would be a matter of finding Jane.

"Pretty town," Linnie said.

Maggie hummed her agreement around the lump in her throat.

"Quaint." Caleb turned onto Main Street and, driving slowly, stooped a little to eye the row of matching Victorian shops, three-story and brick, with melting snow dripping from the corners of their red awnings. "Even the bars are cute." Caleb gave Penny's Pub a disbelieving glance. "Look at that. Without the sign, I would have thought it was a boutique."

"This whole place reminds me of a movie set," Linnie said.

Maggie didn't answer. She trained her gaze on the passing storefronts. The shops blurred.

She'd expected this—this return—to be hard, a time-warp endeavor, plowing into old shame and hurt, heading into the heart of a wreckage. She knew she risked getting recognized, running into Matt Dawson's former teammates and encountering his fans, the ones who revered everything about the young quarterback and considered his expulsion the worst injustice. To them, he'd always be Saint Matthew, taking the big hit for the beleaguered Tigers.

What Maggie *hadn't* expected was the longing. The visceral way she'd experience the mountains and familiar farms and white churches and rushing streams and twisting roads.

This was her home. Or it used to be. But she'd left it, agreed to an exile she didn't deserve. Conceded her territory to bullies and haters and people who felt uncomfortable around her—not because of what she'd done but because of what had been done to her.

Maggie was keenly aware of just how much she'd lost over the course of eight months. How much had been stolen from her.

She ran a hand over Fluffster's head, suddenly grateful for the dog's friendly nature. He whined, snuffled closer, and let her hug him.

Well, she was back. For now. But she couldn't shake the certainty that she didn't belong. And never would again.

Maggie hurried down the campus walkway and kept her head half-turned toward Bosworth Hall when a group approached. A girl was saying something about a ski getting stuck in a lift. The students leaned into one another and laughed.

Maggie felt like an outsider. No, worse than that. An invader. She missed Linnie and Caleb, even though she was the one who'd waved them off, deciding it would be better if she talked to Jane alone. But they were somewhere on campus, walking Fluffster. They'd all agreed to meet in front of the Swan Library in an hour.

Maggie had a good idea of where to start looking. Jane had

mentioned her environmental studies coursework in an email. Most of that major's first-years lived in Nash Hall.

Environmental studies had been Sara Wood's major, too. It probably still was, though Sara would have already moved out of Nash. She'd planned to get an apartment after her freshman year "since the dorms suck"—a criticism Maggie had answered with a shrug. Her own plan had been to apply for a loan so she'd have enough money to move into the dorms her sophomore year. She'd avoided revealing this. Sara would have laughed.

Maggie scowled at the wet walkway, remembering how Sara used to tease her about attending a local university and living at home. Sara had been *allowed* to choose Carlton—the college had meant escaping the Midwest and her family. It had meant excellence plus freedom. For Maggie, it had meant only the former. She'd justified her decision by bringing up Carlton's top-notch English department, by pointing out that she wasn't rich and the only way she could afford a private college was by living with her parents and saving on room and board. But Maggie had sensed the futility of her own argument. She'd simply come across as shy, unadventurous, scared. Scared to leave home.

Or had Sara just worked hard to make her feel that way?

"You're like the baker's daughter," Sara had said once. "The baker's daughter, like any kid from a decent family, gets to choose what she's going to eat on her birthday. And sure, if she wants, she can wander through the bakery and go crazy, picking cakes or pies or tarts or scones, the kinds of treats kids love. But she gets those things every day, whatever sugary sweet she digs. So on her birthday, she says, 'I don't want my candles in a cake. I want them in a plate of lobster ravioli.' Except you didn't. You still went with the cake. See?"

"I love cake," Maggie had snapped, annoyed with the analogy.

"But you might have loved lobster ravioli, too."

Maggie shook off the memory. People were leaving Tanner Center in a rush, probably glad to get out of class and into the sunshine. They looked happy, despite it being a Monday.

Maggie wished it were a Friday, when the campus turned into a ghost town. Practically no one took Friday classes.

She unzipped her jacket and walked faster. It was warmer today. The thaw made the campus noisy with pings, plops, crunches, and splashes. Icicles oozed from eaves. Between short lawns of softening snow and walkways, between the main road and the curb, wherever two places met in a dip, water ran.

Up ahead stood the statue of Ebenezer Carlton. It used to make Maggie smile, how the artist had given the college's founder such a pissed-off look. Not exactly a welcoming expression.

Two girls stood at the statue's base, their heads almost touching. They were watching Maggie and whispering.

Maggie stifled an urge to break into a run. She could see the tidy row of freshman dorms just past the fountain and gazebo. *Nearly there.*

When she reached the first dorm, Finn Hall, four guys were exiting. Talking loudly about a hockey player's injury, they formed a single file to trudge past Maggie. She avoided eye contact and stared straight ahead at the mountains, rolling in their layers, blue by blue by blue, cleanly outlined against one another—a teeming ocean under an empty sky. Off Finn's steep roof, snowmelt dribbled and formed a wet shape on the building's side, like a crouching shadow, but the front bricks shone pinkly in the light, and the windows reflected the day's sparkle. The sun felt hot on her head. Maggie lowered her eyes from the glare and walked past the second hall, McCullers, and toward the third—Nash.

A young woman wearing a gray sweater solved the problem of Maggie's lack of a cardkey. She stepped out just as Maggie got to the doors. With a murmured thank-you, Maggie slipped inside and blinked. It took a moment for her eyes to adjust to the gloom.

The smell of sweat and soap hung in the air. This familiar odor, combined with the familiar, dingy brown tiles, the familiar signs advertising meetings and readings, and the familiar, small whiteboards, colorful with loopy-lettered messages, hearts, and flowers, hit her all at once. She stood stock-still and tried to get her bearings. Everything was the same here, it seemed. Everything except herself.

Holding her coat together at her throat, she hurried past the doors. Sara had lived with her roommate, Tina, on the third floor. Their RA had occupied the largest room on the left-hand side at the far end. Hopefully, the first floor was set up in a similar fashion.

When she reached the last door, Maggie wiped her damp palm on the front of her coat and knocked.

The door opened immediately. "Oh." A freckly woman, glasses askew and reddish braids coming undone, pressed a parted book to her chest and smiled. "I thought you were Flora. She left her key on the dresser."

"Are you the RA?"

She shook her head. "That's Flora. She went to pick up our pot stickers. She'll be back soon . . ." Suddenly, the smile slipped. Her eyes bugged out. A hectic red seeped up her cheeks. She inched back. "Do you want to wait for her?" she asked reluctantly.

Maggie dropped her gaze. "I guess." The floor was streaked with salt from the outside. "I don't know. I'm looking for someone."

"Maggie?"

Down the hall, Sara Wood leaned out of a doorway, her mouth hanging open. She looked like she'd seen a ghost.

Maggie could relate. "What . . ." She shook her head. "What are you doing here?"

"I live here. You know that."

Hardly registering the redhead's mumbled sorry-gotta-go and the closing of the door, Maggie stammered, "But—but you said you were moving off campus."

Sara lifted her chin. "My mom said I had to wait until I'm a junior." Defensively, she added, "But I have a single this year."

She nodded slowly, still reeling from coming face-to-face with Sara Wood, the girl she'd counted as a friend, actually, her *closest* college friend . . . until she'd realized she wasn't.

Sara ran a hand over her silky hair and tucked a dark strand behind her ear. "Well, got to go." She shuffled into her room. "I have a ton to do."

Maggie dazedly followed.

Sara yelped and jerked back when Maggie reached the doorway. "Um . . . nice seeing you." She had both hands on the door, as if preparing to slam it. "Good luck." The words were as final as *get lost.*

Maggie didn't budge. Couldn't. It was as if her feet had taken root on the threshold. A word echoed in her head. The word was *why.*

Sara's eyes flashed. "Stop looking at me like that." When Maggie frowned, bewildered, her old friend continued in a near whisper, "Like I went out of my way to—to *wrong* you or something." She thrust up her chin and crossed her arms. "You blame me, and that's totally unfair."

"You ditched me." *Hooked up with a guy, took off without warning, left me at a party where I knew absolutely no one.* "I don't know why you did that."

"I am *not* responsible for what happened. *I* didn't do anything to you."

She stared at her mutely. Why had she ever wanted to be close to this girl? Maggie knew what good-friend material looked like. Sam, Linnie, Caleb—they were going out of their way to help her. Ran, Colleen, Julia, Hope—they were sweet, too.

Maggie couldn't even claim that she hadn't known better last year. As a kid, she'd formed great relationships with Jen and Shayna. So what had happened to her judgment when she'd started college? Why had she admired Sara's sharp edge? Why hadn't she seen it for what it was? Not wit, not strength, but masked insecurity, weakness cast in meanness.

Maggie was disgusted, but mostly with herself. Her own insecurities had drawn her to such a toxic person. "You did do something," she said at last. "You criticized me for going to the police. And then, when the detective interviewed you, you went on and on about the crush I had on Matt Dawson."

Sara's mouth soundlessly opened and closed like a fish's. "How did you know that?" she finally asked.

"I read the report."

"Well . . ." Sara's gaze darted around the room, as if looking to alight on an excuse, before she flicked back her hair and declared roundly, "It was true. You *did* have a crush on him."

"I barely knew him." A moment from the previous fall came back to her: Sitting in the stadium with Sara and Tina, the three of them huddled between shouting spectators. Maggie had easily spotted Matthew Dawson, standing with his teammates on the sideline, his helmet in the crook of his arm, his blond hair glinting in the sunlight, his number, 35, shining golden on the green game jersey stretched taut across his chest. Thinking aloud, she'd murmured, "Matthew Dawson is the most beautiful man I have ever seen." And Sara had giggled and slapped Tina to get her in on the laughter before answering, "You think so? Ha. You and every other girl here."

The memory made Maggie's skin crawl. Abruptly, she continued, "You made it sound like I'd been pursuing him. Like I wanted him and his buddies to do what they did to me . . ." Emotion roughened her voice. She cleared her throat, fisted her hands in her coat pockets, dug the nails into her palms. *Don't cry.* "I'm looking for someone. Her name is Jane Cannon. She's a freshman. I think she lives in this dorm."

"Never heard of her. And I really have to get back to work. I have an essay due tomorrow, so if you don't mind—"

"I do mind. I want you to help me find this girl's room." *You can do that. That is the least you can do.*

Maybe Sara realized the same, because—after some huffing and puffing and flouncing over to her desk to snatch up a pen and notepad—that's just what she did.

15

IN THE DIM hall, Sara flipped through the student register she'd gotten from the resident director, a woman named Naomi who also lived on the first floor, across from the main entrance. Sara bent her head lower over the pamphlet. "Here she is," she bit out. "Second floor." She jotted the room number on a sticky note, wordlessly handed Maggie the fluorescent pink square, stomped away, then disappeared into her room and slapped the door shut.

Maggie scowled. "Good-bye and good riddance," her mother would have said. Maggie preferred something shorter and said it aloud to the empty corridor: "Fuck you, Sara."

She'd crumpled the sticky note in her hand. After smoothing it open to read it, she headed for the stairwell.

Room 2E was easy to find. She knocked softly.

No one answered.

She knocked again, harder, and waited. A minute passed. She pressed her ear to the door and heard a whole lot of nothing. What if Jane was in class? Linnie and Caleb would be waiting for Maggie by the library soon. She sighed, then tried one more time—a loud rap.

A girl with spiky black hair and bags under her squinting eyes swung open the door, muttering a groggy "Yeah . . . ?" It was clear she'd been napping.

Maggie apologized, then asked, "Are you Jane Cannon?"

She shook her head and said around a huge yawn, "Kimberly."

"I'm looking for Jane." Maggie glanced over the girl's shoulder at a room strewn with clothes. "Is she around?"

Kimberly stretched, her arms making a wide arc that ended with her hands slapping her thighs. Flatly: "She's long gone."

Maggie gasped. Oh God! "Dead?"

"*What?* No." She tilted her head to the side, an impatient gesture. "Moved out. She's back home."

Back home? *Back home?* Where the hell was that? Texas? Missouri? California?

". . . and failing her classes," Kimberly was saying. The broad shoulders came up. "That much was obvious." Drily, she added, "You can't pass your classes if you don't get out of bed."

Maggie chewed on her lower lip. Why had she never guessed that Jane's silence had to do with the possibility that she'd dropped out of school? After all, it's what Maggie had done, though not officially—she'd been granted a leave of absence. But maybe Jane *had* made her leaving official, prompting CC to suspend her email account . . .

Cautiously, Maggie asked, "Did she ever tell you what was wrong?"

"Nope." Kimberly grunted. "Jane was kind of weird."

She grimaced at the assessment—recognized, after everything she'd gone through last year, that the description applied to herself as well. It was hard to stay normal under certain circumstances. "I really need to get in touch with her. Do you have her phone number and home address?" She held her breath, half-expecting Kimberly to shake her head and turn Maggie away.

Instead, she said, "Sure," and trudged across her room, swatted a hoodie off her desk, and yanked open a drawer. She pulled out a notebook and opened it to its first page. "Thought so. Jane lives in Wilson."

Hope flared. "That's outside of Albany, right?" Not far away at all. She, Linnie, and Caleb could drive straight there.

"Close to Saratoga." She picked up what looked like a short essay, made a face at the grade, and turned it over. As she scrawled across the blank side, she said without looking up, "Tell Jane I said hi." Holding out the paper, she added, "She left her ironing board. It's still here if she wants to come and get it. You can tell her that, too."

Maggie didn't realize what she'd expected to find until she and her friends finally reached the Cannon residence, then the truth struck her—she'd assumed the address would lead them to a modest, two-story Colonial, just like a house in Carlton. The one Maggie had grown up in.

But there was nothing middle-class about the Cannons' house.

Linnie, sitting in front, summed it up: "Wow. A mansion."

Caleb gave the steering wheel a nervous drum. "I feel funny parking my car here."

"Like a big brown turd on the side of the road," Linnie murmured.

He frowned. "Hey."

Maggie pulled out her phone. "Half past four." She glanced up at the big brick house. It was old and elegant, but the long windows gave the facade a disapproving aspect, maybe because of the time of day. The glass panes caught the setting sun and glinted redly, like angry eyes. "I'd better do this on my own."

"Yeah, I think you should, too. Jane might not appreciate an audience." Linnie poked Caleb in the shoulder. "Want to take Fluffster to the park we passed?"

The dog obviously recognized the word *park*. He leaned toward Caleb, tail wagging like crazy.

"Let's wait until we find out if anyone's home." He patted his panting dog away from his face. "Looks empty, doesn't it?"

Maggie nodded and chewed on the corner of her lower lip. She hadn't called beforehand—had felt as if it was better to handle this kind of situation in person. She pushed open the door. "I'll ring the bell. If someone lets me in, you guys can feel free to take off."

"You've got my number," Caleb said. "Just call or text when you're done."

"Thanks." Maggie got out and made her way up the paved path.

She rang the doorbell. She'd heard it chime inside, so she

knew it worked, but she went ahead and knocked as well. No one answered. She waited. And waited. After a few minutes, she gave up.

Caleb peered at her ruefully when she slipped back into the car. "No one home?"

Maggie shook her head.

Linnie, eyes fastened on the upper story of the house, said, "Someone's there." While Maggie turned and Caleb leaned sideways to follow her gaze, Linnie added, "Just no one interested in seeing us."

A pale curtain, barely visible in the glinting window, twitched and fell.

"Should I knock again?" Maggie asked.

Still eyeing the window, Linnie said, "Whoever's in there knows you're here. If she wanted to see you, she'd open the door."

"Let's try tomorrow," Caleb said. "Maybe she's sick or something."

"Hmm." Linnie continued to stare up at the house. A strange expression crossed her face, something like skepticism or defeat, but whatever she was thinking, she kept it to herself.

"Maggie!" Dad swept her, along with her duffel bag and half-full Starbucks cup, into a bear hug. "Oh, my goodness, how did you get—wait." He scanned her face. "You okay? It's not your aunt, is it? Don't tell me you had it out with her, too. Poor Minnie's been a wreck. She won't say what the ruckus is over."

Her smile dimmed. "I'm just visiting for a couple of nights." His comments worried her. Mom was good at keeping a cheerful front, even in the worst situations. The fact that Dad (loving and easygoing but, well, kind of oblivious) had clued into the depths of her unhappiness didn't bode well. Mom clearly wasn't on her game. Apparently, she hadn't told Dad she wanted Maggie to move back home, either. But why? "Everything's fine with Wren," she added belatedly. Not really, but hey—she was her mother's daughter. *Everything's fine. Absolutely fine. Nothing to see here, folks. Move along.*

"Your aunt"—he shook his head—"is a contentious woman. So different from your mother." He smiled at her friends standing behind her. "Who do we have here?"

Maggie made the introductions, then called into the house, "Mom?"

Dad crouched to pet Caleb's dog. "She's not home yet, honey. It's Monday night."

"Oh. I forgot." To her friends, she explained: "Book club night at the library." She'd have to find a chance to talk to Mom alone when she got back. And find a way to talk to Jane Cannon tomorrow. Apprehension fluttered in Maggie's stomach. Neither discussion was going to be easy.

"She'll be back a little after nine. Come on in, and I'll get us some drinks." After delivering a parting rub to the dog's side, Dad straightened and waved everyone into the house. "You can only stay a couple of nights?" he asked wistfully.

"Yeah." Maggie toed off her shoes and breathed in the familiar scent of her home, something like cookies and pine.

Linnie wandered around the foyer, hands folded under her chin. Her gaze lingered on the family photos decorating the staircase wall.

Caleb hung back. "If that's okay with you, Mr. Arioli. I've got Fluffster here . . ."

"Don't worry about that," Maggie said. "Dad loves dogs. We always had one when I was growing up."

"Remember how Sandy used to run with me in the morning? Our old golden," he said to Caleb. "Miss that guy. I wish Min would let me get another one. She's not on board with the idea—says dogs tie you down."

"That's true enough," Caleb said. Hands stuffed in his pockets, cheeks ruddy, he walked with Maggie and Linnie into the living room but then went to stand in a corner.

Maggie frowned at him. He looked so uncomfortable. She hadn't thought Caleb had it in him to *be* uncomfortable.

Linnie settled on the edge of the wingback chair and grinned at Caleb.

Maggie wandered to the stack of books on the side table and put down her cup. What author was Mom in love with now?

"Have a seat," her father said. As Caleb sidled along the wall toward the couch, Dad continued, "Pepsi sound good? Cider? Ginger ale? Iced tea?"

"I could go for some cider, thanks," Linnie said.

"Water, please." Caleb cleared his throat. "Just water sounds great, thank you." The dog tried to join him on the couch, and with a squawk of alarm, Caleb pushed him back down to the floor. "Stay."

"Maggie?"

She indicated her coffee cup. "I'm good." As her dad left the room, she rolled her shoulders and neck and yawned. "I am *beat*."

She threw herself into the other armchair. "Can't imagine how tired you must be, Caleb, doing all that driving. I really appreciate it." Fluffster wandered over and snuffled her outstretched hand, and she stroked his neck.

"Oh, no—no, no, it's fine. I'm fine."

Linnie snorted. "Water. Must. Have. Water."

He glared at her. "I'm thirsty."

She smiled slyly and peeked Maggie's way, as if to include her in on the joke.

Maggie stared at her blankly. *What?*

When her father came back with the drinks, he briefly halted just inside the living room, as if struck by a sudden thought.

Linnie accepted her drink with a murmured thanks; Caleb, with more of a strangled sound. And when Dad situated himself at the other end of the couch, Maggie was shocked by his expression. He leaned back and, in a sidelong way, observed Caleb darkly.

Caleb held the glass close to his red face, then abruptly took a sip of water. "Tastes good."

"What flavor is it?" Linnie asked.

He gave her a dirty look.

"So." Dad folded his arms. "Make decent time getting here?"

Maggie nodded slowly, bewildered by his tone. "Six and a half hours."

"Sounds like you were speeding."

"No, no, not at all," Caleb said, patting his flushed face with the glass. The ice cubes clinked. "We didn't hit much traffic."

"Hmm." Dad narrowed his eyes.

Maggie shook her head. *What the hell?* "We skipped lunch, too."

Her father straightened and said in a friendlier voice, "You must be starving."

"A little," Maggie admitted. But with Mom gone, they'd have to cook something for themselves. Dad was useless in the kitchen.

"I was just about to have a bowl of cereal, but we could order a pizza."

"Cereal's fine," Caleb said. "Sir."

Linnie snickered.

Maggie sighed. She was too tired and stressed out to deal with these bizarre tensions. She hadn't talked to Jane yet. And she hadn't talked to Mom yet. Besides finally confronting Sara (which, now that she thought about it, *had* felt pretty cathartic), she'd done little more than knock on doors today. "Actually, I think we'll head to town and get something." To her friends: "Does that work for you?"

"Definitely." Caleb stood quickly. But when his dog rose, his obvious relief vanished. He slapped his forehead. "What about Fluffster?"

"I'll watch him." Her father pulled out his wallet. "Here, sweetie." He passed her a few bills. "Supper's on me."

"Thanks, Dad. I feel bad leaving you behind. Want me to get you something?"

"No, I'm fine. You go." He fluttered a hand, urging them along. His frown returned when he glanced at Caleb. "Drive carefully."

* * *

Sitting in the backseat of the car and muddling over Jane's decision to leave school, Maggie distractedly directed Caleb to Dilly's, choosing it automatically. She and her parents had eaten at Dilly's for as long as she could remember.

But when they got there, the parking lot was full. Caleb slowed by the front doors.

"I'll check on the wait time." Linnie hopped out of the car and hurried inside. A minute later, she returned. "An hour, maybe longer. A couple's celebrating their golden anniversary. Looks like they invited every grandma and grandpa in town."

Caleb shook his head. "I'm starving."

"Me too," Linnie said. "What about that place we passed on the corner?"

"At the top of the hill?" Maggie had to think for a moment before she remembered its name. "Timberline Tavern. Never been there. I think it's just a burger-and-beer joint."

"Beer." Caleb smiled. "I could go for one."

"Just one," Linnie said. "Don't want Mr. Arioli to smell booze on you."

"He wouldn't mind," Maggie said. "Dad likes a Guinness himself now and then."

"Oh, he'll mind. He will mind, baby girl." She winked.

Maggie frowned.

Caleb ignored Linnie. "Let's check it out."

A few minutes later, they entered the bar's dimly lit interior. While Linnie gave her name and their party's number to the hostess, Maggie peered around curiously. The paneled walls, plank floors, and beamed ceiling made her feel as if she'd entered a lodge in the forest. But its smell was definitely that of a restaurant: charred meat and smoke.

Caleb inhaled lustily.

Linnie rubbed her hands together. "No free tables yet, but no line, either. Let's wait at the bar."

It wasn't until Maggie trailed them, passing the booths and tables on her left and, on her right, a handful of guys holding beers, their eyes trained on the games filling two huge television screens, that she realized her mistake.

Her feet slowed, even as her heart began to race.

They never should have picked this restaurant.

16

HEADS BEGAN TO turn. Conversations died. Ahead on the wall was a painted mural. Football players sprinted across a mountain-encircled field in the direction of the end zone. The clouds had been painted to suggest a wispy-white tiger, like a pagan god overseeing the action.

She hadn't entered just any bar. She'd entered one popular with the Tigers and their fans.

Feeling a hard stare, she glanced toward the restaurant side of the joint.

A waitress, poised with a raised water pitcher, glared her way.

Maggie shoved her hands into her jacket pockets and caught up with Caleb and Linnie. The latter was accepting a shot of something when Maggie reached them, and Caleb was asking the bartender what he had on tap.

At Maggie's appearance, Caleb finished ordering and patted the stool next to him. "Have a seat. Nice place. Smells great. What can I get you?"

A bartender slid a dark ale his way. Caleb didn't notice the man's scowl. He was smiling at Maggie.

An escape route. A disguise. "Pepsi sounds good."

He nodded and turned to place the order, but the bartender had stomped to the other end of the curved bar. Caleb smiled apologetically. "I'm sure he'll be back in a minute." Linnie, on his opposite side, murmured something, and he glanced her way with a laugh.

The bartender stood with his wide shoulders bunched up, facing a couple of patrons, a guy in a plaid flannel shirt and a woman wearing a baseball cap. The two of them were looking straight at Maggie.

She lowered her gaze. Dizziness hit her—woozy fear, warm embarrassment. *I have to get out of here.*

Her pulse pounding, she fought the urge to flee and concentrated on the scarred surface of the bar, shivered, and pulled her jacket more tightly across her chest.

Caleb shared a laugh with Linnie, then leaned back as if abruptly aware that Maggie wasn't in on the joke. His smile faded. "You don't have a drink yet. Sorry about that." He called to the bartender, "Excuse me?"

The man didn't turn, but his shoulders jerked.

Caleb gave a shake of his head. "Excuse me? Bartender?"

The man still didn't turn. But he did move. Stiffly, he stepped to the side, kneed open a short gate on the opposite end of the bar, and stormed toward the kitchen entrance, saying loudly on his way out, "*Cunt*."

The music blared. Maggie, hot-faced and motionless with shock, wondered why someone had turned up the volume. Then she realized no one had. It was just that the conversations had ceased. Nothing muffled Taylor Swift gushing about a guy, handsome as hell. The people along the bar weren't looking at Maggie anymore. They'd become very interested in their drinks.

Caleb half-rose, his eyes wide with horrified amazement.

Linnie slammed down her glass and strode to Maggie's side. "Come on. If that fucker can't give you a fucking Pepsi, he can damn well give Caleb and me our drinks on the house." To Caleb, who'd drawn out his wallet, she ordered, "*Put that away*."

A thick-necked man near Maggie snarled, "It's best for all of us if you take your friend and leave. Who knows what she'll do if she doesn't get served to her satisfaction?" He barked a laugh and swatted the person on his left.

His companion chuckled, too. It wasn't a convincing sound. The two men weren't even smiling.

Neither was Caleb. He leaned past Maggie to grab a full glass and hurled the beer in the thick-necked guy's face.

He jumped off his seat, sputtering.

"You're an asshole," Caleb said. At the same time, a big man flew out of the kitchen.

Linnie's laughter was a surprised trill. "Our drinks are on the house, and now your drink is on you." She linked Maggie's arm with her own. "Let's go." She pulled on Caleb's jacket sleeve.

But he shook his head, visibly furious, his glare fixed on the dripping jerk.

The heavyset man, presumably the manager, nervously smoothed the sides of his head and sidled between Caleb and the soaked man.

Patrons watched out of the corners of their eyes. "Hotline Bling" replaced Taylor Swift. The song's bitterness sounded off, the wrong soundtrack to accompany the manager's squeaked apology and the sudden laughter of a group entering the restaurant.

Maggie just wanted to leave. She turned her back on the guy who'd made the ugly joke. He disgusted her. How could he not see that she'd cried rape because six men had raped her? One of those rapists had even *admitted* as much. The way Matt Dawson looked during the hearing returned to her—bent over, hands on the back of his head, weeping and nodding and acknowledging the truth in a broken voice. So did the terror and the sickness she'd experienced sitting in his presence.

She shakily reached into the pocket of her jacket for one of the twenty-dollar bills her dad had given her and set it on the bar. "Caleb." She grazed his shoulder. "Ready?"

"*Yes,*" Linnie answered for him.

Red with anger, Caleb finally spun away from the jerk, who was still standing by the bar, angrily mopping his wet hair with a sleeve.

The manager breathed a sigh of relief and sat heavily on a stool.

They walked single file toward the door. The people they passed looked everywhere—the plates of cooling burgers and fries, their hands, the floor—except at them. Only one person, a bespectacled, brown-haired woman around Maggie's age, didn't avoid eye contact. In a corner booth, she sat with her family. Her gaze was sympathetic.

Maggie appreciated the girl's kind expression. It gave her the courage to walk with her head up and reminded her that not the entire population of Carlton, Vermont, was horrible. For every creep who'd lashed out at Maggie with a tweet, remark, or post, there had been a decent person who'd supported her. Maggie needed to remember that.

It was so hard to remember that.

At the door, she had to pass the group waiting by the hostess. They had fallen silent. Maggie recognized a few players and their pals from that fateful party, their faces forever seared in her memory. Sara Wood stood with them.

And suddenly, the puzzle pieces snapped together, and Maggie saw the big picture. Sara had defended Maggie's attackers to the police for a reason. She'd done it to fit in with their crowd.

Caleb swung open the door and waited for Linnie and Maggie to pass, but Maggie lagged behind, just long enough to scan Sara's pinched face and remark, "Nice friends."

They ended up back at Dilly's.

Some of the anniversary guests had left ("Croaked, most likely," Linnie quipped with a weak smile) and freed up a few tables. The hostess, her sagging bun and half-untucked blouse testaments to a hectic evening, greeted Maggie with a vague, "Hey, Margaret. Didn't see your folks at church yesterday. How are they doing?" She waited long enough to hear "Fine, thanks," then thrust three menus at a hovering employee and ordered him to seat Maggie, Caleb, and Linnie in booth seventeen.

A minute later, the waitress arrived. She poured water, rattled off the specials, took drink orders, and left Maggie, on one side of the booth, staring at Linnie and Caleb on the other.

Maggie wondered if she looked like her friends did: shell-shocked.

They sat without talking for a long moment, peering around blindly, blinking owlishly.

Maggie's hands were still trembling. She wrapped them around the water glass. "Thanks for standing up for me."

"Holy shit," Caleb whispered. Then, louder: "Holy. Shit."

Linnie searched Maggie's face. "You okay?"

She nodded, kind of amazed that she *was* okay. It had been ugly.

But it hadn't killed her.

No one came out to the foyer when they returned home after dinner. Maggie figured out why in the living room. The explanation was on the couch—or, more specifically, on her parents.

Sprawled across Mom's and Dad's laps, Fluffster delivered a halfhearted bark to announce Maggie and her friends, then went back to being the blissed-out recipient of generous petting.

Mom, holding open a slim book in one hand, smiled tremulously. "Honey."

Maggie bent to kiss her mother's cheek.

She dropped her book on the side table so she could add a hug to the exchange, and she murmured in Maggie's ear, "I'm glad you're here. You don't need to go back. Please stay."

"I can't," Maggie whispered.

Mom gave her a look. "I'll give you a few more days there, but I want you home. I'm making the arrangements."

There was a frantic edge to her tone, but she seemed to catch it herself, because she quickly released Maggie. The greetings and conversation she shared with Caleb and Linnie were steady and welcoming: "It's so nice to meet you." "Did you make good time?" "Oh! You checked out the college?" "The campus is lovely, isn't it?" "*Dilly's*? I'm amazed you got a table. Wasn't it packed with the Bauers' anniversary party?"

Even these pleasantries struck Maggie as odd. Her parents had always been protective, and they'd become only more so since last March. Under normal circumstances, her mother would have eyed Caleb with a measure of Dad's distrust, fretted about Linnie, too (considering the things she'd learned about her when she'd stayed with Wren), stressed over the reliability of Caleb's car, and probably worried about the entire concept of a road trip.

Mom was preoccupied. And Maggie knew why.

Maggie nudged open the bedroom door. An enormous snore greeted her. Dad was alone in the room, asleep on his back, his arms sprawled wide. A snorer *and* a bed hog. She softly closed the door. Not the parent she needed to see.

She made her way down the hallway. It was silent. Linnie, in the guest bedroom, must have fallen asleep, too. What about Caleb? He and his dog had settled in the basement den on the pullout couch.

The house felt strange with its added occupants . . . strange in a comforting way. Pleasantly full. And somehow safer, as if

Linnie and Caleb were contributing their kindness to the house, helping to insulate it from the world. Maggie thought about Timberline Tavern. That incident could have ended very differently. Dangerously.

She hadn't told her parents about it—didn't want them to know. What good would telling them do? It would only make them angry and scared and sad.

Downstairs, she headed for the living room, expecting to find Mom still reading on the couch. Instead, she found her sitting cross-legged on the floor, leaning over a family album.

Maggie shoved her hands into her hoodie pockets. "Are you hiding from me?"

Mom rolled her eyes. "Does this look like a covert operation?" She turned a page and clucked. "We used to be so good about getting pictures developed and organized in albums. Then your dad gave me the digital camera for Christmas. When was that? Eight years ago? The next Christmas, he got me an iPhone." She sighed. "I take more pictures than ever but just save them on the computer. A lot of good that does. I hardly ever go back to them." She pulled the album onto her lap and bent to study a snapshot of Maggie as a baby, asleep in the high chair.

Maggie crouched for a better look. Her round baby face was plastered with something disgusting. Mashed broccoli? Asparagus? It was a putrid shade of green. "Ick. What were you feeding me? Soylent green?"

"Peas." Her mom sighed again, damply this time. "You used to love peas."

"You don't have to cry about it. I'll start eating peas again, if you want."

A wet laugh escaped Mom. She closed the album, rubbed her eyes, and sat back, resting her shoulder blades against the seat cushion of the armchair. "Your friends are nice." Her palm smoothed the burgundy cover, and she matched Maggie's nod with one of her own. "Even Linnie. I guess I wasn't prepared to think so, knowing what I did about her."

"But you don't know her." Maggie sat on the floor and picked up another album. Idly opening it, she admitted, "Neither do I." Loving and neglectful, caring and careless, friendly and furious, brave and scared. "Linnie's hard to understand." What would she be like in two days, when they reached her hometown? They'd promised Sam they'd stop there to pick up the letter at Linnie's old neighbor's house. Or at least Caleb and Maggie had promised. Linnie hadn't said a word about the destination. That, at least, was consistent in Linnie's character: a steadfast resistance to looking ahead.

"You could say that about everyone," Mom said, and reopened the album in her lap.

Maggie nodded. No one was ever one thing. Not even Matt Dawson. Those who'd been at the hearing for him and testified (football coach, an old teacher, his parents) had been tearful and incredulous: "Matt's a *terrific* kid." "Respectful, you know?" "He wouldn't—*couldn't*—do something like this. I just can't believe it. I can't picture him hurting anyone, least of all a girl." As character witnesses, these people hadn't been conspirators. It was just that the possibility of Matthew Dawson leading a drunken gang rape had been beyond their comprehension. And Matt Dawson had cried along with them, as if he couldn't believe it himself. But eventually he had confessed. Then even *that* had been dismissed by his fans. A forced confession, they'd insisted. The result of coercion.

She shook off these dismal thoughts and concentrated on the page she'd opened to in the album, jarred when she realized she was looking at a photograph of her grandparents, taken at Thanksgiving. Grandma Heed, smiling at Dad, sat at one end of the dining room table. Opposite her, at the other end, sat Maggie's grandfather, his expression dour. This was not unusual. Behind his back, Mom and Dad had regularly changed his nickname from Gramps to Grumpy. And though Maggie had gotten plenty of attention from her grandmother, even as a young child, she'd sensed that Grumpy Gramps didn't care much for kids.

"What are you looking at?" Mom leaned forward to see the photograph. "Oh."

Maggie caught her lower lip in her teeth and gingerly closed the album.

"No, no," Mom said loudly, "get a good look at our happy memories. Better do it now. Wren's about to obliterate them." Her fingers went to her forehead and rested there, as if to ward off a glare from the sun.

"You're sure the memories were all happy?"

"For me, yes. Sufficiently happy." Her voice was clipped, but it cracked when she continued, "And memories are all I have left of those two."

"You still have Wren. Shouldn't you try to"—Maggie raised her shoulders—"keep her?"

Mom's hand fell to the floor. "I see whose side you're on."

"Don't be like that. I only wish her exhibition wasn't such a problem. After all these years, after you two are finally getting along . . ." She rubbed her eyes. "I hate to think of some fired clay ruining your relationship."

"Fabricating dirty laundry and airing it in everyone's faces." Mom folded her arms and added bitterly, "Family concerns, personal business—just *blaring* it all to the whole world."

Maggie flinched at the choice of the word *fabricating*. "Artists reveal difficult issues. That's, like, their job."

"In Wren's case," Mom said coolly, "it's a job that pays very well, I'm sure."

Maggie gazed at her mutely. Her mother's comments—doubting the truthfulness of what her sister was exposing, wanting any hint of it kept secret, implying Wren was milking the situation to make money—were ugly. And familiar. How often had Maggie been accused of speaking up about matters "better left unsaid," flat-out lying, ruining people's cherished memories, and even setting out to do it for money, though she'd never filed a lawsuit or done anything that would have benefited her financially? "Wren's not trying to make you agree with her or even participate. She's just giving you the heads-up."

"So for the next month, I steer clear, keep my eyes off art magazine covers, and avoid reading the reviews?"

"That's an option."

"And cover my ears if someone stops by to discuss the show?"

"If you have to, yeah."

"And turn off the radio when NPR covers Wren Heed?"

Maggie blew an exasperated sigh. "Depending on how committed you are to avoiding the truth, then yes, I suppose you'll have to stay away from the media, in general, for a couple of weeks."

"So!" Mom's finger struck the air like a baton. "You're convinced that what she's putting out there is the truth."

"I don't think Wren is a liar," she answered cautiously.

"And I am?"

Maggie shook her head. "This is what I know: Aunt Wren has dragged her feet on this project. She's finishing it in the nick of time. It was a hard thing for her to create, to address personally and publicly. Putting the exhibition together . . ." She briefly closed her eyes, remembering Wren that night in the studio, weary yet resolute. "For her, it was a necessary hell."

A tense moment passed, filled only with the dogged ticking of the mantel clock.

Then Mom crumpled. "He was *my dad*, Maggie. I can't—I just can't believe it. He wouldn't. He *couldn't*." She dragged up her gaze and, through tears, stared at Maggie imploringly. "I don't think you understand how this show is going to change everything—how it's going to rewrite my entire life."

"Oh, Mom." Maggie took her hand and squeezed it. "I do know. Last year, I listened to testimony after testimony on six guys' behalf. I couldn't discredit what their families and friends had to say about them. People do good things, wonderful things in their lives. Sometimes they screw up. Terribly. And sometimes their bad behavior becomes a sick habit. But *please*," she exhaled. "*Please* keep in mind: Exonerating Gramps means you're accusing Wren. It's not fair to her. I know how that feels, doing the right thing by exposing a wrong, then getting labeled a liar. It feels shitty."

"People do lie, Margaret. You didn't. But many do."

Many? No. Not in such situations. Maggie couldn't believe

that—wouldn't even change *many* to *some*. There was little to gain by lying. Society, with all its myths and perversions and double standards, made sure of that. She prodded her temples. "Wren doesn't want to lose you. Are you willing to lose her?"

Mom touched Maggie's head and rose to her feet, slowly, staggeringly. "I'm sorry, honey."

After she left, Maggie, exhausted and glum, stayed on the floor, her head propped in a hand. She opened an album and dispiritedly flipped through the photos, again passing the Thanksgiving snapshot. She paused to study it before continuing.

A dull awareness stirred. Something in these pictures seemed . . . off.

More attentively, she plodded through the rest of the photographs. By the end of the album, her inkling had turned into a fully formed thought. She returned to the beginning of the album and went through the photographs again. Then, heart racing, she seized the leather-covered album and pored over its contents.

She slapped it shut and stared straight ahead.

"Shit," she whispered. Why had she never realized this before?

17

THROUGHOUT THE NIGHT, Maggie's discovery consumed her. It invaded her dreams, and she slept fitfully. The next morning, while her parents got ready for work and Caleb and Linnie took the dog for a walk around the neighborhood, Maggie sat the kitchen table, slouched over her coffee and an untouched piece of toast. What was she going to do?

Mom flew into the kitchen. "I'm late." After grabbing her purse, she planted a kiss on the top of Maggie's head and then, wearing an expression that somehow managed both defiance and remorse, hauled her into a hug.

Still sitting, Maggie found her face pressed against her mother's stomach, transporting her to an earlier time when most embraces put her in this position. She fought the urge to burrow and cry.

Mom smoothed her hair. "Listen, sweetheart. I don't want you to confuse what happened to you with whatever's going on with Wren. My sister"—she exhaled heavily—"has always been a handful, drinking, getting high, disrupting everyone's life, basically sleeping around, and raising hell. There's no other way to put this: I hate to say she's a troublemaker, but there you have it."

Maggie thought about Linnie. That night she'd picked her up at the party, when Linnie had compared her history with Maggie's, what was it she'd said? *A bipolar dropout with an ugly history, an addiction or two, and a record, for good measure? I don't qualify for justice. You, though . . . you painted a convincing picture, a classic picture.* Maggie squeezed her eyes shut.

"I'm sorry I ever thought having you stay at my sister's was a bright idea."

"Aunt Wren's been good to me."

"No. She's manipulating you. Tonight, we'll talk more. I'll make the arrangements to get you settled back home."

Maggie sighed against her mother, remembering the previous evening's stressful incident at the bar. Carlton wasn't a welcoming place—not for Maggie. That was why she'd left in the first place. Mom seemed to have forgotten that.

". . . not ready to see Wren," her mother was saying. "Really, I—I just don't want to go there, but it might be hard for you to take the bus, lugging all your stuff, so your dad will probably have to pick you up. We'll figure it out. I've—" Her voice caught. She continued huskily, "I've missed you like crazy. As for Wren, well, I wanted to trust her, but I can't. I simply *can't*. But please . . ." Her hold tightened, and Maggie felt the hand against her head tremble. "Don't ever think I doubt *you*. I've never doubted *you*, Maggie dear. You're not at all like Wren."

Not at all? Maggie pulled away.

Mom glanced at the clock and started. "Shoot. Got to go. See you tonight, sweetheart."

After a hurried kiss, Mom left. Maggie remained at the table. Eventually she'd have to hash it out with her mother. First, there were the photographs. They warranted a discussion. Second, there was Wren. Maggie trusted and respected her aunt. She certainly didn't suspect her of lying. But how to make this clear without Mom accusing her of taking her sister's side?

After traveling all the way to the Cannons' house in Wilson a second time, Maggie found herself in the same situation as the day before—ringing the doorbell, waiting, knocking, waiting. Fruitlessly waiting.

She gave up and returned to the car, parked on the side of the road.

"Nobody's home?" Caleb asked.

"I guess not," she said unhappily, and fastened her seat belt.

"Or, more likely, whoever's home doesn't want to see you," Linnie said from the backseat. She patted Fluffster, curled up next to her. "Ready to give up?"

Caleb frowned. "We've tried only twice."

"And on both occasions," Linnie said impatiently, "not one person in the Cannon household opened the door, so maybe we should take a hint and back off. Jane wants to be left alone. We should respect that."

Maggie moodily gazed up at the brick house. Maybe Linnie was right. She didn't want to harass Jane. That was the *last* thing she wanted. But that flicker of movement in the window the previous day might have been a cat rustling a curtain when it jumped down from the sill, and now it was midday, a time when most houses stood empty. It was perfectly reasonable to assume the same was true of this place. Plus, Jane's failure to write back could be explained if the girl wasn't using her school email account any longer. In other words, Jane could be oblivious to Maggie's attempts to contact her. "If you guys don't mind," she said slowly, "I'd like to come back here again at suppertime. At least then there's a chance Mr. or Mrs. Cannon will be home from work. I—I guess I want Jane to know that I truly did try to get in touch with her."

Linnie huffed. *"Fine."*

Caleb started the car and smiled encouragingly at Maggie. "That sounds like a good plan."

The next three hours, mostly spent walking the dog and looking at strangers' houses, passed slowly. With only a little money and a lot of Fluffster on their hands, they couldn't do much to kill time. They couldn't even visit the village's new dog park. Caleb's pet, without the permit tag verifying his vaccinations, wasn't allowed in. A police officer explained this (and indicated a posted sign that made the rule explicit) before directing them off the premises.

Linnie took the banishment personally. She was pissed; Maggie and Caleb, just embarrassed. They tried to tease her into better spirits. It didn't work.

When Maggie gave her a cheering pat, Linnie wrenched her

arm away and snapped, "Fuck it. I'm going back to the car. It's freezing out, and I'm tired. You guys can explore this shitty town on your own." She stomped down the street.

Maggie stared after her in amazement. "What the hell?"

"Meh." Caleb rubbed his dog's side. "She's just missing her . . ." He shook his head, as if he were reluctant to say aloud what Linnie was missing. His smile was sad. "Try not to take her bad mood personally."

A couple of hours later, they found her asleep (or faking sleep) in the backseat. By then, Maggie half-wished she were doing the same. She felt sapped and discouraged.

But when they returned to the Cannons' place, she had reason to hope. Interior lights warmed the long windows, and the light outside the garage was on, too. A sleek Lexus sat in the driveway. At least one person was home.

"I'll wait here for you," Caleb said quietly as Maggie got out of the car.

"Thanks." She hurried up the walkway and rang the doorbell, then stood at the front door uncertainly, patting her hair and wincing at the damage the day's wind had wreaked. Her cheeks burned from the cold. She blew her nose on a cheap napkin she'd saved from her lunch and shivered inside her coat. She probably looked like a vagrant.

The woman who answered the door clearly thought so as well. "May I help you?" She held the door open at an angle just past a crack. She was tall and stately, a human version of her house.

"Hi." Maggie straightened and lifted her chin, striving to come across as assertive and respectable. "I'm a friend of Jane's. From Carlton. I was wondering if she was in."

"Oh." The door widened, and the woman stepped back. After Maggie entered, the woman shut the door gently, as if to avoid waking someone. "I'm not sure if . . ." She wrung her hands. "My daughter hasn't been feeling great."

"I know. She told me." *And what did she tell you?* There was a lull, during which she and Jane's mother eyed each other. Did Mrs. Cannon know what had happened?

The woman's gaze seemed to indicate a similar quandary. Finally, she walked toward the swirled end of a dark bannister. "Let me see if she's up."

"Oh, that would be great." Maggie smiled in relief. "Thank you."

"Who should I tell her is here?"

"Margaret Arioli."

The older woman's entire bearing changed. "Oh dear." She stepped back from the staircase. Her expression was apologetic, but her hands, half-raised, said, *Halt*. "We're working hard to put that Carlton business behind her."

"She wrote to me, asking for help."

"I realize that." She strode across the foyer and reopened the front door. "But what she needs is professional help. I've arranged for her to see someone starting next week, an excellent therapist in Albany. She's not too happy about that, but I'm doing my best to convince her to go."

"That's good." Maggie edged toward the door. She didn't have a choice. Mrs. Cannon was herding her out. "I don't want to provide therapy. I just thought I could offer her, like, support."

"I see. Well, that's . . . thoughtful." Her tone suggested other-wise. "I know about you, Margaret, and what you went through.

It was in the paper"—she grimaced—"on more than one occasion. You had a tough time last year. Too tough, in my opinion. I don't want Jane . . ." She cleared her throat. "To face a similar ordeal." She palmed her cheek. "I want her to forget and hopefully, someday, start over at a different college. That's the best I can hope for."

Maggie stared at her bleakly. She wanted to ask: What about justice? What about confronting whoever it was who'd hurt her? What about keeping him from targeting others? But Jane's mother looked determined. Over the woman's shoulder, Maggie could see a bit of the hallway at the top of the staircase. She wished Jane would appear and speak for herself—and clarify whether her mom's solution (if it could be called that) was also her own.

"Thank you for visiting." Mrs. Cannon opened the door even wider—a pointed *here's the way out; now leave.*

With a hollow sense of defeat, she trudged outside. "Will you please tell her I stopped by, let her know she can call or write if she wants?"

Without meeting Maggie's gaze, she nodded, then murmured a fast "Thanks and bye now."

Maggie was left facing a closed door. She suspected the woman wouldn't mention a word about her visit to Jane. In fact, Maggie doubted she'd ever hear from Jane Cannon again.

"Well," Linnie said, "*that* was a waste of time."

Maggie turned. She and Caleb had been driving for almost twenty minutes and talking quietly, not wanting to disturb Linnie's sleep.

She struggled up from her backseat sprawl and yawned. A truck hauling logs roared past. Its lights cut into the car, skimming Linnie's delicate features and heavy eyes. She massaged her forehead and faintly groaned. "So Jane's not joining Margaret's crime-fighting team of superheroes?"

The sarcasm rattled Maggie.

Caleb flicked Linnie a frown in the rearview mirror.

Linnie ignored him. She stroked the head of Fluffster, curled on the backseat floor, and smiled humorlessly. "Let's review our mission, see how we've fared. Storming the enemy's camp at Timberline Tavern? No converts there. Pleading with Mrs. Arioli to give poor Wren a fucking break? Wuh-wuh. Enlisting Jane Cannon in the struggle for justice? Nope." She grunted a laugh.

Maggie stared. She closed her mouth.

"Jesus." Caleb stepped on the gas. "What is your problem?"

"I have no problem. In fact, I have the answer. People suck. They don't change. And it's stupid to expect otherwise."

Maggie sat up straighter, not liking the implied insult to herself (a little naive maybe, but not stupid) and her mother (sad and scared, but that didn't mean she sucked—and how the hell did Linnie know about Mom and Wren anyway?). She ordered her shoulders to relax and answered lightly, "Hopefully, we'll have better luck tomorrow in Baldwinsville."

"With *what*? I have no idea why Sam's so hot on my stopping in the old neighborhood."

"But that woman, Mary . . ."

"Tate." Linnie made a sound of disgust. "With the mystery letter. It's a goddamn *letter*! Why doesn't she just mail it?"

"Maybe she's afraid you'll toss it in the garbage if it reaches you that way," Caleb suggested.

Linnie flung back her head and closed her eyes. "We are not stopping in Baldwinsville."

Maggie said, "But we promised Sam—"

"Sam can go fuck himself."

Fluffster whined.

"If there's something important for you to learn from Mrs. Tate," Maggie said haltingly, "shouldn't we—"

In a fierce rush, Linnie interrupted: "I *never* want to go back to that place. I'm not asking you to revisit *your* nightmare. Why would you ask me? Don't make me compare my shit with yours, Margaret. *Don't* make me go there."

The dog barked. Caleb shushed him.

Maggie squeezed her hands together to stop the trembling. Linnie was right. "I'm sorry."

Caleb gave her a sympathetic glance, then sent the sympathy Linnie's way in the rearview mirror. "All anyone hopes for in this car right now is for people to be happier and healthier."

"Speak for yourself!"

The dog whined again.

In a quieter tone, she bit out, "I have no such hope. I am not waiting for joy."

"Then what are you waiting for?" Caleb asked.

Linnie didn't answer. She stared out the window, briefly touching the glass. "Can we just go straight home tomorrow? Without stopping in Baldwinsville? Please?"

"I guess so," Maggie said, "if that's what you want." At Linnie's slight nod, Maggie turned around, frustrated. She folded her arms, stared at the streaming darkness, and willed Linnie's pessimism not to infect her.

For the rest of the drive back to Carlton, no one spoke another word.

18

MAGGIE HAD TEXTED her parents after she and her friends left the Cannons', and when they reached the house, supper was ready and waiting for them. Dad had ordered an enormous pizza and three dozen wings, and he'd picked up cupcakes from Fitz's Bakery, too. He beamed when he presented the dessert, arranged on Mom's Christmas-themed platter. "My Maggie loves Fitz's cupcakes."

"Thanks, Dad," Maggie said, touched but also embarrassed. Her parents had a real knack for making her feel like she was ten years old.

Unfortunately, his efforts to create a festive mood fell flat. Nobody had much to say at the dinner table. Maggie, reluctant to bring up Jane, was vague about how she and her friends had spent their afternoon. Linnie didn't help. Distant and dreary, she picked at her meal and then excused herself from the table without finishing her slice of pizza, mumbling something about not feeling well and calling it a night. Caleb still seemed nervous around Maggie's dad. And though Mom popped a question here and there, her preoccupied expression made it plain she wasn't paying attention to anyone's answers.

Poor Dad just looked confused.

After dinner, Mom waved away Caleb's offer to help clean up, so he took Fluffster outside for a walk. She shooed Dad, too. "Maggie can help," she said tersely.

"Okay . . . ?" With a bewildered frown, Dad tugged the sports page out of the newspaper and escaped into the living room.

While Mom rinsed the plates for the dishwasher, Maggie wrapped up the leftovers and thought about how she'd be leaving for Wren's in the morning—without having seen or talked to Jane. And then there was Linnie, refusing to stop by her old neighborhood to collect the letter . . .

The letter.

Maybe Maggie should write one. She and her friends could swing by the Cannons' place once more on their way back to Wren's, and Maggie could slip the letter into the mail slot. And if that didn't get Jane to contact her, well then, Maggie would just have to make her peace with the situation.

"It's all set," Mom whispered.

She glanced up. "What is?"

"Shh." Standing at the sink, her mother slipped the platter into the sudsy water and peeked over her shoulder toward the dining room. "This Saturday. Your dad will pick you up. He doesn't need to know why. I just told him things weren't working out with

Wren. We'll get you squared away." She scrubbed the frosting off the platter with unnecessary force. "And then we'll have to pray for the best—with my sister, I mean. I keep hoping we'll work through this mess." She drew a shaky breath and continued mournfully, "If only she'd do the right thing and think twice about ruining everyone's lives with her awful art show."

"I can't agree with you on that one . . ."

"You *want* her to ruin my life?"

"I mean about doing the right thing. It *is* the right thing . . . for her." Maggie shrugged. "Probably for everyone."

Mom's laugh was shrill. "Since when is lying right?"

"Oh, Mom." How to bring up what she'd realized from studying the photo albums? This was so difficult! "Are you sure she's—"

Mom released a sob, threw the dishrag into the sink, and fled.

Maggie stared after her. "Well, that went well." Exasperated, she slogged to the sink to finish the dishes, wrinkled her nose at the snowman painted across the platter, and ran his jovial snowball face under the spigot, muttering under her breath, "Everything sucks."

The following morning, Maggie got dressed, packed her duffel bag, and headed downstairs early, hoping to smooth over the previous evening's tension. Though she found her dad in the kitchen drinking his coffee, her mother had apparently left for work. Dumbfounded, she glanced at the clock over the sink. "It's not even seven o'clock."

Dad folded the newspaper. "Sorry, sweetheart. I wish she

were here to see you off. She practically ran out of the house—said something about an early meeting." His expression was troubled.

Maggie's friends trudged into the kitchen, and her father greeted them, then leaned forward in his chair to pet Fluffster. "How about breakfast?" Dad asked. "I can zip over to Fitz's and get us some pastries."

"Thanks, but we need to hit the road." Linnie and Caleb had done a really nice thing, coming with her, driving her here. But Linnie looked sick and exhausted. And Maggie wouldn't ask Caleb to miss more classes and schoolwork. It was time to go.

Dad got to his feet and pulled Maggie into a hug. "I guess I'm picking you up this weekend?"

"No."

"But your mom said—"

"I'm not coming back yet." She squeezed her dad's hand. "But I'd love for you guys to visit me at Wren's."

"That *was* the plan for Thanksgiving. Not certain how that will play out, with your mom in such a tizzy. Plus, your aunt . . . well, I'd rather you visit us here."

She smiled a little. "You don't have to be scared of Wren."

"She's scary," he said simply, but softened the charge with a silly cringe of exaggerated fear. Then he said good-bye to Maggie's friends, shook their hands, and—dead-seriously—warned Caleb, "Drive carefully, and mind the speed limit."

"It's you again."

Maggie jumped. Her hand flew to her throat. "Holy crap, you startled me."

The young woman who'd swung open the front door of the Cannons' house nodded absently. She ran a fingertip over the edge of the envelope Maggie had just slipped through the mail slot. "I wondered if you'd come back."

"Jane?"

She nodded again, barely, and flicked the sleek curtain of her brown hair away from her face—her expertly made-up face. Pale lipstick, hint of blush, lashes darkened with mascara . . .

Maggie blinked up at the girl. Tall, broad-shouldered, calm, cool-eyed. Commanding. Not at all how Maggie had imagined her. After reading those sad emails and learning what Kimberly had revealed about her former roommate, she'd pictured someone wiry, dark, disheveled, nervous . . . *Someone like me.*

"Your friends are waiting." Jane glanced pointedly over Maggie's shoulder. "I won't keep you."

Maggie stuck her hands into her coat pockets and retreated a step. "I wasn't sure if your mom would tell you I stopped by."

Jane raised an eyebrow. "Why wouldn't she?"

"She—she didn't seem all that glad to meet me and said you were having a rough time since . . ." Maggie shrugged lamely. "I was worried you wouldn't know I'd tried to get in touch with you, and I, well, hated for you to think I was blowing you off, especially since it took me such a long time to write back to you."

"I assumed you'd moved on," she said. "Nothing wrong with that. It's what I'm doing." With impatient finality, she added, "I appreciate your stopping by. Good luck with everything." And she took hold of the door, as if preparing to close it.

"Are you going to press charges?" Maggie blurted.

Her face grew shuttered. "After all this time?" She breathed a caustic laugh. "What would be the point?"

"You could inform the univer—"

"I *told* you: I'm putting all that behind me."

"But—but what if the guy who raped you rapes someone else?"

The amber eyes flashed, cracking the cool veneer. "*Don't* say that," she snapped. "I do *not* need to hear that. Isn't there enough on my plate right now without your dishing out a big glob of guilt? If I never see that college again, it will be too soon. I have zero intention of stepping foot on that campus, and no one will make me change my plans, least of all *you*—a dropout! So save your hypocritical bullshit. *You* don't want to go back to Carlton, either!" And then she slammed the door shut.

At least, as they headed back to Wren's cabin, Maggie didn't have to spell out what had happened. Caleb's and Linnie's oh-shit grimaces made it clear they'd gotten the gist of her conversation with Jane. She didn't know if she could have talked about it even if they hadn't. The interaction had drained her, left her feeling pummeled, sick. Depressed. Angry.

She leaned her head against the window. Over the woods skirting the highway, a colorless sky loosened a damp snow, the flakes the size of feathers. Big flakes. Big globs of guilt. Hypocritical bullshit. Maggie squeezed her eyes shut. *Jesus Christ, I only wanted to help.*

"Here."

Maggie turned. A tissue dangled in her face. "Oh." She dried her eyes. "Thanks, Linnie."

"You tried," she said soberly. "That's all you can do." Fluffster whined, and Linnie shushed him and crooned, "It's okay, boy."

Maggie blew her nose. She *had* tried. But she'd failed miserably. With Jane, with Mom. "I didn't accomplish anything. This whole trip . . . a total bust . . ." A sob tripped up her words.

"Oh, no, no, Maggie, hey," Caleb stammered, surprised. He gripped the steering wheel and glanced at her in alarm. "Don't be sad."

"I'm not," she choked out.

"Sure you're not," Linnie murmured.

"I'm mad!" And sad. Okay, so she was both.

Fluffster whined again and poked his head up between the front seats to offer her a lick.

For a long time, Maggie filled the car with the embarrassing sounds of sniffling and crying.

Then, out of the blue, Linnie heaved a huge sigh and growled, "*Fine.* Let's get the fucking letter from Mary Tate."

Maggie sat up. "Oh, Linnie, are you sure?"

"*No.* But whatever."

Wide-eyed, Caleb glanced at her in the rearview mirror. "We're heading to your old neighborhood?"

"*You're* heading to my old neighborhood. You can drop Maggie and me off at Stella's Diner in Syracuse first." She dug out her phone. "Let me pull up the directions. It's on Wolf Street. We'll order a sandwich for you and just hang out until you come get us."

He smiled hopefully. "Who knows? This Mary Tate could have good news. Maybe you'll find out a distant relative left you an inheritance or something."

"Or something," she muttered, her expression inscrutable.

"You can find out. Or give the goddamn letter to Sam." She harrumphed. "I'm sure he'll *love* reading it."

"But—but it's your letter," Caleb said, confused.

"I don't want it." She glared out the window. "Sam wants it. He can fucking well have it." Under her breath, she grumbled, "Bossy, intrusive, patronizing jerk." She leaned forward suddenly, shouldering Fluffster out of her way. "You know what's annoying? Being turned into a project. It's like everyone sees me as some work in progress."

Maggie smiled damply and reached toward the backseat. Linnie took her hand, and Maggie gave her a squeeze. "We all are."

Ice had filled the ruts on Ash Drive. Caleb's car, instead of slurping through mud, rumbled over cold-hardened ridges. Snow trimmed the branches on the straggle of trees, and the lake yawned straight ahead, a mouth full of steel.

"It looks more like February than November," Caleb said.

"It seems like it *should* be February," Linnie said. "Feels like we've been gone forever."

Wren must have seen them drive up. She opened the back door and, arms crossed over her dusty plaid shirt, waited on the frail landing.

There was expectancy in the aunt's wide eyes and parted mouth. Maggie's stomach sank. She wished she could say, *Good news. Mom's sorry. She misses you. She's seen the light and even plans to attend the exhibition.*

But she couldn't.

Wren searched Maggie's face, caught her lower lip in her teeth, and looked away.

When they gathered in the kitchen, the aunt bent to give the dog a pat, then welcomed Maggie with a pat, too. "Did you have fun?" she asked with deliberate cheerfulness. "Do anything special?"

"We tried. Wish it had been more productive."

Caleb nodded distractedly. He hadn't seemed at ease since returning from Mary Tate's. Linnie had noted his shock on their way out of the diner and said, "Nice neighborhood, hmm?" He had only shaken his head. If he'd learned anything important, he hadn't shared it. All he'd said was "I don't think Sam has a right to this letter, Linnie. It's yours." But she'd just rolled her eyes and turned away.

Now Linnie yawned. "I wouldn't call the last three days a barrel of fun. But I'll say this—" She stretched and let an arm land heavily across Maggie's shoulders, pitching her off-balance.

Maggie squeaked.

With a laugh, Linnie hauled her into a tight hug. "Your niece here is pretty awesome." Just as abruptly, she released her, then rested her forearm on her brow like a Victorian maiden preparing to swoon. "*Fucking A*. Am I glad to be back."

19

WHILE MAGGIE WAS unpacking her duffel bag, her father called to make sure she'd gotten back safely. He repeated his offer to collect her on Saturday or "at least for Thanksgiving, honey. It's a family holiday!"

"Wren's family, too," Maggie said. "Is she invited?"

Dad didn't answer right away, then said, "Considering how your mom's feeling about your aunt right now and that whole mess, whatever it is, I would have to say . . . um, no."

"Then I'm sorry. I can't make it."

He didn't ask again.

November slipped by, a frantic spell for the aunt, who was scrambling to mix and apply glazes and fire her last sculpture in time for the exhibition. But for Maggie, the days were quiet and shrouded in snow. Though Dad called every now and then, her mother only texted—and infrequently, at that. Maggie read bitterness and hurt in the stretches of silence. Mom wanted Maggie to team up with her, and Maggie just wouldn't. Taking her mother's side in this conflict was wrong.

The doses of the silent treatment from Mom, the letter Linnie wouldn't read, and Jane Cannon, with her carefully made-up face and styled hair—the snow might as well have fallen on these problems, too. One issue after another, utterly unresolved, frozen under the cloak of cold denial.

On Thanksgiving, Maggie and Wren, lugging store-bought rolls and pies, joined their neighbors.

Maggie expected to find Linnie at the Blakes' but didn't.

"She had a bad episode," Sam confided out of the others' earshot. "Got rushed to the hospital to have her stomach pumped."

"Oh my God." Maggie stared, shocked. "Is she okay?"

He ran a hand over his tired face, muffling part of his "For now, I guess?"

Later, leaning against the window, Kate insisted, "She'll come. I know she will."

Sam wagged his head. "She already called and told you she wouldn't be able to make it, sweetie."

"But we have turkey and mashed potatoes and gravy. She loves mashed potatoes."

It was heartbreaking how long Kate stood with her cheek pressed to the glass, her gaze fixed on the driveway.

Maggie felt a flare of frustration. That Linnie was hurting and battling addictions, Maggie realized. But *why* wasn't she seeking professional help?

Sam finally wheeled his daughter to the dinner table with the promise that she could eat her dessert first. Kate moped through the meal. Maggie felt so sorry for her that, after supper, she hauled some interesting-looking toys upstairs and found Kate in her bedroom. "Want to build Legos with me?"

Kate looked up from her paper dolls. "Those are for babies." She scowled at the toy basket Maggie had set on the floor (like a failed peace offering, she thought ruefully). "I was busy in here using my imagination," Kate said angrily. "Thanks a lot." She scrambled to her feet. "And stop trying to act like my mom." She kicked Maggie in the shin and bolted. From the den: "You're not my mom!"

Maggie glowered after her. She was tempted to trample the paper dolls. Hobbling out of the bedroom, she said under her breath, "I would *never* want to be your mother."

Then she regretted the mutter. Kate was basically a sad kid acting out, *taking* it out on someone else.

Maggie just wished she wasn't that someone.

After the holiday, Maggie texted Linnie to make sure she was okay. Though Linnie responded swiftly, it wasn't much of a response, just a word: *fine*. Then, with her next text, she changed the subject. And Maggie didn't know how to get Linnie to open up. She didn't even know if she *should*.

The last Saturday of the month arrived. The book club was meeting at the shop to pick its next read, an occasion Maggie would have welcomed had Sam not blown her Marge cover. Now she didn't want to go—couldn't drum up the energy to field their questions or even (assuming the girls had done their research on the history of Margaret Arioli) their sympathy and support. *I'm*

221

as much of an avoider as Mom, Linnie, and Jane, she thought gloomily. She texted Ran an excuse, then crawled into bed and drew the covers up over her head.

There was one thing, however, that Maggie *had* to address: her mom's photo albums. Since returning to the cabin, she'd waited for the right moment to discuss her realization with Wren. But that moment just wouldn't arrive. The aunt was almost always busy, even at mealtimes now. She carried her slapped-together sandwiches into the studio and got back to work.

Maggie finally decided she couldn't wait any longer. At the beginning of December, the night before Wren was to leave for New York City, she found the aunt in her studio, poring over some paperwork.

Wren glanced up with a vague smile. "Hey."

Maggie perched on the edge of a chair and stared out the windows. The wind roared against the lake-facing wall. Though it was dark out, the light by the back room's exterior door was on, and in its halo, snowflakes twirled. "Are you worried about the weather?"

"No point. I have to head out, regardless. I just hope parts of the thruway aren't shut down. I don't relish taking the slow, scenic route to New York. Not this time around." She lowered her frown to her papers and turned another page. "I'll be meeting up with a few ceramists. They've got contacts that may help me track down some of these less accessible materials. Worth their weight in gold, and for good reason. Certain high-fire glazes . . ." She whistled softly.

"Pretty?"

"*Gorgeous.*" Patting the papers against her thigh, she glanced around. "Can't think of what else I might need. The truck's packed."

There were no murky shadows in either damp box. Nothing sat on the long table waiting to be trimmed. But the kiln was open, and Maggie spied some bone-dry greenware on its shelves, probably the work Wren had set aside so she could take care of the last sculpture. "It looks so clean in here."

"Sam's doing. Glazing's a messy business—at least as messy as throwing. As soon as I finished the last firing, he helped me wrap and load the sculpture into my truck, then tackled the disaster in here. I think he was glad for the challenge." She hummed a sad note. "He's got a lot on his mind."

Maggie leaned over the table and rested her chin in her hand. "How did the sculpture turn out?"

"It's . . ." The aunt tapped the wheel's base with the toe of her sneaker before finishing flatly, "Done."

Maggie straightened in the chair. "There's something I didn't tell you about my visit to Carlton."

The aunt's mouth curled into a lopsided smile. "You never told me *anything* about the visit." She waved a hand when Maggie started apologizing. "Forget about it. I gathered your mom wasn't open to working things out?"

"No, and I'm sorry about that. I told her you were being more than fair, warning her about the show and telling her to just ignore it if she couldn't deal with it. But she didn't see how that would be an option, since it will probably make the news and all. It was . . ." Maggie tugged at the ends of her hair. "Well, it was obviously a lot easier for her to close her eyes to the situation and lie to herself when no one was putting the truth in the spotlight."

"That's the problem." Wren held the scrolled papers so tightly they crunched. "It's not the truth in her mind. She thinks I'm lying."

"I'm not so sure about that."

"What do you mean?"

A gust roared, rattling the windows. As if awakened by the wind, the furnace turned on with a clank and rush of air. "That night we stayed at the house, I went looking for Mom after the others had gone to bed. I found her in the living room, flipping through the family albums. Mournfully, you know. Like it was the last time she'd be able to see her parents the way she always had."

Wren pinched the bridge of her nose. "A final good-bye?"

"Yeah. She was upset. I tried to discuss the situation with her. It wasn't a productive conversation. Not only didn't I change her mind, she decided I was siding with you."

Pressing the scrunched papers against her chest, the aunt swore softly. "I am *very* sorry about that, Margaret. I was afraid that might happen."

"She wants me back home." Maggie ran a hand over her hair. Apologetically: "She thinks you've been manipulating me."

Wren briefly shut her eyes. "Oh God, worse and worse."

"Well, that's stupid, and I told her so." She pulled a curl straight, then brushed it back. "After we argued, Mom headed upstairs. I stuck around in the living room. The albums were open, so I started going through them, not paying much attention, just thinking about you and Mom. But I noticed something—something strange in the pictures, the ones that included my grandparents. I went through them again, more slowly. It struck me that the whole time I was growing up, Mom never left me alone with Gramps."

"Never?"

"Not that I remember. And in the albums, there isn't a single photo of me bouncing on his knee, sitting by him at the table, playing at his feet. Grandma used to babysit me after school at our house, but I don't have any recollection of his coming along to help. I mean, that's not a huge realization. I guess that information has always been in the back of my mind, but I put it down to what Mom and Dad always said about him, how he was so grumpy. Grumpy Gramps. He *was* grumpy—and distant. But something in those photographs and in my memories of Mom, when she was facing Gramps or even just talking about him outside his presence, makes me think she—"

"Was afraid of him?"

Maggie nodded. "And didn't trust him."

For a moment, Wren frowned at the floor. Abruptly: "Is she conscious of that, do you think?"

Maggie shrugged. "Mom's pretty good at putting problems out of her head and moving on."

"Some people can do that. Forget the past or rewrite it. Or just blank it out. Run away from it. That's what Linnie does."

"Yeah . . ." Maggie remembered Linnie's rant the night they drove home from the Cannons' house. She did do that. And she recommended others do the same. With a tired moan, Maggie got to her feet. "So that's what I realized from those albums. It's what I *think* I learned, anyway. I wanted you to know."

"Thanks, Margaret. I'm glad you told me, though . . ." Her voice trailed off. She sighed.

Maggie nodded. What good did this information do? Unless Mom faced what she subconsciously knew, the truth was like a treasure at the bottom of Lake Ontario. It helped nobody.

20

THE NEXT MORNING, Maggie woke to an empty house. She and the aunt had said their good-byes before bedtime the previous night. Up until the moment Wren began shutting off the studio lights, Maggie had hoped her aunt might invite her to come along on the trip. Instead, she'd given her a brisk, one-armed hug and said, "I left Thomas's and Sam's numbers on the fridge. If anything happens and you can't get ahold of me, call one of them. Help yourself to whatever's in the pantry and fridge. I picked up milk and eggs. Fruit and bread, too. There's soup in the freezer. Eat it up. You good with holding down the fort for a few days?" Maggie had nodded and quit daydreaming about skyscrapers, fine restaurants, galleries, and museums.

Now from her bed, she stared at the wispy flakes floating by the window. No heavy snow or whipping wind this morning. Wren would be okay.

The cabin felt small and safe, tucked into winter like a puppy curled up on a blanket. Not scary or lonely, just quiet. She brought the quilt up to her chin and closed her eyes. Having three days to herself might not be such a bad thing after all. She went back to sleep.

Later in the morning, she showered and made coffee. Standing at the kitchen window, she considered spending the day doing something other than reading and walking (like getting back to Ran, whose last text she hadn't answered yet, or writing a couple of emails to Shayna and Jen, or even throwing on the wheel). She was smiling at this last possibility, when a rumble broke the silence.

A car pulled into Wren's driveway. It was Caleb's.

Maggie clumsily set down her mug, then jerked away from the window. Her hands flew to her throat. Against her warm fingertips, her pulse galloped.

What was he doing here? What did he want?

When she realized what she was thinking, she exhaled a laugh, a tremulous sound pitched high with hysteria. *Christ, Maggie, calm down. It's just Caleb.*

She lowered her shoulders and smoothed back her hair with trembling hands.

The porch steps creaked under Caleb's weight. He knocked.

She shook her head, impatient with herself, with her instinct to panic (*over Caleb, of all people!*). Pinning on a smile, she opened the door. "Hey, good morning." Her voice sounded hoarse. She cleared her throat.

"How's it going?" He shut the door behind him, stepped out

of his damp boots, and crammed his gloves into his pockets. "Wren leave already?" he asked, shrugging off his coat.

"Before I got up."

"She should be fine. The storm passed through by midnight." He hung his coat, then pulled an envelope out of one of its pockets. "I heard the snowplows early this morning."

"You were awake?" She folded her arms across her chest, realizing she wasn't wearing a bra.

"Working on a paper."

Her hoodie was dangling from one of the hooks by the door. While he said something about his geopolitical class, she grabbed the sweatshirt and pulled it on. "Where's Fluffster?" She freed her hair from the neckline.

"Back at the house, sleeping. I probably should be doing the same. That essay kicked my ass."

He did look exhausted. Smudges hung under his eyes.

Feeling calmer, Maggie managed a friendly "How about some coffee?"

"Sounds great." He collapsed into a chair at the table.

After pouring him a cup, Maggie indicated the envelope with a lift of her chin. "What's that?"

"Linnie's letter."

She sat opposite him. "What are you going to do with it?"

He shrugged. "I was hoping you might have a suggestion."

"Well . . ." She cupped the warm mug with both hands and frowned at the envelope. "It's not right to open another person's mail, unless you're a mom or dad and the kid's young and you need to handle things for her, like a bank account or whatever . . ." She bit her bottom lip.

"That's the problem, right? Linnie's not a kid. And you, Sam, and I—we're not the parents." He rubbed the back of his neck. "Visiting her old neighborhood was . . . instructive."

"Rough place?"

"Beyond rough. I mean, Sam told me about Linnie's difficult childhood, but until I actually stopped by Mary Tate's place, I don't know that that information really sank in. I used to think it wouldn't be too hard for Linnie to clean up her act if enough friends rally around her, help and love her." He slumped over his coffee. "But when I got a glimpse of her old world and what she's up against, and when that Mrs. Tate widened the glimpse with a few details . . ." He shook his head.

Oh God, what kind of details? Maggie couldn't bring herself to ask aloud. Linnie had made it plain her childhood had been a nightmare. She set down her mug. "We rally around Linnie because that's what friends do. But she also rallies around *us*." Like how she'd joined in on the road trip. Linnie never had any intention of visiting Baldwinsville. She'd gone just to support Maggie. "Hold on to the letter," she said, "but don't open it."

"Okay." He brushed the table with the side of his hand. "Sam came over when we got back. I, um . . . told him about the trip. I hope that's okay."

She nodded. They were best friends. She figured Caleb had probably given him the highlights, if the trip's depressing events could be called that.

She sighed, mentally tallying up her botched missions.

"You know Sam wants the letter," Caleb continued. "But the more I think about it, the less I want to give it to him. It doesn't seem right."

She stared out the window at the gray sky. Sam would be all over that letter. Then he'd be full of suggestions for Linnie. She felt the certainty of this in her gut. "The letter isn't his to read. Tell Linnie you'll hold on to it for a month, in case she changes her mind, but that you're not opening it. If she wants it, it's hers. If a few weeks pass and she doesn't ask for it, toss it."

"Okay." He raked back his bangs. "I'm glad I asked for your advice."

"Sure." She shrugged.

He smiled shyly at her, then hastily lowered his gaze to his coffee.

But not hastily enough.

Maggie had seen the interest in his eyes. She quickly looked away, too, heat flaring under her skin.

Her chest tightened. With regret and sadness. But mostly with panic: *Oh my God, no. I can't, Caleb. I just can't.*

This instinctive *no* made her sorry for him.

It made her sorry for herself.

If the sound of the waves outside the cabin could cut into her sleep, trip up her thoughts, and yank her back to what had happened, what would a hug do? Or a kiss? Or more? She couldn't imagine handling an intimate relationship.

And finding pleasure? That seemed least likely of all.

A rap on the door made both of them jump. Caleb snatched the letter off the table and hid it under his sweater.

Sam entered with a happy "I've got news!" He stomped his boots, then toed and heeled them off, leaving white clumps of snow on the small rug.

"What is it?" Caleb asked. He sounded put out.

Sam grinned. "*Huge* news."

"Tell us, and I'll get you some coffee." Maggie went to the shelf to collect Sam's favorite mug. She was glad he'd shown up. Relieved. It struck her that Sam had become like a brother to her.

He shed his coat and dragged off his hat. Dark hair poked around his head in wild tufts. Cupping his fingers in front of his mouth, he blew on his skin. "Freezing out there." He rubbed his hands together. "So!" He fell into a chair and slapped the table. "My news," he said with relish. "My incredibly awesome news." And then he wiggled his eyebrows and leaned forward.

Caleb smiled grudgingly. "Yes . . . ?"

"The School of the Art Institute in Chicago."

"Chicago?" Maggie repeated, bringing his coffee to the table.

Sam nodded, an exaggerated up-and-down motion of his head.

"What about it?" Caleb asked impatiently.

"Wren has a friend who teaches there, another sculptor. She asked her if I could send her my portfolio. It's not complete. I still haven't finished my last project, but I put together images of some other work, a few ceramic pieces, mostly paintings and drawings."

Maggie smiled a little at the wonder blooming in his face. "She liked it?"

"She *loved* it. And she shopped it around her department, made some calls . . ." He turned to gaze dreamily out the window. "They're offering me a full scholarship if I want it."

"Holy shit," Caleb breathed.

"That's amazing," Maggie said. *But what about Kate? What*

about Linnie? What about your original plan to attend Alfred University? Belatedly, she added, "Congratulations."

"Want to come over?" Sam asked hopefully. "And read her email and see how the sculpture's coming along?"

"Hell, yeah," Caleb said.

After Sam gulped down his coffee, they took Caleb's car to Sam's house and took turns sitting in front of his computer to read the email and check out the winning portfolio. Then they followed him into the workshop to admire the sculpture still under way.

What Maggie and Caleb *didn't* do: ask about the logistics of juggling college with a young daughter or wonder aloud about Linnie.

Sam didn't mention these matters, either, not even when Kate arrived home from school, bounded past her grandfather, and stormed the workshop.

She let Caleb swoop her up and, suspended in the air, squealed when Sam tickled her. As soon as Caleb returned her to the floor, she stopped laughing and glared at Maggie. "What is she doing here?"

"We're just hanging out, Squirt," Sam said.

Thomas, jangling his keys, paused in the doorway. "What's up?" he asked, smiling curiously.

"Nothing." Sam's gaze slid away from his dad's. He stuck his hands into the back pockets of his jeans.

Maggie and Caleb shared a glance.

So Sam hadn't told Thomas yet. Maggie supposed not even Wren knew. And Linnie? Not likely.

21

WREN DIDN'T KNOCK on the Blakes' door. Striding right into the great room, she announced, "We're here!" Then she tossed her messenger bag onto a deep chair and flung herself into the chair's twin. "And I'm *hungry*."

Thomas's voice drifted their way from upstairs: "Hey, Hungry. Be down in a minute."

Maggie perched on the edge of an ottoman. Her aunt might have been hungry. But she *looked* wiped out.

It was Sunday. Maggie hadn't expected Wren home until late. She'd been surprised when the truck roared up the cabin's driveway just a few minutes ago, kicking up clouds of snow. After dropping her small suitcase on the kitchen floor, the aunt had hauled Maggie into a tight hug and said, "Grab your coat. We're heading next door."

Now Maggie frowned at Wren, limp in the armchair, her head back, eyes closed. Her aunt hadn't said a word about the exhibition, merely mentioned Sam's invitation to supper.

What supper? The unlit kitchen was clean, not a pot or pan in sight. "So how did it go?" Maggie asked.

Wren opened bleary eyes. "Good. Bad. Frankly, I don't even know. And at this point, I don't give a shit. I'm just so glad it's over." With a sigh, she sat up, dragged herself to her feet, and crossed to the windows.

Vermilion saturated the sky. The setting sun lit up the peninsula—blurred the whole length of Devil's Tongue in a fiery glow. "When I gaze out this way from my studio," Wren murmured, "a sunset like this feels personal, a treat whipped up especially for me. From here, though . . ." She stepped back from the window and ran a hand along the side of a rocker, its cherry grain reddened by the waning light. "Everything here, inside and out, still belongs to Muriel."

A distant screech erupted.

Maggie tensed. She knew that howl.

Thomas appeared on the upper landing. "What's going on?"

"How the hell am I supposed to know?" Wren flapped her arms. "Sam called me on my cell when I was driving back, invited Margaret and me over for supper, said, 'Come around six.' Here we are." She sent her thumb over her shoulder to indicate the kitchen. "So where's my supper?"

"Beats me. I was at the college, catching up on a stack of essays, when Sam called and told me the same."

They turned to Maggie, eyebrows raised.

She hummed noncommittally. She could guess Sam's

objective—and also the reason for Kate's tantrum. But it was his news to share.

Thomas kneaded his forehead. "Want a drink?"

"I want food, but I'll temporarily settle for a drink." She sat heavily at the island, smiled at Maggie, and patted the stool next to her.

A moment later, Sam hurried down the stairs. "Sorry about that." He shooed his father away from the pantry. "I've got dinner, Dad. Take a seat. I'm just a little behind schedule. I see you got drinks, that's good, that's g—"

A door crashed open upstairs. "I hate you!" Kate screamed. The door slammed shut. This was followed by another slam. Then a third.

Thomas started speaking. A fourth slam interrupted him. They waited for a fifth. When it didn't come, Wren whistled, a soft sound of awe. "Feisty."

Thomas stared aghast at his son. "What happened?"

He yanked a box of dried pasta out of the cupboard. "Kate's a little miffed." Olive oil, artichoke hearts, cured olives, and roasted red peppers—he transferred an armful of cans and jars to the island.

"Hate to see what she's like when she's really angry," the aunt said.

Maggie took a shaky sip of iced tea. *I've seen that, and it's not pretty.*

He smiled weakly. "Check out my sculpture, Wren. Tell me what you think."

"Okay." She picked up her Pepsi can and, like a person preparing to lug a heavy burden, collected herself off the stool.

Thomas trailed her.

In a sidelong way, Sam watched them cross the room. As soon as they disappeared into the workshop, he turned to Maggie, his eyes huge. "This isn't going so well."

"Kate's not thrilled about Chicago?"

"I didn't even mention Chicago at first, just sat her on my lap, opened up some websites I'd found, showed her a bunch of cool destinations—Lincoln Park Zoo, The Bean, Navy Pier, John Hancock Observatory. I figured I'd, you know, butter her up at first . . ."

"Sweeten the pot?"

He sighed. "Didn't work. She got mulish right away, let me rave and gush on my own, then announced, 'I'm not going.'"

"Could she have overheard you talking about the school with someone?"

"I don't think so. But maybe? I've been careful." He pulled a sauté pan and the stockpot out of a lower cabinet.

"She's smart." *An evil genius.*

"She's pissed." He worked silently for a moment, smashing and chopping cloves of garlic. "When I took the plunge and told her my amazing news"—his smile was sickly—"and spread a map, just to point out how reasonably close Chicago is to here, she asked about the big ponds. And I was like, 'Ha, ha. Those aren't ponds. They're lakes. See? Lake Ontario, Lake Michigan.'" He shook his head. "She ran into Dad's room and glared at the water. Then she lost it. She just . . ." He stopped chopping and blinked at the cutting board. "Lost it."

"It's got to be hard." Linnie left the apartment—essentially left *Kate*—and then Sam and his daughter left the apartment, and now, at last settled in a new home, Kate was being asked to leave again. That had to suck. Of course, Sam could arrange to keep her with Thomas. Between Sam's dad and Wren, Kate would be well cared for. But that wasn't the same as happy. And yet, how many students dragged their kids off to college? How many students even had kids?

She didn't voice her thoughts. Sam looked thoroughly miserable, as if the realities of his situation had finally caught up with him.

Her aunt and Thomas were still in the workshop. She could hear them talking but couldn't make out what they were saying. "Your dad and Wren don't know yet?"

"Nope." His shoulders jerked up. "Should I even bother telling them?"

Maggie chewed on the corner of her bottom lip. She didn't have a good answer. Pushing away her empty glass, she stood. "Put me to work. What can I do?"

They prepared dinner side by side without talking much. Sam asked Maggie only to rough-chop the artichoke hearts and slice the olives. Sam's father and Wren returned to the great room, breaking the moody silence with a few flattering remarks about the sculpture.

Sam mustered a sad semblance of a smile. Wren and Thomas didn't seem to notice his lack of enthusiasm. By the time the water reached a boil, they'd settled on the couch with some bread and cheese and were laughing easily. Wren mentioned she'd seen someone at the exhibition for the first time in seventeen years. And Thomas asked questions about people Maggie had never heard of.

Sam poured the linguine into the boiling water and stood over the steam with a wooden spoon, tapping the stiff strands into the pot.

There was a rattling sound at the door, then a loud rap.

"What the heck . . . ?" Thomas said. He shared a perplexed glance with Wren, strode across the room, and paused by a window to peer toward the front of the house. "Oh."

As soon as Sam's dad unlocked the door, a wide-eyed Linnie shot into the house with a panicked, "Kate? Where's Kate? What happened?"

"Mom!" Kate stormed down the stairs, descending so quickly and weeping so wildly tears flew off her face. Maggie, though clear across the great room, took an automatic step back. Linnie caught the small hurricane, and Thomas and Wren closed in with pats and tuts and soothing murmurs.

Sam gave the gathering a sour glance. With his wooden spoon, he swatted down the few remaining strands poking out of the pot.

"Jesus, Sam," Linnie breathed, holding Kate close. "What did you do to her?"

Sam slapped the spoon on the counter. "What kind of question is that? What do I ever do but love her and take care of her?"

An implied condemnation hovered in the lull that followed. Linnie, stricken, dropped her gaze. Kate, still sobbing, adhered herself to her mother's legs. Linnie touched the small shoulders, then crouched to pull her daughter into her arms. Wren and Thomas discreetly looked away, then shuffled to the couch.

After a moment of hesitation, Wren smoothed the cushion at her side. "Come on over here, you two. Come sit with me."

Sam's dad held up a slice of bread. "Want a little snack, honey? I can get you some butter and jam . . ."

"No!" Kate wailed into Linnie's hair.

Sam growled and slammed the pan onto the stovetop.

Maggie felt like a pointless prop in an otherwise meaningful play. She sidled along the wall to the front door, which had been left slightly ajar, then widened the crack and let the cold touch her face. Snow was falling again, a thin weaving of it, like a net ensnaring the evening air. Veiled by the weather, the lake spread black and vast. It held a stillness, a curious quality of patient expectation. She peered around the side of the house and, in the waning twilight, made out the Saab. Kyle wasn't sitting inside it. Linnie must have borrowed his car. Maggie shut the door.

Over Kate's sobbing, Linnie was saying to Thomas, ". . . just got back from Caleb's when she called my cell. I could hardly make out her words, she was crying so hard, but obviously, I came right away." She cast Sam a defensive glare.

He made a face at the minced garlic he was stirring around the pan.

"Daddy's making me leave," Kate wailed. "Two whole lakes that way!" She pointed to the towering windows overlooking the lake.

Linnie slowly shook her head, confused. Then she, Wren, and Thomas turned to Sam with frowns.

Sam poured a good half bottle of white wine into the pan, where it hissed, boiled, and spat, then he added the cutting board's piles of chopped ingredients. He stirred once and finally faced the others.

Kate sniffed loudly.

"Does this have to do with your exciting news?" Thomas asked.

Sam smiled bitterly, probably over his father's choice of adjective. "School of the Art Institute of Chicago offered me a full ride."

Besides Wren's surprised squawk, the announcement didn't generate much of a response. Thomas's and Linnie's frowns persisted.

Linnie pulled her pale hair away from her face. "I thought you were set on going to Alfred."

He shrugged. "Hard to turn down an opportunity like this."

"Chicago?" Thomas cupped his forehead. "I didn't even know you applied there."

Wren half-raised a hand. "Does this have anything to do with Becky Min?"

"Becky *who*?" Thomas asked.

"Min"—she whisked the air his way without looking at him—"the sculptor. She teaches there."

Sam nodded. "She said some nice things about my portfolio, asked if she could share it and get back to me." He set the wooden spoon on the island carefully. "The offer was what she came back with."

"A full ride." Wren clucked, a satisfied sound. "Wow."

"So you arranged this?" Thomas asked with an edge of asperity.

"I'd hardly say I arranged anything. I wanted Becky to see Sam's work because I'm, you know . . ." She gave an embarrassed shrug. "Proud of him."

Linnie straightened out of her crouch, though she kept a hand on Kate's head. "Thanks, Sam. Thanks for checking with the rest of us before hiring the movers."

"The movers? But I—I didn't," he stammered. Then, scowl restored: "Don't be an asshole. I haven't made a decision yet."

"But you go ahead and freak Kate out with the news? Thought, 'Hey, why not traumatize her with the prospect?' What are you—an idiot? Couldn't you have run it by your dad first? Or *me*? What about me? Don't I get a say in where you take my daughter?"

"Two whole lakes." Kate sniffed again.

"Oh. I see." He crossed his arms. "Now you want a say."

She shuffled her daughter behind her, a protective gesture that brought a disgusted grimace to Sam's face. "Don't use that tone with me," she snapped.

"What will you do? Call social services and demand sole custody? Huh. Would they even entertain your call when you obviously don't know what custody means?" His hand landed on the island as a fist. "It means *parenting*, not just showing up every so often."

"Sam," Thomas said warningly, taking a step forward.

"Here we go again." Linnie threw her arms out at her sides, grand master–like. "Another episode of Sam Blake's production of Linnie the Bad Mother." She hugged herself and glared. "You have *no fucking clue* what a bad mother looks like."

He returned the glare. "But I do know what a good mother looks like—not *remotely* like you!"

Linnie's angry flush disappeared. Her face emptied of color altogether.

Wren shook her head. "Not cool, Sam."

Maggie, palms on her cheeks, shuffled closer. "Linnie's had a rough time of it lately and maybe—"

"Lately? How about *always*?" Sam's hands swung up to pound

the air. He strode across the dining area and stood in the workshop doorway. Past him, deeper in the room, Maggie could make out the dark outline of his sculpture. With his back to the others, he muttered, "She's the only one allowed to hurt in this family. The winner of the suckiest childhood. I am so fucking tired of hearing about Linnie's horrible past, Linnie's awful suffering, Linnie's night terrors, drinking problem, drug problem, cutting problem, and *goddamn depression*. I lost my mother. But do I get to wallow? Fuck no. Linnie's sad situation is the *only* situation." He whirled around to skewer her with some narrow-eyed rage. "You're so selfish—so wrapped up in your own problems. Do you ever think about what *I* went through?"

Linnie moaned softly. Her face was wet with tears. She gave her cheeks an absent swipe. "I was there. I know what you went through because I was dragged through it and made to pay for it." She ran her hands down her coat and began buttoning it up. "If it hadn't been for your mom's passing, I wouldn't have stuck around here at all. I wouldn't have dropped out of high school. I wouldn't have given up my dream to get the hell out of this shit-town and do something interesting with my life. I wouldn't have seen my fucking future go down the drain. I gave up everything, *everything*—even the privilege to do what I felt was best with my own body—because *you* wanted me to. You know what I think, Sam? I think you deliberately trapped me."

There was a piercing silence.

Then the smoke alarm blared.

22

THOMAS HOLLERED. WREN screamed. Everyone made for the stove. Maggie reached it first and twisted off the burners. It was too late to save the food. Waving at the black cloud, she squinted at the pans they'd forgotten.

Sam's hands fell on his head. *"Shit."*

The ingredients smoldered in a blackened mess. Maggie flicked on the fan in the hood, Linnie opened the window over the sink, and Thomas climbed a stool to shut off the alarm.

Wren, sidling over to the sink and putting her arm around Linnie, eyed Sam's father askance. "Careful up there, old man."

He gave her a look but took the hand Sam raised to help balance him on his way down.

Sam blew an explosive sigh, then turned to Linnie, his expression sad and abashed. "I'm sorry."

"I am, too," Linnie said, her voice trembling.

Sam rubbed his eyes with the heels of his hands. "I never meant—"

"Yeah, you did," Linnie choked out, through a strange laughed cry, "and so did I. What I said, though, it wasn't the whole story. Sometimes I hated you, but sometimes . . . I didn't. And don't."

Wren patted her back.

Acrid smoke wafted around the kitchen. Thomas coughed and then leaned over the sink to inhale the cold air blowing through the window.

"Well, I guess we'll . . ." Sam flapped a hand and finished dispiritedly, "Figure something out." He went back to inspecting the disaster on the stovetop.

"Should we call for a pizza?" Thomas asked.

"Good idea," Wren said.

Maggie patted her hair, weirded out by the shift from murderous tension to "let's order a pizza." She looked around and realized something: One of them was missing. "Where's Kate?"

Sam stopped scraping burnt ingredients into the garbage disposal to glance over his shoulder, his eyebrows raised.

Linnie stepped out of Wren's one-armed hug and called for her daughter.

Thomas put down his beer. "She was building with Legos in the playroom earlier. I'll check in there." He trudged through the dining area toward the basement door. When he headed down, he called, "Kate?"

"She's probably in her room." Sam washed and dried his hands. "I'll go look. My phone's up there. Pepperoni okay with everyone?"

"Get half with spinach and mushrooms, will you? Actually . . ." Wren took a hesitant step forward. "Mind showing me the email from Becky?"

"Sure." He smiled tiredly. "Laptop's in the den. Come on up."

When everyone else disappeared, Maggie turned to Linnie.

She was frowning. "Do you hear that?"

Maggie raised her head and heard a soft whine.

"Oh. I must have left the door open." Linnie headed that way.

Maggie grabbed her wrist. "You did, but I closed it."

Linnie's eyes widened. Without a word, she tore her hand free, ran for the front door, and whipped it open. "Kate!"

Darkness had fallen. In one of the trees along Wayside, the moon shone, gibbous and ringed and blurred by snow. It looked like an animal's watchful eye.

Linnie fumbled with the switches by the door until the exterior light unrolled a short carpet of illumination across the snow. The prints of small sneakers drew a path in the direction of the lake.

"Oh *no*." Linnie sprang outside.

Maggie started following but stopped when she realized she wasn't wearing shoes. Trembling, she stumbled back, ran for the boots she'd left by the door to the garage, and yelled for Sam as she grabbed her coat off the back of the chair.

He flew down the stairs, his face filling with dread. "Is it Kate?"

Wren descended more slowly. "What's going on?"

"Kate left." Maggie made for the door. "Took off for the lake,

I think." She didn't wait for them to follow, just ran after Linnie, straight into the night.

Kate's and Linnie's prints made dotted lines that disappeared into the darkness. Maggie paused, surrounded by the cacophony of wind and water. She concentrated on the winks of the first stars until her eyes adjusted to the darkness. Then she moved forward again, more tentatively now, straining to find tracks in the moon's pale shimmer.

Snowflakes, small and hard, spangled the air. A gust swept her hair into her face. Smooth snow stretched ahead in bluish, seamless phosphorescence. She'd lost the footprints. Looking up, she shouted for Linnie.

"Here!" The faint response didn't drift from the short beach below or the woods to the right. It floated from the left, where the land narrowed and jutted out over the water.

"Wait up!" Sam called. A flashlight beam, then two arcs of light whipped up alongside her.

"Which way?" her aunt demanded, resting a hand on Thomas's arm.

"The bluff," Maggie said.

"*Shit.*" Sam lurched ahead, and his flashlight drew a brilliant zigzag through the darkness. "Linnie! Kate!"

Linnie's answer came from farther away this time.

Sam ran after the sound of her voice.

Maggie followed him. The flashlight's narrow beam up ahead struck her as impossibly frail, a mere pinprick of shine in the blackness.

A branch caught her coat. One tree, another, another—she

ran under their boughs. Between the trees, moonlight pooled and sifted. The branches cast shadows like shawls. The snow was thinner here. Maggie slipped and nearly fell on an icy patch. A moment later, she *did* fall, tripping over a rock.

She staggered to her feet. The trees thickened to a stand, even as the ground on which they grew narrowed. Thomas and Wren had fallen behind. Sam had sped ahead. So Maggie entered the thicket alone and almost blindly, with only the moonlight dappling the ground and lake.

The water stretched close and loud on either side. Waves glugged over ice and shale. With her hands out to help her feel her way forward, Maggie rushed through the wilderness of Devil's Tongue.

Her feet were cold and wet in her boots. The trees towered around her, sentinels guarding a secret place. They penned her in. *How many? Four, five, six.* They circled her. She breathed fast, stumbled, used her fingers like claws in her panic and haste, tore through the vines and branches, caught a handful of thorns, winced. Her palms hurt. She was hurt. *Hurt, hurry, get away, away, call Mom. Shirt, underwear, jeans, fast, faster, my phone, shit, where is my phone?*

A sob overrode her gasping breath. It was her own sob.

The sound dragged her back to the present.

Kate. Where was Kate? She seized a trunk and held herself steady.

In that second, Wren caught up to her and wrapped her in a steely hug. "*Jesus Christ*, Margaret. Didn't you hear me hollering for you to stop? You don't run like a maniac through a stretch like this, not unless you want to plunge into Lake Ontario." She gave her a little shake, then released her.

Huffing and half-bent, Thomas reached them. "Oh my God," he panted. A glowing beam shuddered and then disappeared as he stuffed the flashlight into his coat pocket. His arms fell across Maggie's and Wren's shoulders, as if to brace himself as much as to protect them.

Sam's voice cut through the crash of waves: "We're here!"

Thomas craned his neck to the side. *"Where?"*

"Down here!"

Not farther along then. Below. They inched their way to the right edge of the bluff, Sam's father holding aside branches with his arm for them, Wren cursing as she stumbled over a rock, Maggie still disoriented and sweating, despite the cold.

"Did you find her, son?"

It was Linnie who answered, directly below where they stood. "Yes." An indecipherable exchange followed: a soft question, a low retort, a child's querulous demand. Then Linnie again, louder this time: "We've got her."

23

IN THE COPPER glow of the cabin's kitchen, Wren murmured, "Oh, good." She tapped the screen of her phone. "Thomas wrote. Here's our hospital update." She read aloud, "'No hypothermia, mild frostbite on her right hand, nothing serious, ready for home and hot cocoa. Linnie's sleeping over.'"

While the aunt texted back, Maggie dropped her forehead in her hand. *Hot cocoa?* She flared her eyes at the table.

Her aunt set down the phone. "Well, it was an interesting plan—to stow away on the first pirate ship that swung by Devil's Tongue. Didn't work, but, hey, there's the cocoa. Plus, her mom's sticking close."

Maggie grunted.

The aunt smiled. "Think a time-out's more in order?" When

Maggie shrugged, Wren shook her head and leaned back in her chair. "All kids want attention. It's nice when it comes in the form of praise, but they'll take what they can get and do just about anything to win it. Throw a temper tantrum, get attention. Run away, get attention." She scrubbed her face and let her fingertips rest on her eyes. "Kate's no different." Heaving herself up from the table, she added tartly, "Besides, what were Sam and Linnie thinking, ranting and raving in front of Kate?"

"That was dumb."

"Dumb and mean." The aunt folded her arms. "Whatever mistakes those two made with each other, they're not Kate's fault. Keep up that bullshit, and they'll have trouble on their hands and no one to blame but themselves."

Too late. Maggie also got to her feet but couldn't muster the energy to do more than that. She stood there, gripping the back of the chair and staring at the table without seeing it.

Instead, she saw bits and pieces of the long night: the snow, thin and stinging, a shivering Kate, the waves battering the bluff, Sam's terrified eyes, Linnie's shocked face, the snarl of branches, and herself—once again completely falling apart. Like a boat wrecked on the reefs of the shallows.

". . . use some sleep. Hmm? Maggie? *Maggie?*"

She started. "Sorry?"

The aunt gazed at her in alarm. "I think we'd better call it a night. Come on." She braced Maggie with a one-armed hug and steered her out of the kitchen. "Let's get you to bed." She turned off the kitchen lights. When they reached the hallway, she said softly, "Good night, sweetheart."

"'Night."

The aunt waited at the foot of the steep stairs as Maggie headed up, then asked abruptly, "You okay?"

"Yes." *No.*

That was what she'd learned tonight. Still so not-okay.

Maggie woke to a *drip, drip, drip* along the eaves and down the roof, wet snow's slide and plop. Spring sounds for a winter barely started.

She pressed her hands together. Her palms ached from the brambles. Where else? Lower, her right hip and knees—they hurt from the fall. And her head. That hurt, too.

She wished she could keep sleeping, just blank out the previous night—Kate's disappearance, Sam and Linnie's fight. Her own fucking head trip. *Oh God.* She burrowed deeper under the blankets.

That moment on the bluff—the memory, experience, fact of it—drained her. It had been weeks since she'd suffered that kind of relapse. She had begun to hope she never would again. Only the previous morning, she'd thought, *Look at me. I'm sleeping better. I can stay alone in Wren's cabin and not be afraid. I have good friends. There's some rough shit going on with Mom and Linnie and Jane, but I'm trying to make things better. Because I can. Because I'm up for the challenge. Because I'm stable and normal enough to help.*

Then just hours later, there it was again: the past tearing into the present, and so predictably, herself, getting swallowed by the old fear and pain and *being back there.*

She hated it. She hated that she hadn't seen it coming.

From downstairs came Wren's cautious voice: "Honey? You all right?"

Maggie dried her face with the flat sheet. "Yeah. Just tired."

The aunt was silent for a moment. "I made blueberry scones if you want some. They're pretty bad, hard as rocks, actually, but tolerable if you dunk them in coffee."

Maggie closed her eyes. "Thanks. I'll be down in a bit."

Eventually, she did make it to the table with one of the scones and a cup of coffee. Her head swam. When was the last time she'd eaten? Yesterday. Lunchtime. She'd had a bowl of soup while checking the messages on her phone. Dad had called. She'd planned to return the call last night. She should touch base with him and write back to Ran, too, who'd texted her a couple of days ago. And she should check on Linnie—make sure everything was okay with her and Sam and Kate. She should . . .

She put her head on the table.

"Hey." Wren walked into the kitchen. Her hand fell on Maggie's hair. She threaded her fingers through some curls. "My hair is just like yours. Wild." Lightly, she continued, "Sometimes I study you and think, if I'd ever had a daughter, she probably would have looked a lot like you . . . with Min and me being twins and all. And if I'd had an affair with your dad, my daughter might have looked *exactly* like you."

Maggie laughed, a rough sound but still a laugh.

Wren gave her one last pat, then headed for the coffeepot. Pouring a cup, she said without turning, "Want to try out the wheel again? Kate's not here to pick on you."

"I—I've got some emails to answer. And texts and stuff."

"Maybe tonight, then."

Maggie nodded and heaved herself up from the table.

The aunt caught up with her in the hallway. "Forgot your phone, Margaret."

Avoiding Wren's eyes, she accepted the phone with a mumbled thank-you, then climbed the stairs to the loft and tossed her phone on the floor. Her messages could wait until later. She crawled back into bed.

"Move over."

At the nudge on her shoulder, Maggie awoke with a start. "What—" She twisted around and sprang back.

An inch from Maggie's face, Linnie smiled. "Wren thought you could use some company. She said you've been blue all week."

Had an entire week passed? Maggie waved away the invasion of pale hair and scrubbed at the lingering tickle on her nose. "Company's nice." The words sounded rough, snagged on sleep and emotion. She cleared her throat and slid over to make room. "How's Kate?"

"Kate is a girl getting what she wants. Or thinks she wants."

"You and Sam playing house again?"

"Oh God, that appears to be the case." She groaned a laugh. After a minute, she said, "She's at school right now. I have to pick her up in a few hours."

So it was probably around noon. On . . . Thursday? Maggie prodded her face. Swollen eyes, gouged palms—the aches registered in a bracing way. *Pull yourself together.* She had to get up. She would. Soon. Eventually.

Linnie brought one of Maggie's ringlets close for an inspection and then wound the curl around her finger until the frizz was pressed out and the strands were smoothed to a sheen. "You remind me of myself a long time ago. Caught and nearly gutted."

Maggie thought about this. "How did you get loose?"

"I just learned to avoid the hook. What did my old therapist say?" She mimicked a prying expression. "'You've detached, Linnie.'" She rolled her eyes. "No shit." She released Maggie's curl, rolled onto her back, and raised her head an inch to free her own hair. After spreading it out over the pillow, she relaxed with a noisy exhalation. "Anything swimming too fast or too slow in my vicinity looks like bait, so I don't bite." Her forearm fell across her forehead. "Avoid, avoid, avoid, Margaret. That's my mantra."

The words planted a sickness in Maggie's belly. Avoidance. Of everything? A musty basement, keening wind, stand of trees, crashing waves—all triggers. What would the next one be? "Then how do you know what's safe?"

"You don't. You surge ahead, faster and faster. That's what I do. But it's no good. I have to try something different—see a doctor, get back into therapy, straighten myself out . . . stop. I know I do." She closed her eyes and thrust up her chin, exposing her neck. "Just stop. I'm so tired."

The roof began to ping with rain. "Do you think you can get better?" Maggie asked. The question for the oracle: *Can you? Can I?*

Linnie opened her eyes and stared hard at the ceiling.

Maggie saw her swallow. Fear was plain in Linnie's face. Was she remembering Sunday night and Kate's running away?

"A week ago," Linnie said gruffly, "I would have told you no, it's hopeless. I'd given up, given up on *myself*—decided if I couldn't help but be a shitty mom like mine was, Kate shouldn't have to witness it. But Kate . . ." Sadness and affection loosened her features. Her lip trembled. She caught it in her teeth. After a moment, she said in a choked voice, "Kate won't give up on me. So I'll get better . . . because I have to. Because I love her."

To the sound of rain drumming the roof, Maggie and Linnie fell asleep side by side. It was a short-lived nap. Maggie jerked awake when the aunt called from downstairs, "Margaret! Some friends here to see you."

Surprised, Maggie struggled out of her cocoon of blankets.

"Who . . . ?" Her brow creased in sleepy confusion, Linnie pushed herself up more slowly and armed her hair away from her flushed face.

Ran appeared at the top of the stairs. Her gaze flitted to Linnie, then back to Maggie. "Mind if we come up?" she asked anxiously.

I mind. Today I really do mind. "Of course not." She rubbed her eyes and tried to rally her spirits. *Oh God, I am so not up for this.* "How's it going?"

"Fine, good . . . yeah. We're, uh, good." She quickly climbed the rest of the stairs and then, as Hope, Julia, and Colleen followed, stood off to the side, wrapped her ponytail around her wrist, and glanced around searchingly, as if the right words were around here somewhere and she just had to track them down to know what to say. It was a strange look for Ran Kita.

"That's good," Maggie murmured lamely. She didn't know what to say, either.

The four girls stood in a huddle on the opposite side of the room, close to the stairs, so that their heads didn't hit the angled ceiling. They smiled stiffly. Maggie smiled stiffly back.

Linnie glanced at Maggie, her eyebrows raised.

"Oh. This is Linnie." Maggie introduced the girls, as well, and they exchanged greetings.

Another lull followed. Maggie checked an impulse to groan. This was why she'd created Marge. Marge didn't have a past that made chatty girls quiet and uncomfortable.

Hope gave her shaved head a scrub. "Nice room."

"Thanks," Maggie said.

"Great view," Colleen said. "Of the lake, I mean. Over there." She pointed toward the windows behind Maggie's and Linnie's heads. Then, as if realizing how unnecessary it was to direct everyone's attention to the lake's location, she snatched back her hand, tucked it into her armpit, and laughed—a sickly hahaha.

Julia sucked in her lips.

Maggie sat up taller against the headboard and hugged her legs to her chest. "You guys want to sit?" They looked like prisoners facing a firing squad.

Linnie drew up her legs, too. "There's plenty of room."

"Thanks." Ran swung her arms and sidled closer. Gingerly, she perched on the edge of the bed. Without looking directly at Maggie, she said, "We've missed you at book club."

"Oh, yeah, well . . ." Maggie pleated the top of the flat sheet. "It's been kind of . . . hectic here. Sorry."

Hope sat heavily next to Ran. She slouched forward and clasped her hands.

Julia and Colleen sat cross-legged on the floor.

Julia tucked her hair behind her ears. "We hated to think you were avoiding us."

Colleen nodded. "And we felt really bad, learning what we did about you when we googled your name."

Hope gave her knee a small kick.

Colleen frowned and whispered, "*What?*"

"I wasn't really avoiding you," Maggie said. Only this. This weirdness. "I just didn't want to talk about . . . you know." She shrugged.

"I don't blame you." Ran twisted the ponytail into a tight coil. "You shouldn't feel like you have to."

"If you don't want to," Julia said.

"But if you ever do, you, like, totally can." Ran stood suddenly and crossed to the window that overlooked the woods. "With us, I mean."

"We're here for you," Colleen added.

Julia nodded. "You're not alone."

Hope planted her hands on her knees. Fiercely, she said, "You are *never* alone."

"Thanks." Maggie tried to smile.

Ran folded her arms. She toed the floor in a little sweep and said briskly, "There's this book coming out next month that's supposed to be really good. It's called *The Bear and the Nightingale*. I think we should read it."

"What's it about?" Maggie asked, grateful for the change of subject.

"Magic and fairy tales. It takes place on the edge of the Russian wilderness. This winter demon lurks . . ."

Ran told them about the book, and the conversation stayed

on the safe subject of fantasy novels. They didn't talk for long. After a few minutes, Ran checked her phone and said, "We'd better get going."

"Julia has to babysit her brothers," Colleen explained.

The departure (a flurry of see-you-soons and tentative pats and little waves) was awkward—but not as awkward as the visit's beginning had been.

"Your friends are nice," Linnie observed afterward.

"They are. They're really sweet." Maggie felt a fluttery lightness in her chest. She'd made it through the post-Marge reunion. More than that, she didn't have to be Marge anymore. She didn't have to hide and pretend. "You should go with me the next time."

"To your book club?"

Maggie nodded.

"Okay." Linnie smiled. "I like books." She drew out her phone, absently glanced at it, then yelped, "Shit! I've got to pick up Kate." She scrambled out of bed. "Hurry up. You're coming, too."

"I am?" She grimaced. Kate wasn't going to be happy to see her. The kid never was. On the other hand, going with Linnie gave Maggie something to do, and *doing* something with someone suddenly seemed smarter—and healthier—than *not* doing anything all by herself.

Maybe Linnie suspected the same, because she said, "Yes, you are."

24

THE SAAB WAS sitting outside the cabin.

"Still driving Kyle's car?" Maggie asked, surprised.

"Where he is right now, well . . . let's just say he won't have any use for a car."

"Ooooh." Yikes.

She smiled. "Buckle up, Margaret."

At the elementary school, Linnie swiftly parked and jogged up to the building. She reappeared a minute later, smiling down at her daughter and holding her hand.

Kate looked annoyed when she spied Maggie in the front seat, but she didn't make any cutting remarks, just delivered a kick to the back of Maggie's seat as they drove away from the school.

Instead of driving north, in the direction of Wren's cabin, Linnie headed south.

"Where are we going?" Maggie asked, then turned around to scowl at Kate when the girl kicked her seat again.

"Allenport." Linnie stared straight ahead. "I have to stop by Caleb's."

When they got there, despite the wet, cold weather, they found him outside, leaning against a post on the porch. He was talking to Sam.

As soon as Linnie parked on the side of the road, Kate peeled out of the car, holding a spiral notebook. It flapped like a wing. She raced up to her dad.

He caught her and gave her a jostling hug. "Now *this* is a nice surprise."

"Surprise!" Kate shouted, and giggled when he carried her down from the porch, hugely bouncing her with each step.

Caleb followed and gave Maggie a cheerful nod. "How's it going?"

"Good." Tolerable. She smiled wanly. "How about you?"

"Great."

Sam snorted. "Caleb's always great." He set his daughter back on her feet and held her against his side, palming the dark head. "What's up?" he asked Linnie.

She shrugged and shoved her hands into her coat pockets, then she sat heavily on a middle step, exhaling a sound like a high-pitched *phoof*. "I'm beat," she said to no one in particular.

"So am I," Sam said. Kate wiggled out from under his palm. For a second, he didn't seem to know what to do with his hand.

Then he closed it into a fist and held it against his heart. "It's been a long week." His frown flickered over his daughter.

With the spiral notebook tucked under her arm, Kate jogged up the stairs past her mother. On the landing, she spun around and ordered Caleb to catch her. As soon as he did, she laughed. "Put me down!" Then she trotted back up the stairs and said, "Catch me again, Caleb!"

The notebook slipped away from her on the second leap.

Maggie collected it and wiped off the old snow streaking its cover. "Want me to hold this for you?"

"*No.*" As if Maggie were planning a confiscation, Kate pounced and grabbed the notebook. "This is my book of secrets."

"Oh." Another book by Kate Blake. Exciting. "Okay." She turned back to Linnie.

Kate sidled between them and pressed the notebook against her chest. "Want to know what today's secret is?"

"Sure. What's today's secret?"

"*Duh.* I can't tell you. It's a secret."

The others found this funny. Maggie smiled. It was kind of funny. But mostly it was annoying.

Linnie stood. "I'm getting cold. Let's go in."

When Caleb got to the door, he bent to pick up a bag and explained, "Leftovers. Sam and I went to Mythos for lunch. Hungry?"

Maggie thought about it. "Actually, yes. Starving."

"Me too," Linnie said.

He beamed. "We'd better feed you, then." And he waved them all in.

One of Caleb's housemates lounged in the living room. It was

Jack, the weight lifter Maggie had met the first time she'd visited the place.

A mostly empty bowl of popcorn rested on his stomach. "How's it going?" he asked, turning off the television. He passed Sam the remote and tossed popcorn to Fluffster. When Kate got on the floor and opened her mouth, he laughed and attempted a few dunk shots on her as well. The dog sniffed around and cleaned up the misses. Yawning, Jack rose. "Naptime. See you guys." He trudged out of the room, just as Caleb returned from the kitchen, carrying a plate and two forks.

Kate threw herself on a dingy couch and stretched, hands reaching toward one end, toes pointing toward the other. "All mine. You guys have to share those two little couches."

While Sam and Caleb got into a conversation about a professor, Maggie and Linnie shared the plate of Greek food. Afterward, Linnie stood and wandered around, stopped by the coffee table to flip open an abandoned physics textbook, then picked up some playing cards spread there. She absently turned them all in the same direction, tapped them into a tight pack, cut the deck, and neatly wove the cards in a way that made them look zippered. She added a flourish at the end by springing the cards together. "The faro shuffle." She smiled. "A trick." She left the deck on the table and fell back, sprawling next to Maggie.

Kate, still hogging a couch, patted the cushion. "Up. Up, Fluffster!"

The dog ran out of the room.

With a screech of his name, Kate shot off the couch and pounded after him.

"Stay downstairs, Kate!" Sam called.

Maggie heard Kate's feet on the stairs and waited for Sam or Linnie to order her back down. They didn't. She sighed.

Linnie looked distracted. She got to her feet again and went to the window just as the sun found a crack in the clouds. The light appeared to rush down to meet her. Fingerprints and grime smeared the panes, but the shine sifted through the smudges, and licked Linnie's hair into a radiance, like threads of precious metal. She lightly touched the glass, then, almost violently, whirled around. "Okay." She slapped her hands on her hips. "Where is it?"

Sam stopped talking midsentence and stared at her blankly.

"I'm not talking to you," she told him impatiently.

"It?" Caleb asked, confused. But then his eyes widened, and his lips began to curl into a smile.

"Oh!" Sam grinned. "*It.*"

"Yes. It." Glaring outside again, she folded her arms and added witheringly, "I know you still have that thing, Caleb. You probably planned to save it until my dying day. God forbid you give up hope." She flicked him a pitying glance, but there was a grudging affection in her voice when she added, "Forever hopeful Caleb."

He winked at Maggie. "It's in my room."

Linnie swatted the air. "Go get it." As Caleb made for the stairs, she turned her glare on Sam. "And I'll read it in my own time, when I'm good and ready, *without* an audience, thank you very much."

"What?" Sam held up his hands. "I didn't even say anything."

She sniffed and went back to scowling at the sun-silvered clouds.

Sam surreptitiously turned to Maggie and mouthed, *Yay!*

After Linnie dropped her off at the cabin, Maggie went in search of Wren.

Linnie's willingness to read the letter and face its news, no matter how potentially grim, made Maggie feel optimistic. She wanted to talk to Wren about it.

But the aunt wasn't in the studio, and her bedroom door was closed. Maggie wasn't surprised. Wren had been feeling wiped out lately, juggling all the media inquiries about the exhibition. She was probably resting.

Maggie trudged up to the loft. She tried to read but couldn't concentrate. She tried to nap but couldn't fall asleep. After a while, she wandered back to the kitchen and fell into a chair at the table. It was suppertime, but she was still full from the leftover spanakopitas.

She checked her phone. Her father had texted, so she wrote back to let him know she was fine. She hesitated, then texted her mother as well, just to say she missed her. Her email was still crammed with the new and unread. She had to get rid of some of them. She tapped the icon and discovered, right at the tippy-top, a message from Jane Cannon.

Maggie was dumbfounded.

With a shake of her head, she opened the message.

I'll go back if you go back.

That's it. That was all it said.

Maggie sat in the chair for the longest time, mentally replaying the handful of words and automatically rejecting them, her refusal repeating like a refrain, *I can't go back, I can't go back*. She might have done this for the rest of the evening if the door hadn't suddenly flown open, ushering in a thin scattering of snowflakes.

Linnie stood there, the night behind her. Her expression was unfamiliar, un-Linnie-like, an exercise in Os, rounded mouth and eyes.

Crap. Maggie set the phone on the table. "Bad news?"

"Just . . . weird." Linnie blindly closed the door behind her. "Margaret, I—I have a sister."

"A sister?"

"Half sister, from my dad's side."

"Your dad?"

"And not even a younger sister."

"Not even younger?"

Linnie smiled, her old self again. "You sound like a parrot."

Maggie, still discombobulated from Jane's email, struggled to process Linnie's news. "Wow," she finally managed. "Tell me about her."

"I didn't know she existed. *A sister*." She strode to the table, sat on the edge of a chair, then immediately stood again. "The letter was from her. She gave it to my old neighbor, hoping that Mary would be able to get in touch with me and pass it along."

"Did she say anything about herself?"

"You won't believe it."

* * *

Maggie slept poorly. She couldn't stop thinking about Jane's email—Jane's challenge. In the morning, she hauled herself out of bed, searched for her cardigan in the tangle of clothes on the floor, and focused on Linnie's happier news about her half sister.

Danielle Pinsky was thirteen years older than Linnie. She'd been adopted at birth to become the only child of Adam and Rael Pinsky of Syracuse and was now a surgeon at Syracuse Hillside Hospital. Her research into her origins had led her to Linnie's old neighborhood, the last place her birth father had lived. There, thanks to Mary Tate, she'd learned about Linnie. She hoped to meet her and gave her email address and phone number, so Linnie could contact her.

"Do you want to meet her?" Maggie had asked.

"I—I think I do," Linnie had stammered. "But not by myself."

"I'll go with you," she'd offered, hearing in her own words an unintentional echo of Jane's *I'll go back if you go back.*

Now, giving up on finding her cardigan, she grabbed her hoodie instead.

On her way downstairs for a cup of coffee, she heard a commotion: the rev of an engine, Wren shouting a greeting from the porch, the thud of a closed door, and voices in the driveway. Maggie reached the kitchen at the same time the back door opened. *"Mom?"*

"Honey." Wild-haired, red-eyed, her mother hurried across the room and pulled Maggie into a choking embrace.

Maggie drew back. "What's going on? You look . . . upset." She looked like hell.

Mom self-consciously smoothed her hair.

Maggie checked her pocket and found a hairband. "Here."

"Thanks." She drew the disaster into a ponytail. Then her hands collapsed at her sides, and she sighed, so heavily her body seemed to shrink a little from the exhalation.

Wren passed her a cup of coffee.

Without meeting her sister's eyes, Mom accepted it with another murmured thanks.

It clearly wasn't reconciliation with Wren that had brought Mom here so early. Maggie glanced at the time on the microwave. Ten o'clock. *Jesus.* "You must have left home in the middle of the night."

"I wasn't sleeping anyway. I texted Janice to let her know I didn't feel well enough to go to work, which is true"—she paused to glare, as if daring anyone to suggest otherwise—"then I left."

A fear seized Maggie. "Is Dad okay?"

Mom brushed a hand across her eyes. "He's fine."

The kitchen door opened. "Morning." Linnie kicked off her sneakers without bothering to untie them. "Sam here?"

"In the studio," Wren said. "He came over extra early—after driving Kate to school."

"Making up for taking off yesterday afternoon?"

"Yep."

"Ah."

No one seemed to have anything else to say.

Linnie gave Maggie a what's-going-on look.

She shrugged.

Linnie turned to Mom. "So how's it going, Mrs. Arioli?"

She answered with a distracted shake of her head. Which wasn't much of an answer.

"What about you?" Maggie asked apologetically. Linnie had shown up, probably hoping to talk more about her half sister, and here she was receiving a cool reception. "How are you doing?" Her voice sounded loud in the quiet kitchen.

Linnie's smile slipped. "Fine." She retreated toward the door. "I just stopped by to chat," she explained to Wren, "but I can always come back later, if you have things you need to take care of."

"Don't go," Maggie said hastily, sitting at the table. *Don't leave me to face the sisters' awkwardness alone.* "Join us."

"Please do." Mom set down her brimming mug and dropped into a chair. "You might be able to help. After all, I believe you were there."

"Where?" Linnie sat.

"Timberline Tavern."

Understanding dawned. "Oh," Maggie said. "There."

Frowning, Wren poured two cups of coffee. "Timberline Tavern?"

Mom surged forward and slapped the table. "The local sports bar that refused to serve my daughter a stinkin' Pepsi."

Wren looked sharply at Maggie. *"What?"*

She sighed. "Just the bartender."

The aunt put a mug in front of Linnie and one in front of Maggie and then sat where her own cup was waiting for her. "Why wouldn't he wait on you, Margaret?"

Mom slapped the table again. "Because Carlton's a shitty dump filled with assholes and fucking morons who care more about football than kindness and justice and common decency."

Maggie's mouth fell open. *Did Mom just drop the f-bomb? On all of Carlton?*

"You told me you went to Dilly's," Mom continued accusingly.

"We did. Afterward."

"Why didn't you say anything about what happened before?"

"Guess I didn't see any point in upsetting you. No one got hurt. How did you find out?"

"Tammy McDaniel." At Maggie's blank look, Mom clarified, "Brown hair? Glasses?" She waved a hand: immaterial. "Tammy and her mother visit the library once a week." Her hand landed on her forehead. "That I ended up hearing about this atrocity from an acquaintance and not my own daughter . . ." Tears filled her eyes. "That *astonishes* me."

Linnie smoothed the tabletop with her fingertips. "But your daughter handled it. Much better than I would have."

Maggie smiled vaguely. "Thanks, Linnie." She was thinking about the bespectacled girl. She remembered her. She remembered her sympathy.

"Well." Mom fell back in her chair. "That's it for me. I'm done."

Maggie frowned. "Done?"

"With the tavern?" Wren asked.

"With Carlton."

"The college?" Linnie asked.

"Not just the damn college. Carlton cliques, Carlton Tigers, Carlton fans, the endless parade of Carlton creeps. I *hate* Carlton."

"That's not true. You've got great friends there. And colleagues." Maggie shook her head. "You can't lump the whole town together over one incident."

Wren raised her mug. "It's tempting, though." She took a long sip.

"If only it were the one incident. But it's been months and months of bullshit." Mom rubbed her eyes with her fists, a curiously childish gesture.

Maggie didn't know how to react. This wasn't her old mother, the soothing, church-board-treasurer-at-Saint-Luke's, look-on-the-bright-side Minerva Arioli. Three-quarters of a year had reduced her to this: a frailer, unhappier person.

Maggie was still learning what those months had cost her personally. But the toll wasn't hers alone. The hurt was shared, compounded in others . . . in Mom and Dad, especially. She remembered something her mother had said once—years ago at the doctor's, when they'd waited in the office for the nurse to return with the vaccinations and Maggie had been sick with dread. "I'd take them for you in a flash if I could, little Mags." And Maggie hadn't doubted for a second that her mother had meant it. All these years, in every hurtful situation, her mother would have shielded Maggie from the pain if she could have. But it wasn't possible. Parents couldn't take life's blows and stings for their children. And that was the terrible truth.

Mom raised her face from her hands. "Your dad and I talked about it. We're moving."

Maggie stared. It took a moment for her to add a voice to her amazement. "You can't move."

"Sure we can. Your dad's a CPA. I'm a librarian. We can work anywhere."

"Carlton's home." *My home.*

"It's . . ." Mom gazed morosely out the window. "Poisoned."

Wren sighed. "You want to keep her safe."

"I want to try."

Linnie averted her face, but Maggie read the expression before she hid it: *Good luck with that.*

"You're a great mom, Min," the aunt murmured.

Mom swallowed. "A parent can only be so good. There's too much danger out there." She folded her hands together tightly. "But I can do better than our parents did."

There was a concession in those words. Wren had heard it, too. Pain worked over her features. She reached across the table and covered Mom's folded hands with both of her own.

"Don't make any hasty decisions about Carlton," Maggie said.

"If we stay or move—who cares?" Mom asked sadly. "You don't want to be there, either."

Maggie mumbled something about not acting rashly and lowered her gaze to her cup of coffee. But she was thinking about Jane Cannon's email. About Jane's future. And her own. *I'll go back if you go back.*

25

WITH THE EXCUSE of taking a walk, Maggie and Linnie escaped the tension in the cabin. Lake Ontario sparkled under the late-morning sun. The ice fringing the shore had mostly melted, and across the east end's crop of rocks, the snow had turned tensile, streaked with seaweed and pockmarked with the recent rain. It was almost Christmas, but the weather looked like it was gearing up for spring.

Holding on to a bent pine by the rocks, Maggie stretched out a leg and tested a clump with her boot. The snow detached from its berth. It slapped the water and turned in a drunken reel. Maggie drew back, shoved her hands into her coat pockets, and caught up with Linnie.

They walked into a gust. Their hair flew up, threaded together, and swirled around.

Linnie grabbed her strands and pinned them over her shoulder. When they reached the lake's edge, she said, "I wrote to Danielle."

"That's awesome." Maggie's unzipped jacked fluttered open. She caught the sides and folded them over her chest like a shawl. "Did she write back yet?"

Linnie smiled shyly. "Almost right away. She sounded . . . happy. We're meeting for supper at the Dinosaur Bar-B-Que Sunday night." She reached out a hand, and as Maggie took it, she asked, "You still willing to go with me?" After Maggie nodded, she continued, "We'll have to leave here by quarter of six."

"Are you excited?"

"Nervous." Leaning forward, she released Maggie's hand and narrowed her eyes on the lake.

"What is it?" Maggie followed the direction of her gaze.

"I'm looking for Toronto. Wren swears, on a perfectly clear day, you can make out the teeniest tiniest speck of civilization on the opposite shore."

She squinted at the horizon, then gave up with a "Huh." The lake might have been an ocean. The distance made her think about Sam. "What's going on with the art institute?"

"Your aunt told Sam to hold off on a decision and just work on finishing his sculpture." A smile quivered on her lips. "You know—the brain sculpture. Wren said if it comes out of the kiln looking cool, he'll have some images to add to his portfolio. She wants him to send the portfolio to Alfred, see if what happened with Chicago might happen there, too."

"That's a great idea." Sam could commute to Alfred—which

made it more doable than Chicago. "Wren went to Alfred. I wonder if she'll pull a few strings."

"I wouldn't be surprised . . . though I suppose Sam's plenty good enough to get into the college without her help."

"But he has to be able to afford it."

"Yeah." Linnie exhaled. "That's the tricky part."

Maggie folded her arms and peered across the lake. Sam's future, Linnie's, her own—all like Toronto. There, but impossible to decipher.

Now even her parents' future looked uncertain. Would they move?

A seagull picked its way along the shore. Maggie observed its progress without really seeing it. She was worried about Mom.

Her mother was not happy. She especially wasn't happy with Carlton. And how much *less* happy she'd be if Maggie told her that she was considering returning to college there. *Considering* it. She hadn't decided yet. Nor had she written back to Jane.

A return had never been part of Mom's plan. Maggie knew that. The business of a sabbatical had been her mother's way of making an eventual transfer to another college easier. To a safer college. *The Safe University*. As if there were such a place.

One thing was for sure: If she strolled into the cabin right now and mentioned a hankering for a women-only college in Alaska, Mom would be thrilled.

Maggie shivered and smoothed down her wind-ruffled jacket so she could zip it.

"You're getting cold," Linnie said. "Want to go in?"

"Not yet." Anxious to put off her mother for a little longer, she said, "It's neat to think about this Danielle, like, out of the blue—boom. Family."

Linnie nodded once. She was gazing at the other end of the beach, where snow webbed the marshy stretch between the aunt's property and the Blakes'. The wind battered the straggle of brittle brush there, and the brown remains of goldenrod and cattails shuddered stiffly. Across the marsh, Devil's Tongue cut into the lake, a riot of rocks and thicket and trees. What had the mapmaker labeled it? Something about a graveyard for ships.

Linnie finally said, "It *is* neat, and, of course, I hope she's nice . . . but if she's not?" Her shoulders came up. "I already have a family. Kate, Sam, Thomas." She smiled fleetingly. "You, Wren, Caleb . . ." Her voice died. A frown drew two lines between her eyebrows.

Abruptly, she continued, "I realized that there." She indicated the wild bluff with a lift of her chin. Fear flashed across her face. "A lot of people have been rooting for me, covering for me. Helping me when I felt helpless. Fighting for me . . ." She looked away sharply. "Well, now I'm fighting for myself."

Mom decided to stay for the weekend. When Linnie left and Maggie returned to the cabin, her mother announced the news, an unconvincing smile pasted on her face.

Friday passed, then Saturday, and hour upon hour, Mom's fake smile persisted. Fixing meals with Wren, setting the table, walking with Maggie on the beach—during every activity, she stayed almost maniacally cheerful.

It was obvious, however, that she was steering clear of difficult subjects. She didn't mention again her plan to leave Carlton.

And she didn't ask Wren about the exhibition or how the sculptures had been received. And she certainly didn't say a word about their childhood. Her attempt to restore her and her sister's relationship while avoiding certain topics struck Maggie as comparable to someone using tape to fix a shattered platter—one missing big pieces. It wasn't going to work.

Maggie watched her mother with concern. Artificially chipper, jumpy with nerves, Mom seemed as fragile as the snow Maggie had tested on the rocks Friday morning. How easily the white chunk had answered the merest pressure of her foot and broken free.

Maggie's mother, with her brittle smile, seemed just as likely to fall apart.

On Sunday morning, Mom stood at the sink window, fidgeted with her purse strap, and patted her hair, which was coiled into as neat a bun as an abundance of frizzy curls allowed. "I hope Wren's not long." She glanced at her watch. "I've got to finish reading a novel for tomorrow's meeting."

"You're leading the book club discussion?" Maggie crouched by Mom's feet, batted her aside, and reached into the cupboard.

"I'm supposed to."

She grabbed the bottle of Mr. Clean and a bucket. First the kitchen, then the bathroom, then everywhere else. She wanted to finish before Linnie picked her up. They had their dinner date with Linnie's sister tonight.

Her mother checked her watch again. "What in the world is your aunt doing in that studio? I wish she'd hurry." She folded her arms and scowled out the window.

"Adam's got Wren on the phone," Maggie explained. "Whenever that happens, it can take a while." At Mom's baffled look, she explained, "I don't really know who he is—an agent, maybe?— just that he handles her projects, conferences . . ." She waved a hand. "Stuff."

"Oh." Mom turned quickly and went back to frowning out the window.

Maggie sighed and settled the bucket in the sink. Her mother didn't want to hear about the art stuff. In fact, at least in Maggie's hearing, the only questions she'd asked Wren that related to her work had to do with a mug on the counter and the curly-handled vase on the bookshelf behind the couch. It was as if Mom had mentally recast her sister, from a ceramist to simply a potter. Pots were safe. Sculptures—not so much. As for the studio, Maggie suspected her mother would never step foot in that space again. Too afraid of what she might find.

She poured some cleaning liquid into the bucket, turned on the spigot, and watched bubbles form under the water's rush. "What novel are you doing this week?"

"*Carry On.*"

"Oh, I love that book." Maggie smiled. "I've read it twice." Rainbow Rowell was one of her favorite authors. "If I were heading back with you, I'd come." She shut off the water, transferred the filled bucket to the floor, and strode to the closet outside the kitchen. From the hallway, she added, "It'd be fun to hear what others have to say about it." She collected the mop and returned to the kitchen. "How are you liking it so far?"

Her mother didn't answer. She'd obviously lost the thread of their conversation. Peering out the window, she said, "Who . . . ?"

A small blue car was turning off Ash Drive. It crept toward the cabin. The slow speed suggested the driver was a stranger, uncertain of his surroundings. After the car door opened, a thin man emerged.

Maggie frowned. "I have no idea."

He made his way around the messy drive, where rain had frozen into pearly pits. The morning sky was more silver than gray, the sun shrouded but discernible behind the clouds. The stranger's red hair was a shout of color. His breath clouded the air around his bespectacled face.

Mom answered the door, her expression questioning.

His eyes lit up at the sight of her, and before she got a chance to inquire if she could help him, he burst out with a hearty "Hello!" and thrust out a hand. As Mom limply took it, he gushed, "I am so happy to meet you. Thrilled! And I appreciate your willingness to talk to me—on a Sunday, no less. I realize it isn't at all your thing."

Mom took a step, retreating into the door. It banged the wall and bounced against her back. Her hand, once released, fluttered to her cheek. "No, no, I'm afraid—"

He frowned at her tone of regret, then threw up a flat palm, like a cornered suspect proving his lack of a weapon, and said hurriedly, "I won't steal much of your time. Promise." He sidled to the kitchen table and opened a briefcase. Yanking out his laptop, notes, and phone, he continued swiftly, "This is a lucky break. I'm grateful and honored and want you to know I'm a big fan—"

"But I—I'm not—" Mom stammered, just as Maggie, behind her, said, "She's not—"

"Huge!" he interrupted. "So much so I actually drove all the way to New York just to see your work firsthand, and I can honestly tell you it was like no exhibit I've attended before, which is saying something, you know, since that's my gig, covering this sort of thing. But what struck me about your show was how, well, *emotional* it was. I can't remember ever—*ever*—standing in a gallery where so many people were reduced to tears. The whole thing—electric! And difficult—but necessary. Truly. In particular, I want to focus on three pieces, what I consider, if you don't mind my saying so, the real masterpieces of the collection." He tugged a folder out of the briefcase, stepped to the side to find a clear spot on the table on which to open it, and tripped on the chair next to him. In his scramble to right himself, he dropped the folder.

Three large photographs spilled across the floor.

Mom stooped to gather them. Eyes wide and unblinking, she slowly rose. The photographs trembled in her hands.

The top one captured in blown-up detail the culminating sculpture of Wren's collection. Maggie recognized the hollowed heads and folded slabs of clay and the four subjects, threatened, threatening, blind, free.

"Holy crap. I'm sorry about that." One hand gripping his red hair, the journalist muttered some self-castigation under his breath and, glancing apologetically at Mom, made to relieve her of the photographs.

She clung to them and stepped back. A whimper escaped her. She didn't seem to notice she was crying—didn't seem to notice anything besides the photographs, not Maggie's hand, resting on her shoulder, not the journalist, flustered and apologetic. Mom shakily went through the photos, tears falling unchecked.

Footsteps pounded down the hall. Wren halted in the kitchen doorway. "Michael Brady?"

The journalist's beleaguered expression turned purely confounded. He stared at the aunt, gaped at Mom, and glanced back at Wren with some fast blinking.

Mom shuddered but didn't turn at the sound of Wren's voice.

"That's my sister," the aunt explained, striding into the kitchen. "I apologize. Forgot all about the interview and—" Abreast of Mom, she cut off her own words with a squeak and moved quickly, hands out, as if to seize the photographs. But Mom pressed them against her chest and released a sob. "Jesus Christ, Min, I'm sorry." Then, with a ferocious glare at the hapless journalist, she barked, "I *wish* you hadn't shared those." Wren didn't seem to know where to turn or what to do. "This is harrowing stuff for my sister."

He flinched. "I'm sorry. I—I didn't know. I thought she was you . . ."

A high-pitched note sounded. From Mom. A laugh like the peal of a siren. "Harrowing . . . for me. Harrowing for *me*?" Tears coursed down her cheeks. "Oh, Wren, Wren . . ." She moaned and wavered. "I'm so—so sorr—" Her eyes rolled back. Her knees buckled. The photographs swooped to the floor again.

Wren and Maggie yelped, lunged, and caught her. And cracked their heads together in the process.

26

MAGGIE RUBBED THE bump on her head and looked up from her menu.

Linnie and her half sister had the same eyes, in shape if not shade. But Danielle Pinsky was darker than Linnie, her skin olive-toned. She was taller, too, and disconcertingly direct. Danielle didn't look at the menu. She didn't glance at the Genesee River, gray and rushing outside the window by their table. Maggie guessed she also wasn't paying much attention to *her* or the smoky sweetness wafting through the restaurant or the gleaming wooden floors. She was entirely and warmly focused on Linnie.

And Linnie was smiling back. She looked dazed.

Since their initial handshake, Danielle had made no effort to mask her delight with Linnie. *Enchanted* was not too strong a word.

Linnie and Danielle. Mom and Wren. It was turning out to be a good day for sisters. An emotional day. A hard one. But good. Maggie was glad to be out with Linnie. Her mother and aunt needed time alone. They'd have the next couple of days as well. Maggie had agreed to drive to Carlton in the morning and cover Monday's library book club discussion in Mom's place.

Danielle closed the menu. "We have the same laugh. There's something similar in how we laugh, don't you think? The suddenness of it." She glanced distractedly at the waitress who'd appeared to take their order. After Maggie requested her pulled barbecue chicken sandwich and fries, and Linnie said absently, "I suppose I'll have that, too," her sister said quickly, "Make that three, please," and then leaned forward. "Enough about me. Tell me more about you."

Linnie's clasped hands came up to her chin. "Well . . . hmm." She peeked at Maggie. So far, Linnie had peppered her sister with questions. She was genuinely curious about Danielle—Maggie didn't doubt that for a second. But she also was clearly reluctant to talk about her own life.

Maggie nodded encouragingly, but Linnie still seemed at a loss for words. Finally, Maggie blurted, "Linnie's one of the smartest people I know."

Linnie gave her a grateful smile.

"I can tell," Danielle said, her expression admiring. "You even *look* smart."

Linnie laughed.

"There's my laugh again." She took hold of the edge of the table. "What do you like to do, Linnie?"

"Read."

"You too?"

Maggie smiled. More than one reader at the same table. Inconceivable.

"What kinds of things?"

"Pretty much everything, but poetry's my favorite. Right now, I'm into Mary Ruefle and Anne Carson."

Danielle's hands came up, a gesture that said, *See? My sister's brilliant.* "Do you also write?"

"Just poetry." She gave a self-conscious shrug. "Maggie's like that, too. Really into books."

"Not a writer, though," Maggie said.

The sisters started discussing authors. Did you read so-and-so's this, not that one but his latest? I did, and what about his first one? Then Danielle asked, "Are you majoring in English?"

"I haven't gone to college yet." Lowering her gaze to the table, Linnie smoothed her napkin. "Didn't even graduate from high school"—she glanced up and wrung the napkin like a wet washcloth—"though I'm signed up to take the GED in the spring."

"Oh." Danielle frowned, confused.

"I got pregnant my junior year and dropped out." She released the napkin. "I have a five-year-old. Her name is Kate."

Danielle's mouth fell open and stayed that way. When she finally got some words out, there were only two: "A daughter."

Linnie nodded once.

Tears filled Danielle's eyes.

Linnie's hands flew to her cheeks. "I'm sorry to disappoint—"

"Disappoint?" The sister fumbled with her napkin and pressed it hard against her eyes. Then she settled a fierce look on Linnie. "A niece. I have a niece. A sister *and* a niece." Napkin to the face

again, a muffled apology, then: "I can't believe I went for so long . . ." She cleared her throat and continued huskily, "Wondering about you—praying you'd let me meet you, just so damn blown away that I had a biological relation." She blew her nose into her napkin. "Not that I'm ungrateful. I know I was lucky to get adopted. And I love my parents. I couldn't love them more if they'd brought me into the world. But to find out about you was . . . something else. And now I learn there are two of you. Two people who share my blood. It's—it's just . . ." She exhaled shakily. "Amazing."

Linnie started crying, too.

They shared a look, then sobbed a laugh. The same laugh: sudden and surprised.

Maggie couldn't stop herself. She began to sniffle as well.

Danielle wiped her eyes on her sleeve. "Tell me about my niece. Kate. Does she look like you?"

"More like her dad. But she's really . . ."

Maggie waited. *Stubborn?*

"Terrific," Linnie finished on a sigh.

"Smart?"

"Oh gosh, so smart."

"And probably beautiful."

"Just darling."

"What else?"

"Super creative, funny, and sweet."

"May I meet her?"

"Of course."

"Right now? Today?"

Linnie laughed. "Sure."

"Tell me more about her."

And Linnie did, saying quite a few things that didn't match the Kate that Maggie had gotten to know. Not that she thought Linnie was lying—just that Maggie was realizing that there was a side of Kate that she didn't get to see.

Maggie thought about the people she knew, close and far, new and old, alive and dead, and followed the chains of love that linked them, sometimes beautifully, sometimes not. When two people shared love, they noticed the best in each other. But love could also keep a person from seeing the truth . . . from noticing the bad. Maggie supposed the cliché about love being blind was true. And what a dangerous circumstance that could be.

But what a wonderful thing, too.

The next day, Maggie softly closed the back door behind her. Her mother and Wren were still sleeping, and she didn't want to wake them. She'd warned them the night before that she'd be heading to Carlton first thing in the morning; she just hadn't mentioned *how* early—or, for that matter, why so early.

Pink formed fluffy clumps across the sky. The rosy clouds reminded Maggie of a girl's slippers. As she made her way to the driveway, the wind swooped her hair up from behind and prodded her in the direction of the lake. She resisted the nudge. This wasn't a day for beach walks. After she got into Mom's car and started the engine, she sent a brief text: *Be there by two. Keep an eye out for me. Maggie*

Just a reminder. Last night, she'd sent some longer messages—emails to a few different people. And she'd received responses.

As she traveled toward home, she thought about Linnie and

Danielle. Over dessert the previous evening, they had discussed the possibility of a Christmas Eve party—just the Pinsky family, Linnie, the Blakes, and Maggie's small family. Maggie wondered about Caleb. Maybe, if he was around, he'd come.

Before she knew it, she was halfway to Carlton. The drive wasn't difficult at all. Easy enough to go back and forth on some weekends to see Wren, Linnie, Sam, and her book club friends. She didn't want to miss any more meetings.

There was a lot to do before making her way to the library tonight. Dad knew to expect her for supper. They would probably dine early at Dilly's. And then, in the morning, Maggie would return to Wren's. Mom planned to go back to Carlton on Wednesday. Last night, Maggie had called her mother's boss to let her know that she'd be covering the book club discussion and that Mom wouldn't be back to work until Thursday. Janice must have gotten the impression from Maggie's discreet explanation that Minerva Arioli had suffered a nervous breakdown because all she'd said was, "Poor Min. I'm not surprised. Tell her to take as much time off as she needs. With her losing her folks and then that awful business you went through last year and Min being such a trouper, staying so strong and upbeat, well, it was all bound to catch up with her eventually." Maggie hadn't corrected her. Janice was mostly right.

The next time Maggie glanced at the time it was half past one. Almost there. She took the Wilson exit.

She had no difficulty finding the Cannons' house. And this time, it wasn't hard to track down Jane, either. Despite the cold, Jane was waiting for her outside by the front door, hunched in a black winter coat and sitting on a brick step.

Maggie parked on the side of the road.

Jane nodded. She looked determined, and Maggie was relieved about that. They were going to Carlton to press charges.

As she slipped out of the car, she remembered the first time she'd met Linnie, also perched on a front step.

Jane, Maggie: girls who'd barely crossed the threshold of childhood—who hadn't even made it through their teen years—before getting knocked down. And Linnie had been even younger.

But Maggie hadn't *stayed* down.

"Hey." She smiled and trudged up the paved walkway. "Our appointment's at three-thirty. It'll take us over an hour to get there. Ready?"

"Yeah." Jane smiled a little. Her face was free of makeup and full of resolve. "Thanks for coming with me today. But what about next year? Are you going back? Did you decide?"

Maggie put out a hand and helped Jane get on her feet. "I'm in."

ACKNOWLEDGMENTS

Several friends' support saw me through this novel, from the research to the writing, and I am obliged to them.

Special thanks to my outstanding editor, Liz Szabla, who has an unerring sense of what's working in a narrative and what isn't. She encouraged me to dig deeper into some parts of Maggie's story and wisely advised me to leave matters messy when it came to a few others. I couldn't ask for a better editor. Her insights are exceptional and invaluable to me.

Heartfelt thanks to my marvelous agent, Rebecca Stead, who is nothing less than a blessing. I am grateful for her guidance, intelligence, wit, and warmth. Also, right up to the eleventh hour, she put her writerly talent to excellent use for my benefit. (Thank you, dear Rebecca.)

A huge thanks to everyone at Feiwel and Friends, including Morgan Rath, Melinda Ackell, Liz Dresner, Katie Klimowicz, Anna Poon, and Kim Waymer. What a terrific team.

Thanks to Amber Christopher-Buscemi, my wonderful writing partner, who read an early draft of the manuscript and provided sage advice. Thanks to my smart friend Anna Symons, who puts up with my brainstorming, listens closely, and counsels well. And thanks to the psychology professor (and my longtime friend) Amy Gaesser, who answered my questions about PTSD and recommended some superb books in the course of my research.

Speaking of books, I consulted many. A few nonfiction works proved particularly helpful, including Dr. Bessel van der Kolk's *The Body Keeps the Score*, a thorough examination of trauma and its lasting effects on survivors. Alice Sebold's *Lucky* is a brave memoir about a sexual assault and its harrowing aftermath. I found it deeply moving, as I did Jon Krakauer's *Missoula*, an illuminating investigation into campus rape. Krakauer deepened my understanding of how sexual assault cases may play out in the criminal justice system, how a university's adjudication process will handle such cases differently, and the controversies and challenges that arise in both arenas. These works confront the difficult subjects of rape, trauma, and abuse with compassion and honesty, and they taught me a great deal.

For their generous spirits and countless kindnesses, I am grateful to Jennifer L. Johnson, Jennifer R. Johnson, Allie Johnson, Gwen Oosterhouse, Diane Palmer, Adrienne Kirby, Maarit Vaga, Marsha Rivers, Sharon Stewart, Shannon Stewart, Sharon Root, Nicole Slick, Rita Walton, Erin Lyon, James Tate Hill, my pottery pal Sylvia Johnson, my terrific siblings Robbie Ostrom and Noelle Swanson, the rest of my family, and my students, who keep me on my toes and teach me at least as much as I teach them.

Most of all, warmest thanks to Michael, Lily, and Quinn—my sweethearts.